THE 6 STEP PLAN

KANDICE HEMENWAY

To A.

For romance book club, for telling me to do this, for unlocking my brain, for notes on notes, for bee inspiration, for endless encouragement.

This would never have happened without you.

To R.

My forever best friend, my relentless caretaker, my definition of romance.

I love you always.

CONTENTS

CONTENT WARNINGS

Chronic Illness (management and pain descriptions): central theme

Ableism (internalized and from previous partner): central theme

Sexually Explicit Content: on page

Parental Abandonment: referenced, not on page

Violet has lupus. We get a front row seat to the challenges her condition creates for her, both physically and mentally. At the beginning of our story, Violet has yet to make peace with her condition. She struggles with frustration at her limitations, feeling like a burden, and believing in the value of her contributions to her relationships. While certainly not every person with chronic illness experiences these struggles, they are common. It is my dearest hope that this story might be validating for those who've had this experience, enlightening for those who haven't, and healing for those currently struggling.

CHAPTER 1

VIOLET

My eyes fluttered open to the pulse of pain radiating from my hips and knees. Not the start I was hoping for. A morning evaluation was my standard practice, and I could already tell today's results would not be encouraging.

Everything hurt. Fingers. Wrists. Ankles. Hips. The joints were stiff and sore, like they hadn't moved in years. I half expected to hear them creak as I flexed.

God, I was exhausted. Not sleepy. Not tired. Utterly spent—as if someone had opened the drain and flushed every ounce of energy from my body. This level of fatigue was difficult to explain to people. It wasn't the same as a long day or a bad night's sleep. This exhaustion was bone-deep, wringing out every cell. Like in movies when someone's life-force is getting siphoned and they turn into a skeleton right there on the spot. That was me now—a skeleton with swollen joints.

I rolled to my back, and my breath hitched as an intense ache bloomed across my middle. My hand drifted to my lower ribs, gingerly finding the swelling, hot and tender, protruding from my chest. Inflammation in the cartilage of my rib cage—one of my oldest, weirdest, and most hated symptoms. When it flared up, it could be relatively minor with a prickling sensation and a bit of discomfort, or it could look like half a softball stuck under my skin, causing blinding pain and impeding my ability to breathe. Today was…medium…I guess.

Medium. So very eloquent. I was great with the words today. As a professional words expert, I was well-qualified to make these evaluations. I mentally placed a "needs work" note on my internal monologue, but I didn't have high hopes. My brain was wading through dense fog in search of fragments of thoughts, and I wasn't convinced it could put the pieces together even if it were to find them.

Focus on the checklist, Violet.

Joint and muscle aches. *Yes.* Fatigue. *Big yes.* Brain fog. *Densely foggy.* Ribs. *Damn. Maybe more than medium.*

Fever? I placed a palm against my forehead. *I don't know. Probably.*

Rash? Moving my hand to my cheek, I didn't even need the mirror to know it would be bright red. The heat in my skin announced the raised splotches forming downward-pointing triangles on both cheeks like some sort of sad lupus clown. They called it a butterfly rash because of the way it unfolded somewhat symmetrically across the cheeks like a butterfly's open wings, but that imagery always seemed a little too pleasant for the reality. Sad lupus clown was a far better fit.

Looked like check marks across the board, symptom-wise. I was in a flare. It didn't come as a great shock. I'd felt kind of off yesterday but held on to hope it was a blip and I'd wake up feeling improved this morning.

No such luck.

The situation demanded drugs—both Regular Meds (immunosuppressants, symptom reducers, and supplements) and Get Rid Of This Flare Meds (steroids). But I needed to feed myself something so the pharmacy I was about to consume didn't turn my stomach. I also really needed to pee. That could go to the front of the line.

Pee. Food. Meds. What else?

I didn't have any pressing deadlines. I was working on edits for a manuscript in which the client used the word *moist* seventy-four times —so not exactly making notes on the next Great American Novel. This round of notes wasn't due for a couple of days. It could wait.

What else?

Evan. I was supposed to have dinner with Evan tonight. Ramen at my favorite spot. Well, one of my favorite spots. I was a connoisseur of ramen, so I had at least four favorite spots, each with its own special strengths. Tonight's ramen place had the best marinated eggs— perfectly jammy yolks and exactly the right amount of salt. An absolute delight.

Eggs…why am I thinking about eggs? Right. Ramen with Evan. Text him to cancel.

Evan. Pee. Food. Meds. Nap.

Grabbing my phone, I fired off a quick text.

Bad day. Rain check tonight?

His response came in seconds.

EVAN

Of course. You ok? Need anything?

I'm okay. Taking meds and heading back to bed. I'm sorry.

No worries. Take care of yourself.

He didn't need many words from me to understand, a fact I appreciated on days like this.

With an embarrassing amount of effort, I made it out of bed, performed my restroom ministrations, snagged a package of peanut butter crackers (a go-to for low-effort food), took a fistful of pills, and slid fuzzy socks onto my icicle feet before climbing back into bed. The single circuit around my apartment had cost me. Even more pain. Even less energy. Nothing else to do but hunker down and ride it out.

I huddled under my blankets, attempting to create a cocoon of safety. Too bad the thing I needed protecting from—my turncoat defective body—was sharing the cocoon with me. I closed my eyes, a tear spilling down my cheek.

I was so tired of this.

I had my first symptoms—aching knees, a rash on my chest, and the weirdo rib thing—when I was in middle school in a small West Texas town. Not the cute kind with charming downtown shops and a plucky mayor. The kind with one blinking stop light, a convenience store, and dirt. My parents were good people and did their best with what they had, but we weren't exactly flush with resources. Mom drove me in to see a parade of doctors in Odessa, but my symptoms were inconsistent, and when they finally disappeared, Mom and Dad were relieved to chalk it up to a fluke and move on with life.

Unfortunately, that was only the beginning. When I was twenty and in my junior year at the University of Texas, the situation escalated. I missed classes. I saw more doctors. But my presentation was unusual, and answers remained elusive. I basically stumbled through my last two years of school, relying on the goodwill of sympathetic professors and sheer determination to get my degree and escape my blinking-light town.

I wouldn't get a diagnosis and treatment plan until I was twenty-five. Now, three years later, I was making progress. My daily life was still affected but not completely derailed by my condition. Flares were shorter, fewer, and further between. But they would never be gone. Days lying in bed being crushed by pain and exhaustion would always be a reality.

This was forever.

I blinked as the tears came faster, then screwed my eyes shut and willed my body to sleep through the ache.

———

I woke from my nap to rustling coming from my kitchen.

He can't help himself.

I tested my limbs, chanced a deep breath, and concluded I was feeling a bit better.

We'll call it a win.

Grabbing a scrunchie from my nightstand, I wrangled my mane, gave my button-up pajama set a once-over to make sure everything was closed, and shuffled my fuzzy sock feet down the hallway, finding Evan unloading bags in the kitchen.

He…needed a haircut. Wavy and chestnut brown, his hair was slightly shorter on the sides and back but had grown a little overlong on top. It flopped over his brow as he reached across the counter.

Maybe the haircut can wait.

Objectively? He was gorgeous.

His features were strong—square jaw, high cheekbones, prominent brow—but they were all a bit rounded at the edges, as if the gentleness inside of him had reached out to soften them. He had warm brown eyes and an easy smile with three deep dimples that appeared one at a time as it widened, like a Richter scale of happiness.

Anticipation of those dimples appearing at the sight of me was enough to send a little flutter through my belly.

Good grief. You can shut that right down, ma'am.

I hadn't had those kinds of thoughts in a while. This flare had my brain addled and my defenses down. Giving myself no more time to ruminate on illicit topics, I stepped quickly out of the hallway and into my tiny great room.

His smile grew as he spotted me until two dimples creased his cheeks. "Good morning, sunshine. How ya feeling?"

"I'm okay. A little better than this morning." Coming to stand beside him, I gestured to his haul. "You didn't have to do this, Ev—"

He gently laid his palm over my mouth. "I'm here to help. Let's not waste energy on arguing. Agreed?" Having abandoned my wayward thoughts, I didn't dwell for one single second on how my lips tingled at his touch. I nodded and he released me. "Good. Now are we setting up shop back in bed or on the couch?"

"Couch."

He started to move, then hesitated, running a thumb over my cheek and drawing a sigh from me. Whatever unauthorized paths my mind was trying to lead me down today, his touch would always be comforting. I fought the urge to lean into his palm.

"You're pretty red. It's bad today, huh? Where are you?"

I hated that question. I was historically unreliable with the pain scale. I tended to undershoot because I didn't want to be dramatic. Ideally, I'd never have to try to come up with a number at all. "I don't know. Five or six?"

"So seven?"

My expression must have broadcasted both that I was annoyed and that he was correct.

He grinned. "Let's get you to the couch, rickety." Taking one of my hands in his, he wrapped his other around my waist, supporting me as he walked me to the couch. "You all roided up?"

The way he referred to my steroids always made me smile. Like I was out there flexing my guns and throwing some cars. The contrast to reality was striking. My frame was slight and my muscle tone squishy, rigorously forged from approximately half a dozen gym trips over the last decade and many, many, *many* hours curled up reading. I was being half carried the six steps to my sofa. A juicer, I was not.

"I started a round this morning." He deposited me on the couch and burritoed me in a fuzzy blanket before disappearing down the hall, emerging a few moments later with my stainless steel water cup.

My apartment was essentially a dollhouse. You could make it from the front door to the back wall in sixteen steps. Entryway—two steps. Great room, with living room to the left and eat-in kitchen to the right —eight steps. Hall—six steps. It had one bedroom, one bathroom, and a laundry closet. *Luxury!* In fairness, my decorating choices likely contributed to the dollhouse feel. My interior design priorities were character and coziness, so my belongings were a collection of flea market finds and three thousand blankets. Evan called it an elderly hermit's fever dream. He was right. And I loved it.

Light streamed through the window of the living room. It was summer, so it was harder to tell, but didn't seem like evening light. "What time is it?" It was a Wednesday. He probably should've been at work.

"Almost four. I cut out early so I could grab a few things." He bustled about, making my water, adding ice to the cup from the freezer then opening the refrigerator. "You're out of lemon wedges."

"Yeah. I don't even have more lemons to cut. I need to get some—"

He stuck a hand out from behind the refrigerator door, holding a produce bag. "Got ya covered. I'll cut extra before I leave." He cut a few slices to add to the cup he was making now. "All right. Brace your-self. I've got a new entry, and this one is a winner." We had an ongoing game, Weird Shit I Saw In Austin. Our city never disappointed, but I could tell by the way he bounced from foot to foot that this would be a particularly good one. "A guy on a motorcycle...with a sidecar... where the passenger was a dog...wearing riding goggles."

"No way."

"I shit you not. See for yourself." He pulled his phone from his pocket and tossed it to the couch. I freed my arms from their burrito blanket confines, keyed in his password, and opened his camera roll. Sure enough, a photo of a beagle wearing riding goggles in a sidecar was his latest image.

"Oh my god, he's perfect. Seven points for originality and an extra point for extreme cuteness."

"I think it deserves a nine, but I'll agree to eight." He closed the lid on my cup and held up a takeout bag. "Do you want your ramen now or later?"

"You brought ramen?"

"From the good egg place…with an extra egg. You hungry?"

Warmth suffused my chest, and my stomach rumbled. He was the best best friend ever. "Starving. I managed a package of crackers earlier but haven't eaten since."

"Then dinner is coming right up. I also put a couple of bowls of soup from the deli in the refrigerator for tomorrow."

He assembled my ramen and delivered it and my water before returning to the kitchen island for his own. He'd done so much today. Gratitude and guilt welled up inside of me. He was always doing so much, always making sure his people were taken care of. It was one of his loveliest qualities, but it also stretched him too thin at times. I, on the other hand, was the textbook definition of high maintenance. I hated putting him out like this, taking advantage of our friendship.

He settled on the couch with his dinner.

"I'm so grateful for all of this, really, but you didn't need to go to so much trouble."

"I thought we agreed to no arguing about this." He continued before I could protest. "We take care of each other, Vi. That's not trouble. It's what we do."

Begrudgingly, I let the subject drop. He meant what he said. We did take care of each other. But I could never take care of him enough to balance the scales.

He dug into his bowl. "So what's the latest at work?"

The mere mention of it had my gut pinching with anxiety.

Sometimes my job wasn't so bad. Yes, there was the manuscript that didn't use a single contraction because the author wanted it to sound "literary." And the one that was 450,000 precious-words-that-couldn't-be-parted-with long. I had navigated seas of adverbs and paper-thin plots. But they weren't all like that. I also got to work with some truly talented authors. Authors who were reaching for the same dreams I'd once entertained. Authors I envied.

This week, however, had been particularly rough.

"Mostly I spent the week trying to come up with a constructive way to say, 'Yes. You are correct. No one will ever see this twist coming. Because it doesn't make any sense.'"

He snorted into his soup. "And?"

Clearing my throat, I slipped into my Writer Whisperer Voice. "You've achieved the shock factor for sure. Ideally, you want your twist to feel both surprising and inevitable. I recommend going back through the story and working in clues that point toward this. Not so much that you give it all away, but enough that it gives that unavoidable feeling to your reveal. It's a tightrope, but I think you can find the balance."

His mouth hitched at the corner. "Deft as always."

"We'll see. She's…temperamental. I'm kind of expecting a nastygram in response."

Why some people paid to have their work edited and then got mad at me when I did exactly that, I would never understand, but it happened more than you'd think. And I was definitely waiting for that other shoe to drop in this situation.

Evan bristled. "And where's Gemma in this? She should be running interference for you. Or at least backing you up." We both knew that wouldn't happen.

Gemma was my boss. She used to edit herself, but over the last few months, she'd shifted basically all of her workload to me and my counterpart—in addition to our own. That was annoying, but tolerable. Less tolerable was her habit of throwing us under the bus with clients.

"I'll add that to my wish list."

Setting his bowl on the coffee table, he squared his shoulders. *Here we go.*

"I think you should quit."

I didn't even attempt to contain my eye roll. "You know I can't—"

"You could though. You hate this job."

"Hate is a strong word. Editing is not a job to hate. Plenty of people love it."

"But you're not one of them. And even if you were, your boss is an asshole."

I opened my mouth to argue but quickly snapped it shut. There was no argument to be had on that front. My boss *was* an asshole. I shoveled in another bite of ramen instead.

"Exactly." He nodded at my no-response response. "So quit."

"It's not that easy. The money is decent. I can work from home. The schedule is flexible." I'd repeated those things to myself so many times they'd become a mantra. So many chronically ill people would kill for this position. I should be grateful. "That's not waiting around every corner."

"But how do you know that if you won't even look? You have to explore your options, at least. You could work for someone else. Or freelance—work for yourself." He hesitated. "Maybe even start writing again."

I tamped down a twinge of longing. Writing may have been my dream once, my first love, but if my illness had taught me anything, it was that swinging for the fences wasn't a game I was made for. I needed to keep my plans small and manageable.

He backpedaled, lifting his hands in surrender. "Or not. I'm just saying you don't have to accept a job that makes you miserable. You're brilliant. You can do anything. You don't have to settle. You could—"

I sighed and dropped my spoon into my empty bowl. "I thought we agreed to no arguing?"

His brow wrinkled in concern. "I'm sorry. You're right. I stand by what I said, but I shouldn't have pushed when you're already feeling bad."

"I know you're trying to help. But I need to be done for today."

"Good enough." He took my empty bowl and put it on the coffee table, then pulled my feet onto his lap. I snuggled down under my blanket while he switched on the TV and selected the profile labeled *E&V's Bingewatch.*

Guilt gnawed at me. Guilt over being a burden. Guilt over hating (yes, that was the right word) my job. Guilt over not doing more to change my situation. Guilt over not being content with what I had. But with a full belly of ramen, the soothing drone of comfort television, and the soothing presence of Evan, my tension eased.

I didn't realize I'd drifted off until he half sat on the couch next to my hips and gently squeezed my shoulder. "Hey. It's late. I've gotta head out." My blurry eyes brought him into focus. "I did the dishes and left more lemon wedges in the fridge."

"Thank you." It came out as a croak.

"About next week. Do you think you'll still feel up to going? I don't want you to feel obligated. It'll be fine if you can't make it."

I cleared my throat. "No. I think it'll be okay. Or I hope it will. It's more than a week away. I can't make any promises, but I really do want to be there. Can we play it by ear?"

"Of course. I'll check on you tomorrow. Get some more rest." He dropped a kiss on my cheek and left, locking up behind him.

CHAPTER 2

EVAN

"VI. I'M HERE."

She appeared from the kitchen. Forest green lace hugged her soft curves. Her auburn curls were swept back, a few pieces escaping around her face and neck. Her wide, mossy eyes met mine, freezing me where I stood. I looked at those eyes all the time, but something about the smoky makeup she wore tonight made them feel like tractor beams. Her red-painted lips stretched into a brilliant smile, her face lit with happiness at seeing me. Something in my chest tightened.

That's…weird.

"Two minutes." She held up two fingers then spun on her heel toward her room.

I was unprepared for the back of that dress. It swept down, revealing a long expanse of her pale, freckled skin and scooping just in time to outline her heart-shaped backside as it swayed down the hall, carried on pointy black heels. Something tightened several inches lower than my chest.

Fuck. Me.

As soon as she crossed the threshold of her room I turned and doubled over, bracing my hands on the entry table and squeezing my eyes shut.

Jesus, Evan. Stop ogling your best friend's ass like a goddamn creeper. What is wrong with you?

Her voice rang out from her room. "I just have to put on earrings and grab my clutch."

"Take your time." *All the time you need, please.*

Fortunately, by the time she reappeared, I'd righted myself, and my inappropriate thoughts were crowded out by concern. She seemed better than she had last week—the light was back in her eyes—but I needed to be sure. I reached for her as she got close. "Are you sure you're up for this?"

Her smile was soft, but her response was confident. "Yes. Definitely. It wasn't so bad this time. It only lasted a couple of days, and I'm feeling much better. I want to go." She leaned in to nudge my arm with hers. "I've been saving spoons. I'm good. Promise."

Chronically ill people spent more time, thought, and conversation on energy management than I ever could have imagined without knowing Vi, but being her friend, I'd become well-versed in the issues and the lingo. Spoons were units of energy. Running low was bad and running out could be a disaster, so she tracked and managed them closely. She'd been saving spoons—conserving energy—so she'd have enough to spend on supporting me tonight.

It meant more to me than I was willing to tell her right now. She may have been conserving spoons, but she wasn't far out from a flare. She didn't need to stress. And if I told her how anxious I was about tonight, she'd definitely stress.

Still, she deserved my appreciation. "Thank you. I'm really glad you'll be there." She also deserved to hear how great she looked—from her friend, not the perv who had walked in here. "Besides, you clean up nice. It would be a shame to let all this"—I gestured wildly in her general direction—"go to waste."

She beamed and I offered my arm. "Shall we?"

———

Adrenaline was thrumming through me by the time our Uber dropped us in front of The Driskill. This was an annual shindig, ostensibly an opportunity to recognize outstanding work from the previous year, but in truth as much an opportunity to schmooze with industry people as a celebration. I'd been attending every year since I graduated college and went to work for my firm, Violet always my plus-one, but this year was different.

I'd known I wanted to be an architect since I was a kid with LEGO, obsessed with the thrill of seeing buildings I imagined in 1:42 scale and populated by plastic yellow people. So I got my degree in architecture and went to work for my dream company, The Andrews Group, right out of school. The day the offer came in, Violet and I pooled our cash and bought the most expensive bottle of champagne we could afford. It was awful. And one of the best nights I could remember.

It had been a long journey from LEGO to here, and I still had a long way to go, but tonight was a big milestone—maybe a huge one.

We stepped inside the wood-and-leaded-glass double doors, the polished stone floor in front of us flanked on either side by rows of gilded columns.

Damn, I loved this building. It was an Austin landmark. Designed by Jasper Preston and built in 1886, it was the oldest operating hotel in the city and dripped with history. A building like this was the holy grail of my profession, a design people were still using, enjoying, and writing about over a century later.

This was the kind of work I wanted to do—work that had significance, shaping my city for generations. If tonight went well, I might get more exciting opportunities. It wouldn't be a project like this, obviously, but it would be a real start. I just needed to win.

I flexed my hand to calm the twitch.

"You okay?"

I startled at her question and shoved my hands into my pockets. "Yeah. Of course. Why do you ask?"

"Because you're quiet. You barely said a word on the way over. And we've been here for a whole minute, and you haven't mentioned Jasper Preston or the stained glass ceiling." Her smile was knowing… and a little smug.

Huffing a quiet laugh, I forced a smile back, trying to shake off my tension. "I didn't realize my tour guide services were so important to you."

"Vitally."

My smile came easier. "Then buckle up."

I regaled her with facts about the thirteen-story annex that opened in 1930 as we found the bag check and waited in the short line, but I couldn't kick the feeling of restlessness.

Placing her hand on my arm, she held my gaze. "Hey. You're going to be okay. Win or lose, you're great at this, and being recognized tonight is proof of that."

The band squeezing my chest loosened a tic. It was amazing how a touch and a few words from her made me feel calmer. I took a steadying breath. She was right. I'd be okay either way. I needed to relax and enjoy the evening.

We climbed the grand staircase to the mezzanine, where the cocktails and mingling portion of the evening would take place. Spanning the second floor of the hotel, it had the same stone flooring and columns as the lobby, detailed moldings on the walls and ceiling, and a balcony overlooking 6th Avenue. It made me giddy.

We snagged a couple of flutes of champagne from a passing tray (much tastier than our celebratory bottle as broke twenty-two-year-olds) and made our way through the room.

Let the schmoozing begin.

After about a lap and a half, something over my shoulder made Violet's eyes go wide and her lips curl in over her teeth. "Incoming."

I turned in time to mutter a curse and hear Violet muffle a laugh before we were face to face with Bradley Stetson (absolutely not his real name), fellow architect at Andrews and bane of my professional existence. He wore dark jeans that may as well have been painted on, a black pearl-snap shirt and blazer, a belt buckle the size of a dinner plate, a comically tall cowboy hat, and boots. I swear I heard spurs as he sauntered up, hand extended.

"Howdy, y'all."

"Brad."

"Evan." His eyes trailed over Violet. "And who is this lovely lady?"

I placed a protective hand on the small of her back as she shook his hand with a smile.

"Violet." She was unfailingly polite.

I was not. "You've met, actually. Multiple times."

"Oh, well, I'll have to beg your pardon, then. I can't imagine how I didn't remember meeting such a beautiful lady." His laugh was grating. "Listen, Evan. I wanted to congratulate you on the nomination tonight. Having your name listed near such talent must feel like a really big deal to you. You keep working hard, pal."

He didn't even wait for a reply. Having delivered his jab, he patted me on the shoulder, tipped his hat toward Violet, and moseyed on down the road.

I rolled my eyes so hard I could see my brain. "That guy looks more like a cartoon every time I see him."

Batting big doe-eyes, Vi let loose her West Texas accent. "But, Evan, he's just following the Lord. The higher the hat, the closer to Jesus."

"Pretty sure it's the higher the *hair*, the closer to Jesus."

"And the size of that belt buckle." She fanned herself dramatically. "Butter my biscuits. That's how you know he's a gen-u-ine cowboy."

"That man has never been on a horse in his life. And did you hear him? 'Howdy, y'all.'"

"He's embracing our culture."

"He's lived here two years! He's from Orlando. That's not even part of the South." Mischief flared in her eyes, and I knew what was coming, so I cut her off at the pass. "No. I will not have this argument with you tonight, Violet June Ward. The South stretches along the Eastern Seaboard from Charlottesville down to Gainesville—not an inch further—and you damn well know it."

That broke her. Her persona fell away, and she tried to contain her giggles. I couldn't help but join her. When our laughter receded, she laid a hand on my arm. "Don't let him get to you about the award."

"I don't give a damn what he says to me about the award or anything else. I do care that he treated you like nothing—pretending he didn't even remember you when I know for a fact he's asked Nancy about you."

"Well, your concern for my honor is mighty gentlemanly, Mr. Marshall." She wrapped her hand around my arm. "Now, might I trouble you to refresh a lady's beverage?"

"It would be my pleasure, Miss Ward."

The next hour proceeded mostly as expected. We suffered through shoptalk. We caught up with friendly acquaintances. We quietly mocked the boys' club at the bar. It was pretty much business as usual, but as the night progressed, so did my nerves. I felt edgy and frayed. As long as Violet stayed close, I was able to keep it together, but I was treating her like a damn security blanket. The ceremony couldn't come quick enough.

———

"Congratulations." Paul clapped me on the shoulder.

Paul and Nancy Andrews were the best in the business. A husband-and-wife team (he was the architect, she was the designer), they'd built the firm together from the ground up, and now it was an Austin institution.

"And it was an excellent show you put on."

When they called my name during the ceremony, my first instinct was to look to Violet for confirmation. Her expression was bursting with excitement and pride. My chest expanded like a balloon. For a second, that look on her face was the only award I cared about.

Then she pushed me out of my chair.

I'd recovered, gaining my composure before my ass hit the floor, but there was flailing involved. Vi was clearly mortified by the laughter rolling through the audience as I made my way to the stage, but I couldn't have cared less. It was the biggest success of my career to date. I was untouchable.

"You did give him quite the sendoff." Nancy squeezed first Violet then me in a warm embrace. "We're so proud of you."

Violet blushed as her nose wrinkled, her tell for embarrassment or discomfort. "He was just sitting there! I was trying to get him moving. A little too aggressively, I guess." Her eyes caught mine, and her face softened. "But of course I'm *so* proud of him, too."

The chest-expanding sensation was back. If Vi was proud of me, the rest of the world could go to hell. Okay, maybe not my bosses who were standing right here. But everybody else…

Clearing his throat, Paul nodded toward the bar. "Let's go get some drinks."

We took orders and set off. "I can't tell you how proud Nancy and I are of you. You're a damn fine architect. I'm glad you're working for Andrews instead of our competition." He chuckled and then sobered.

"But even if you weren't, I couldn't help being proud of you tonight. You deserved it."

If there was anyone besides Violet whose pride mattered to me, it was Paul. My relationship with my dad was strained at best. He left when my sisters and I were young, and his spotty presence in our lives had caused more disappointment than anything else. Over the years, Paul had become a mentor, investing in me personally as well as professionally. There wasn't much I wouldn't do to make sure his investment paid off.

We stepped to the front of the line and placed our orders. Paul leaned an elbow on the bar top. "I'm out early next week, but come see me when you have time on Thursday. I've got some things to talk to you about."

"What kind of things?"

"The kind we'll talk about on Thursday."

Great. I definitely wouldn't spend the next five days wondering about that cryptic lede.

The bartender slid four glasses across the bar. I sampled my old-fashioned, and Paul dropped a tip in the jar. "So, when are you going to lock that girl down? Marry her? Start making a few kids?"

I choked on my drink.

We'd gone from zero to making babies in three seconds flat. I had to hand it to him. I didn't normally get flustered, but he had me on my heels. That question was nothing new in my life. When your best friend was a girl friend it kinda went with the territory, and I'd gotten it about Vi and me more times than I could count. But usually not so bluntly...and never from Paul.

"I don't—we don't... It isn't that way between Vi and me."

"Are you sure? Because from where I'm sitting, you've got a beautiful woman on your arm who you adore and who adores you right back. And you're sitting around with your thumb up your ass."

I could not believe I was having this conversation. "Of course I'm sure. Violet and I have been friends for ten years. If there was going to be something else between us, it would have happened already. It's not our thing. She's my friend—my best friend."

"And Nancy is mine. Has been for forty years. Nothing better in the world than being married to your best friend."

"Sure, but you're also in love with her. I'm not in love with Violet." As I said the words, I caught sight of her across the room, her face lit with laughter, and my chest clenched. Damn. The stress was getting to me tonight.

"Ah. Well. My mistake, then."

As we made it back and handed the ladies their drinks, I was still trying to figure out what had just happened—what could have prompted Paul to ask me that. Of course I loved Violet. More than anyone. But there was a huge difference between loving someone and being *in love* with someone—a universe of difference. And yes, she was an objectively attractive woman, but that didn't mean I was attracted *to her*. I'd almost never felt anything like that about Violet—other than tonight—which was probably a fluke because it was a big night with lots of stress…and because of that dress.

Violet interrupted my turbulent thoughts. "Hey, before I forget, your mom wants you to call her when you get home tonight."

"My…" I tried to pick up the thread of the conversation.

"Yeah. I texted her to let her know you won, and she told me to make you call when you got in." She turned back to Nancy to continue their conversation.

"Sure thing."

———

After making a stop at Violet's so I could see her home safely, the Uber dropped me at my place. We lived close enough I could have walked, and I normally did. But I didn't have it in me tonight. I felt like I could sleep for a week.

I went straight for the kitchen, tossing my keys on the island and shedding my suit jacket. No idea where that ended up. I grabbed a glass from the cabinet, filled it at the tap, and downed the entire thing before filling another.

What a weird fucking night.

A great night, of course. The award was a major achievement. Paul's encouragement meant the world to me.

But Vi…

Shake it off, man.

I threw back the second glass of water, wiped my mouth with the back of my hand, and set the glass in the sink.

I needed to get some sleep and put this great, weird, emotionally charged night in the rearview. But first…

I pulled my phone from my pocket and tapped my mom's contact. She answered after half a ring.

"Baby! You kicked ass!" Donna Marshall. Never one to mince words or withhold praise, especially with her kids.

"Yeah, Mom. I kicked ass."

"I'm so proud of you, Ev." She couldn't hear my smile, but I knew she'd feel it. "Did you and Violet have a good time?"

"Yeah. The event was great. But I'm pretty gassed. Ready to get to bed." I trudged toward my bedroom to do just that. "How was your day? Did the exterminator guy come?"

"Uh…yes. He made it by." There was a hesitation in that statement. She was hedging.

"Mom…"

"It's nothing you need to worry about tonight. I mean it. We can talk it through later."

"Or we can talk about it right now, so it doesn't keep me up all night. Tell me what he said, Mom."

"Stubborn as a damn mule."

"Everything I know, I learned from you."

"I only accept that truth when it suits me."

I almost caved to a laugh but held the silence. I did learn from her, and I could do this all night.

Her beleaguered sigh rattled through the earpiece. Victory.

"Extensive termite damage."

"Shit." I dropped to the edge of my bed and rubbed at the headache forming between my eyes.

"Exactly. The list is getting long. Too long."

Mom still lived in the house I grew up in. It was such a great place—a 1920s Victorian—and an awesome home to grow up in, but to say it needed work was an understatement. She was a single mom of three. She worked hard, raised her kids, put us all through school, and was now helping support my younger sister, Lauren, and her little girl, Tabitha, who moved back in with her last year. It's not that she didn't do her best to take care of the place, but she'd had other priorities for the last three decades or so. It was too much neglect for a house that old though, and it was starting to show the effects.

There had to be something I could do. "We'll figure it out."

"*I* will figure it out. I'm talking to some people and sorting out my options. You don't need to worry about it."

Sure. I'll just go ahead and stop worrying. That wasn't going to happen, but I wouldn't get anywhere arguing with her tonight.

"Fine. But at least keep me in the loop, okay?"

"I promise."

We said I love you's and goodbyes, and I collapsed back onto my bed. I knew what kind of options she'd discover. Bad ones. The list of problems with the house was getting more extensive and more dire. She couldn't keep living there as-is. She couldn't afford the repairs. She owned the house, which was an advantage, but with the house's condition, it would be difficult to sell it for anything reasonable. Certainly not enough to get her, my sister, and my niece into a new place.

My headache intensified.

This fucking night.

I dragged myself off the bed and forced myself to change. I would not make the situation worse by sleeping in my suit.

She couldn't lose the house. It would be devastating financially, not to mention emotionally. I didn't know how yet, but I would find a way to get those repairs done. I'd call in favors. Or take classes and do it myself. *Okay. That's the exhaustion talking.* I'd need to do better than that.

With my suit hanging where it belonged, I climbed into bed, pulled out my notebook, and scrawled *Save the House* at the top of the first blank page.

Time for a plan.

CHAPTER 3
VIOLET

LINA

Laaaake house! 24th–26th. Everybody in?

EVAN

Hell yes.

Yaayyyy!!! Yes! Very very in! 

NICO

I am currently referring all calendar inquiries to my illustrious fiancé as the wedding schedule has become too cumbersome for me to track and I do not care to have my ass handed to me for double-booking.

JAMIE

Lol. Weirdo.

No wedding conflicts. We are free and will definitely be there!

NICO

The judge has spoken.

LINA

😒

Remy? We can't see you nod via txt bud.

REMY

Yeah. Thanks for that. I was on a call. I'm there.

LINA

You used your words. So proud.

REMY

JAMIE

Who's got what, food-wise?

REMY

I'll take burgers and dogs for Fri night.

EVAN

Vi and I can do snacks and sandwich stuff.

Yes!

LINA

I'll bring fixings for Rem's stuff. And eggs and bacon for breakfasts.

JAMIE

We'll take dinner on Saturday. And bring some tamales for breakfast and snacking as well.

I'll also bring bubbles and OJ!

LINA

Other than that BYOB. I'm not paying to keep you assholes in beer all weekend like last time.

Looking at you Evan.

EVAN

That was Nico! I took two beers. TWO. Nico forgot his and took half your damn case!

NICO

I plead the 5th.

LINA

You are the literal worst.

NICO

You love me.

LINA

JAMIE

Nico's kleptomania aside…I think that covers everything.

I can't wait!!! Lina, please tell your parents we say thank you!!!!

EVERYONE

I danced in my chair as I set my phone back on my dining table/desk.

The lake house belonged to Lina's extraordinarily generous family. They essentially gave us unrestricted access to it when her parents weren't there themselves, and we gratefully took them up on it, heading out there a few times a year. It was an incredible vacation home and over the years had become the backdrop for some of my favorite memories with my favorite people.

Evan, Nico, Lina, and I met in the dorms our freshman year. Lina and I were roommates. Nico lived a few doors down from Evan. We formed our little group and carried each other through undergrad. Four years later, we gained another member when Nico met Remy in law school, and he fused right in. Sometimes it was hard to remember he hadn't been with us since the beginning. Finally, we added Jamie when Nico (who was apparently the official on-ramp to our cohort) met and fell in love with her three years ago.

The promise of time away with them felt like an oasis materializing on the horizon, the appearance of which was not a moment too soon. But those hopeful-oasis feelings evaporated like a mirage when I opened my email to a shouty capitals subject line topping the list of new messages.

I expected this was coming from the moment I sent the feedback about her plot twist, but a quick skim told me it was worse than I'd anticipated. Eight—no, nine—paragraphs laced with more shouty capitals and a plethora of exclamation points (and not the good kind) sent to me and Gemma.

My stomach sank lower and lower as I read the torrent of spite. Starting with a litany of my many incompetencies, she then moved into a full character assassination. I was talentless, idiotic, and cruel—a hack who could only justify my existence by unfairly denigrating authors who were more gifted than I could ever hope to be. We then moved into the threats portion of the missive, demanding my termination.

My jaw clenched as frustration bubbled to the surface. This was outrageous. All I had done was my job, and I'd gotten this in return. It wasn't right. And I didn't have to accept it. I would professionally defend myself and then sever our working relationship.

I moved to hit reply, but before I could, a response from Gemma came through. I opened it, bracing for her betrayal.

> *So sorry for what you've gone through with Violet…clearly unacceptable…have faith that I will deal with her appropriately…*

The frustration boiled over. I stood and paced into the kitchen, my fingernails digging into the flesh of my palms.

I was done. This work was so close and yet so far from what I truly wanted. The tedious projects. The difficult clients. That was all manageable, if unfulfilling. But Gemma was the last straw. She demanded too much and gave far too little, and I was officially overdrawn.

I'm going to find a new job.

A weight lifted from my shoulders. Excitement surged through me as I grabbed my resolve with both hands.

Evan was right. I could make a change, and I would.

I had a solid portfolio. I could apply for other jobs or even start free-lancing.

Or...

Before I could rationalize my way out of it, I strode to my computer, closed the email window, and opened a new browser tab.

How to become a novelist

That search was largely unhelpful, returning listicles and tips for beginners, but I was undeterred.

Jobs for novelists

These results were more promising. I fell down a rabbit hole, clicking links and scribbling ideas. Forty minutes and five search terms later, I stumbled upon an article about a fellowship for unpublished authors with fairly big names attached to it and clicked through to the website to investigate.

It was a six-month program in Boston. Advanced courses taught by well-respected authors, editors, and other industry professionals. A cohort to develop stories with. Premium networking opportunities.

Could I actually do something like this? It sounded incredible but it had to be hyper-competitive. They only ran the program every other year, and the classes were small. Not to mention the fact that applications (along with a short story submission) were due in just over three weeks, which would be a breakneck pace for writing some-thing decent.

And even if I could get in, could I keep up? My body could fly off the rails at any moment. They probably wouldn't accommodate that.

I scanned the list of contributors and stopped mid-scroll.

Miranda Shultz.

Miranda Shultz, my absolute idol, was one of the mentors. My eyes darted to the bookshelf in my living room stacked with her books—every one she'd ever published—read and reread countless times. Her writing was enthralling, the best the mystery genre had to offer. Learning from her was literally the stuff of my dreams. If that wasn't enough to entice me, nothing was.

My pointer hovered over the How to Apply button. It probably wouldn't work out…but maybe, if I got out of my own way for once, it could. Evan's words echoed in my mind.

"You're brilliant. You can do anything. You don't have to settle."

I clicked.

CHAPTER 4

EVAN

Paul's *"come see me when you have time on Thursday"* had turned out to be every bit the mindfuck I'd anticipated. Fortunately, confidence in my position prevented me from jumping to worst-case scenarios, but that still left a lot of possibilities, and I'd spent the last five days obsessing over every one.

I'd resisted the urge to storm his office first thing this morning, but now, at 1:15 p.m., I'd come to the end of my restraint.

I knocked, poking my head into his open door, hoping I didn't look as nervous as I felt. "Is now a good time?"

From behind his wooden desk, Paul waved me in, gesturing toward one of the chairs sitting opposite him as he shuffled the sketches he'd been looking through to the side. "Sure is. Take a seat."

The office was bright and spacious but not grand, well appointed but utilitarian. Paul Andrews wasn't one for flash.

Once I was seated, he leaned back in his chair and steepled his fingers at his chin, regarding me for a long moment before he spoke. "Lucia Torres is retiring. Wants to spend time traveling."

That...wasn't what I'd expected to hear. Luce was my department head in the commercial division. She was a great boss and a great architect. The company would miss her, but good for her if she was cashing out to go find some adventure.

I wasn't sure why a heads-up on the org change required a meeting with me. Apparently the reason should have been obvious because Paul was studying me expectantly.

"We're looking to promote her replacement from within. Someone who can bring fresh ideas and energy to the table." I straightened in my seat as the meaning of his words sunk in. "I think it should be you. You're young for the role, but the work you're doing represents the direction we want this department to go. Last weekend was proof enough of that. You're excellent at leading teams, and I'm confident you could grow into the managerial side of things with some mentorship." He grabbed a manila file folder and passed it to me over his desk. "This is a job description and compensation information for the role. Salary range, benefits, bonus structure, including a pretty generous signing— well, in your case, promotion—bonus."

I flipped open the front folder and scanned the compensation page. The numbers were sizable. I could barely believe this was a real conversation we were having. We were talking about more zeroes than I'd ever seen in my life and a whole department to run. It would be a huge leap for my career.

"What do you think? Are you interested in throwing your hat in the ring?"

My head snapped up. "Are you kidding? Of course I am."

"I thought you might be." *Yeah. Understatement.* A smile twitched at the corner of his mouth, but then he sobered. "You're not the only one in the running. Obviously, my opinion carries weight, as does Nancy's— she's behind you too—but the executive team makes these decisions together. You've got to convince them. I'm not going to overturn the will of the group to put my candidate in the role."

Of course he wouldn't. Paul was never the rule-with-an-iron-fist type. He and Nancy believed in the value of a team, and they respected the people they put in place. "Understood. Who else is being considered?"

"It's between you and Brad."

Of fucking course. It took every ounce of self-control I possessed not to react to that. It made sense. That caricature of a human was good at his job—annoyingly so—and he had more years of experience than I did. I had a longer tenure at Andrews and was better-liked by my colleagues, but winning a popularity contest was not going to get me this job.

"What can I do to show them I'm the best choice?"

With what looked like pride, he tapped his desk with his knuckles. "Now *that* is the right question." He stood and walked to the window, hands in his pockets. "The award last Saturday was a huge step in that direction. But what they really need to see from you is leadership and the ability to deal with high-profile projects." He turned to face me. "The city sent us a Request for Proposal last week for a new municipal building and community center downtown. The project is huge, and it's yours. You put together the team, you lead the proposal creation, you pitch it."

Holy shit. This meeting was blowing my mind at every turn. A downtown municipal building? That was a huge opportunity. "I don't even know what to say. Thank you so much."

"It's not a favor. Luce and I agree you've earned the opportunity. You're more than capable. And if you win the bid, you'll not only find yourself with a potentially career-making project, but a very strong case for department head."

I leaned back in my chair, certain I looked shell-shocked because I absolutely was. "No pressure."

He rumbled a laugh and clasped me on the shoulder. "No pressure."

My phone was in my hand as soon as I made it back to my office.

You're about to hate me.

VI

Why?

> Because I just had the wildest meeting of my career but I can't tell you about it till I get out of here.

> That's hours from now! You were right. I do hate you.

> Sorry. Couldn't be helped. I was going to explode if I didn't talk about it.

> I'm not sure this counts as talking about it, but if it kept you from spontaneous combustion so be it. Call me as soon as you leave! And it better be good news.

> I think it could be great news.

I spread the contents of the manila folder across my desk and pored over every detail. There was more than enough to get excited about here—leading this project, a chance to run the department, a significant pay increase. It was everything I'd been working toward. But my eyes kept drifting back to a single line item: *Signing Bonus*.

This was the answer to my problem. If I could land this job, that bonus would more than pay for the repairs on the house. Mom, Lauren, and Tabitha would be taken care of. This was my chance to fix the whole mess for them, and I wouldn't let them down.

———

It was a perfect Saturday to be at the park. The sky was bright blue and filled with puffy clouds. The temperature was mild. Well maybe not *mild*, but it didn't burn like the pit of hell, and at this time of year, that was really all you could ask for. We even had a light breeze working. It rustled Violet's skirt around her legs as we sat our picnic supplies down.

Her sundress was white with tiny white flowers stitched into the fabric. It tied behind her neck, hugged her breasts and stomach, then floated away from her hips, ending above her knees. Apparently I was noticing all of her dresses now, and I had no idea what to do with that fact.

I spread our blanket, claiming our favorite spot at Butler Metro. Situated on the edge of one of the lawns, it was away from the thick of the action but still had a view of Lady Bird Lake and downtown Austin. We spread our blanket next to a thick copse of trees, where we could count on shade till mid-afternoon.

"So have you designed Austin's newest addition yet?" She pulled out our books and the little round pillow she brought for her head while I grabbed water for us both from the cooler.

"Not quite. Just studying the request for now. Making notes. There's a project briefing meeting in a couple of weeks where we'll get more information. I'll really be able to dig in then."

"You mean to tell me you have no initial sketches?" She nudged me as we settled into our spots.

She knew me too well. I had a pile of sketches a dozen deep already. "Maybe a few."

Her hum was knowing as she pulled a hair tie off her wrist and piled her hair into a curly bun on top of her head. My eyes traced the constellation of newly uncovered freckles trailing down her neck to the curve of her shoulder—

Really, man?

This—whatever this infatuation with her was—was supposed to be an anomaly. One night of stress-induced attraction at the banquet. But here we were in the light of day, and I was mapping her freckles.

Maybe I needed to get laid. I hadn't had sex in months, not since Liz and I broke up. I wasn't pining or anything. We were only together a few months, and she was great, but it became clear to both of us that there wasn't really a future there, and we parted as friends. It was nothing that should've kept me in an extended dry spell. But I hadn't been able to find much interest in anyone since.

Until now. And I needed to snap the hell out of it.

"So…speaking of projects, I have news." The tension in her voice had me immediately on high alert. It didn't necessarily sound like a Bad News intro, but it was definitely serious.

"What's up?"

"It's big news. Well, maybe it's big, but also maybe it's nothing. Right now, it's exactly nothing. So you have to promise not to make a big deal. Because it may or may not even materialize into something, so we don't need to put the cart before the horse."

I laid a hand on her knee. "Vi."

"I know." She took a deep breath and sat up straighter. "I'm applying for a writing fellowship."

"Seriously? That's amazing!" I was shocked in the best way. I'd been after her forever to do something like this, but she'd always seemed completely closed to the idea. "I have a thousand questions. What's the program? How does it work? How did you find it? When do you start?"

"I don't yet. I haven't even submitted my application, much less been accepted. Which is why I didn't want you to make a big deal."

"It's a huge deal!"

"You have made my case."

I lifted my hands in surrender. "Fine. I'll rein it in. But I still want details."

A smile pulled at her lips. "It's amazing. I found it online while I was rage-searching how to become a novelist."

"Nice. Gemma?"

"Who else? Anyway, it's super intensive. But the learning and networking opportunities are unbelievable…"

She gushed about the details, but my brain snagged on "six months" and "Boston." That was a lot of time and a lot of miles, and I didn't like the sound of it…or the vaguely sick feeling settling in my gut.

But the way her face lit up as she talked about it had me pushing that aside.

Of course I loved this for her. Seeing her excited and speaking with authority—it reminded me of the Vi I met in college. She was self-assured back then, ready to take on the world with her quiet confidence. But being sick for so long had done a number on her. At some point, she lost faith in herself—stopped taking risks or pushing for the things she wanted. And I got it. It was part self-preservation, part energy management. She had bigger problems to worry about. But at least some of it was that she felt smaller than she once had, and that was the part I hated.

Now she was looking at me with a glint in her eye I recognized. She was inspired. And I would do everything in my power to help her hold on to it. Even if the thought of her going opened a pit in my stomach.

"It sounds awesome."

"Doesn't it? They only host it every other year. It's crazy competitive, so I probably won't even get in."

I grabbed her hand, a tingle racing across my skin where we touched. "Of course you'll get in. You're brilliant."

Her answering smile was blinding, triggering that now-familiar tightening in my chest, but this time it was accompanied by an overwhelming urge to lean in and capture her smile with my mouth.

Violet's lips were full, but her mouth was narrow, so when her lips parted in surprise, they formed an almost perfect O. But they weren't parted in surprise now. They were stretched with happiness. Happiness I wanted to taste.

Fueled by desire and idiocy, I leaned in.

She gasped and froze, eyes wide with alarm.

Oh shit. What did I just do? "Vi?"

She looked down, grasping at her top. "Oh my god. No! Get out! Get out!"

"Of course. I'm—" *Wait.* She wasn't even looking at me. I had no clue what was going on, but it didn't seem connected to my lapse in judgment. Whatever it was, her distress was growing by the second. "Violet. What's wrong?" I reached out to her, but she was already gone, scrambling away and disappearing behind a group of bushes.

What in the hell…?

Her panicked voice reached me a moment later with a call for help, and I was up and moving like my ass was on fire.

I turned the corner around the bushes and skidded to a stop in front of her. Her face had gone pale, her eyes wide as saucers. In her hands by her neck were the untied straps from her top. She spoke in a rush. "There's a bee in my dress, and it won't come out."

"A what?" Her undone top was not helping my effort to make sense of the situation.

"A bee! You have to get it out." She spun and gave me her back. "Unzip! Unzip!"

Without another thought, I did as I was told, reaching for her zipper and pulling it down with one quick tug. While her dress fell open from her shoulder blades to her hips, she held her top slightly away from her body, trying to encourage the insect invader to escape. One or the other might have preserved some coverage but together, Violet was effectively topless in front of me…and I could see *everything*.

My eyes scraped across her bare skin. Those captivating freckles dusting her shoulders. The column of her spine. The soft dip of her waist. The curve of her perfect, perky breasts leading to…

Holy lord, what are those?

Over her nipples were…stickers, I guess? They were pale pink and looked like lacy little hearts and were so fucking sexy I nearly choked on my tongue. I could not understand why boob stickers covering the part I so desperately wanted to see were doing it for me, but here we were. Blood rushed south, making my dick swell.

She is in crisis, you asshole. Do not get a boner. Do not get a boner. Do not get a boner.

The lack of blood to my brain was making me lightheaded. I was now a fall risk with an inappropriate erection.

"It's not leaving." Her rising panic snapped me back to my senses, and I tore my gaze away from the feast of things I had absolutely no business looking at.

The little bastard did not want to vacate her top—not that I could blame him. He was going to have to be forcibly removed, and as her hands were still full keeping her effective nudity from becoming complete nudity, it was on me to fish this bee out of her dress without condemning myself to hell in the process.

Should be fine.

I screwed my eyes shut and slid my hand into her open dress, skimming it around her ribs to the front where the bee was holing up. My thumb grazed the bottom of her breast.

Do not think about how perfectly it would fill your palm.

Yeah. That was going to go about as well as *do not get a boner*. Spoiler: I had a boner.

A flutter by my fingers prompted me to cup my hand, and I swiped, sending the culprit flying out of the side of her dress. Violet squeaked, and the bee buzzed away as we fell into silence. A flush spread across her skin, and I swore to myself I would not think about it later.

"Are you…uh…are you okay? Did it sting you?"

Her voice was as shaky as I felt. "No. I don't think so."

"Good." Zipping her up with efficient strokes, I forced lightness into my voice. "Great. Don't see how he was in there that long without stinging you…so…yeah…that's great. You should be all set here. I'll let you…uh…adjust."

Then like an absolute coward, I fled before she could see the tent I was pitching.

By the time she returned to our blanket, I'd calmed down—not completely, but enough to be able to hide it at least. She sat down beside me.

"Well. That was an adventure." She cleared her throat with lingering embarrassment, so I did my best to ease it.

"What are friends for if not bee rescue missions?"

Her nose scrunched. "I guess. But I'm sorry you had to…"

"No worries. Seriously. It's not a big deal." And it wasn't. My rogue attraction to her aside, she needed help, and I'd helped her—nothing she needed to be embarrassed about. "We're adults, Vi. What's a little skin when your life is on the line?"

She laughed, tension cracking and falling away, as she leaned in to nudge my arm with hers.

Relief rolled through me at the gesture. "But really, you're okay?"

"Yes. Sting-free and put back together."

"Good. Now let's get you out of here before the murder hornets show up."

CHAPTER 5

VIOLET

With the windows down, the music up, and Evan singing at the top of his lungs, stress melted off of me with every mile we put behind us. Body stress, work stress, fellowship application stress—none of it could touch me this weekend. The lake house may have been only forty minutes outside of town, but it felt like another world, and I was more than ready to escape to it.

We turned onto the private drive and spotted the house lit up like a beacon, white stucco facade glowing in the late afternoon sun. It was a sprawling villa right on the Lake Travis waterfront with a terracotta tile roof, arched windows, and an enormous wooden front door. Grand would have been an understatement.

Gravel crunched under our tires as we rolled to a stop. Climbing out of the passenger side of Evan's 4Runner, I stretched, taking a lungful of air and drinking in the scents of cedar and water as he pulled our things from the trunk. Bags in hand, we climbed the front steps, greeted by the muffled sounds of music and laughter.

"Definitely sounds like they waited for us." I opened the front door, maneuvering my suitcase to the side and holding it for Evan who was managing our cooler in addition to his bag.

With five bedrooms, a resort-style pool, chef's kitchen, and bathtubs big enough to sail in, this place was a level of luxury I could've scarcely imagined where I came from. The first time Lina brought us, I was scared to touch anything, nervous to even be taking up space where I clearly didn't belong. But those fears melted quickly in the face of her family's hospitality. Now, after years of vacations and long weekends and holidays, stepping over this threshold evoked a sense of coming home.

"When has Lina ever waited for anyone?" He hauled our cargo through the entry and into the great room. Decorated to reflect its hacienda-style architecture, the house was brimming with warmth and whimsy—bold colors, painted pottery, vibrant tile work, rich textiles. They made this outrageously fancy place feel casual and homey.

"You're heeeere!" Lina threw her arms open and hopped off her stool. Even dressed for the lake she was effortlessly fashionable, with some kind of magical glamour that originated directly from her rather than anything she put on. She was as brassy as she was beautiful, which was saying a lot—since her deep brown eyes, striking features, and killer curves basically made her a modern-day, sable-haired Venus. "Come get a drink. You need to catch up."

Never let it be said that Lina didn't have her priorities in order. She may not have waited for anyone, but she wasn't about to leave someone behind.

"I just walked in the door. Can I at least say hello to everyone first?"

Jamie bumped Lina out of the way and wrapped me in a hug. "Was traffic bad? I was worried you were going to get stuck."

"No. It really wasn't. I think we barely beat the rush."

"And thank god for that. We've been waiting on you to hit the pool. Go get changed." Lina smacked my bottom in encouragement.

"You have a bee in your bonnet today—more than usual."

"The weekend, Vi. It calls to me. I need us all in the pool with drinks in hand, or I'll never be at peace."

"Lord." Jamie rolled her eyes. The direct inverse of Lina, Jamie's look was more storybook princess, soft and sweet with blonde hair, blue eyes, and fairer skin. But she had a spine of steel and a sharp wit underneath. If Lina broadcasted her brass, Jamie's snuck up on you like a fairytale ninja. I adored them both. "Let's move it along before she devolves into a Shakespearean tragedy. Evan and Violet, y'all go get changed and unpacked. We'll unload your cooler." She nudged Nico and he dutifully relieved Evan of the cooler in question. "Rem, you go get the grill started. I'm already getting hungry." He gave one firm nod. "Lina, you're in charge of those drinks you need everyone to have." With a very enthusiastic yes, she headed toward the booze.

Within seconds, everyone had been dispatched on their respective assignments.

Behold, the power of a second-grade teacher.

———

As I tossed my bottle of sunscreen to Evan, I had to admit, Lina was right. Life was better now that we were all by the pool with drinks in hand.

She, Nico, and Jamie were already in the water. Remy was finishing prep in the outdoor kitchen. And Evan and I were putting our things down by the loungers under giant striped umbrellas.

I took a sip of my beer and sat it on the table, then turned to find Evan standing in exactly the same spot, staring down at the bottle of sunscreen in his hand like he'd never seen one before.

"Can you help me with that?"

He flinched, snapped back from whatever tangent his mind had been off on. "Yeah. Yep. Of course." He dipped his chin toward the lounger. "Take a seat."

I sat and he settled in behind me, squirting the lotion onto his hands and running them over the tops of my shoulders. There was a tension in his movements as he worked the lotion into the skin of my neck and upper back. They were firm and precise. Efficient. Not rough, but certainly not gentle. The whole thing felt a little strange, especially since he was also unusually quiet.

He cleared his throat.

"You okay?" I looked back over my shoulder but, behind his sunglasses, his eyes were unreadable.

"Just a scratch in my throat."

"Oh. Do you need a drink?" I reached for my bottle, leaning back and over him to reach the table.

"No! I mean, no need. My hands are dirty. I'll get some when I'm finished."

Okay…

As I straightened to face the pool again, his hands returned, skimming over my shoulder blades and then drifting lower where they slipped under the back string of my top. A tingle raced down my spine and reflexively, stupidly, *noticeably*, I sucked in a breath. He froze.

Oh god. Keep it in your pants, Violet. You cannot ask him to put on your sunscreen and then make it weird.

I took a deep, steadying breath. "I love the way this sunscreen smells." *Good save?*

Another throat clear. But his hands started moving again. "It's nice."

"It's new. I—"

"All done." He patted my shoulder twice and stood, dropping the bottle to the chair. "You've got it from here, right?"

"Uh. Sure. Of course." I turned to talk to him, but he was already walking past me toward the pool.

Damn. What was I doing? I hadn't indulged this ridiculous crush in years.

We met our freshman year during a hallway bowling incident (a game that involves a stack of empty beer cans, a densely packed ball of aluminum foil, and none of the protective gear that combination necessitates). We connected immediately, but we were both seeing other people, so our relationship was forged squarely in the friend zone. When my romantic entanglement imploded a few months later, feelings for him crept in, and by the end of that first year, I was pining.

But by then he was also my best friend in the world—far too important to me to jeopardize over a crush—so I put a stop to it. I resolved to snuff out my infatuation, and I was successful. (Mostly.) I tucked away my romantic feelings. (Mostly.) And even when he and his girlfriend broke up the following year, I didn't get sucked in to fantasies that he'd see what he'd been missing all along and declare his love for me at any minute. (Almost entirely.)

In the intervening years, I'd had it under control. He had a string of girlfriends. I had a couple of forays into the dating world that didn't go very well for unrelated reasons. But like the end of that first year, our relationship statuses were irrelevant. We were strictly friends. And it was easiest when I committed to that truth.

Not that I never had those kinds of thoughts about him. They did occasionally surface. But they didn't color my daily interactions with him. They were more like lightning bugs. Tiny flickers that occasionally popped up when the circumstances were just right. Pleasant, but passing.

Only lately, the lightning bugs had multiplied and were threatening a mutiny.

I needed to regain control. I'd boxed up these feelings once. I could do it again.

Folding his long body onto the seat next to me, Remy took a pull of his beer. The quiet stretched—space for me to talk if I wanted.

When Nico first introduced us to Remy, I thought he was brooding or maybe shy. But as it turned out, he wasn't either. He was just quieter, understated.

"I'm good."

He lifted a thick brow, the barest hint of humor in his piercing blue eyes. "Are you sure? You've been sitting with that bottle of sunscreen for a few minutes now. I can give you more alone time with it if you need."

I snorted. "I'm sure. But thank you." *For making me feel better.* How he did it with so few words was a mystery to me, seeing as I couldn't accomplish anything with that low a word count. I waved the sunscreen bottle. "I'm gonna finish with this and let it soak in. I'll swim in a few."

Nodding slowly, he took one more long drink, then stood and headed for the pool.

———

The sky was lit in oranges, pinks, and purples. A breeze rustled the trees and made tiny waves across the surface of the water. In dry clothes and full from dinner, the guys went to smoke cigars around the fire pit while Lina, Jamie, and I lounged by the pool.

Jamie took a giant gulp of her cocktail. "God, I love summer. Don't get me wrong, I love my kids too, but the recharge before the next batch of tiny dictators arrives is necessary."

"It's kind of great that you have a chunk of time off leading up to the wedding. Not having to juggle school in that run-up has to help."

Lina waggled her brows. "She also doesn't have to juggle it in the aftermath."

"What aftermath? It's a wedding, not a natural disaster."

"Please. If there's not aftermath, she's not doing it right...or Nico isn't."

A shocked laugh burst out of me, but Jamie looked like the cat who got the cream as she raised her glass. "To aftermath."

Lina followed with her own glass. "Hear, hear."

I added mine to the group and we clinked.

Jamie settled back into her lounger. "Speaking of aftermath…I'm saving both of your plus-one spots, regardless, but do either of you have dates lined up?"

"Nope." Popping the p, Lina jammed her straw through the ice in her glass. "There are no eligible wedding dates in the greater Austin area. Believe me, I've checked."

Jamie's brow furrowed. "Didn't you have a date last Saturday? The girl with the cute dog in her pictures?"

"Sure did. And I think I would have preferred a date with the dog."

Oh no. She'd been looking forward to that one. She was putting on an unaffected front, but I knew better. "Was it really that bad?"

Her shoulders slumped on a sigh, a tiny crack in her facade. "Not really. But it wasn't good either. She was nice, but she was so timid. I felt like I was bowling her over the whole time." She waved the unpleasantness away. "It's for the best, though. I don't want to have to babysit someone at the wedding. I'm going to party and dance and if I find a cute enough guest, take them back to my room for some fun."

"Well, hopefully there will be a decent pool for you." Lina saluted her with a tip of her glass, and Jamie cut her eyes toward me. "What about you, Vi?"

"Uh. No. I'm happy to fly solo as well. More time to devote to you."

Humming, she nursed her drink. "So my brother's in town. He's going to come hang out with us for a while tomorrow."

"That's great." Jamie talked about her brother a lot. He lived in Houston, so our paths had never intersected. It would be nice to finally meet him and put a face to the name.

She looked at me expectantly, her lip caught in her teeth. "I've been wanting to introduce you…" *Oh…oh nooo.* This was a trap, and I'd walked right into it. "I think you'd really hit it off."

"Ooh, fun. A setup." Lina wiggled in her seat. Easy for her to be excited when she wasn't the one in the crosshairs. Traitor.

This was not a road I was looking to go down. Not with anyone, much less with Jamie's brother. The stakes would be even higher, the fallout even worse. "Jamie…"

"Hear me out." She sat up, sloshing a bit of her drink over the rim, but it wasn't enough to deter her. "He's so great—sweet and smart and handsome…"

"I'm sure he is. Maybe Lina—"

I was not above using my friends as human shields, but my deflection effort was in vain. Lina scoffed a "nice try" while Jamie plowed ahead. "He's not her type. But I know you would get along so well with him."

I had to shut this down. I appreciated her enthusiasm, and the fact that she wanted to set me up with her brother was an honor, but it could not happen. "I'm sure we will, too. As friends. I'm just not interested in anyone. I am romantically unavailable."

Reluctantly and with a healthy serving of disappointment, Jamie gave a small nod of acceptance. She may not like the answer, but she wasn't going to push.

Lina, on the other hand, was fundamentally incapable of not pushing. She turned to face me, elbow planted on the armrest and chin cradled in her palm. "Let's discuss why that is, shall we?"

Out of the frying pan, and into the fire. "It's…not worth it."

Lina's brow arched, her skepticism plain. From my other side, Jamie's voice was soft. "Sometimes it is."

"Yes. Of course it is sometimes." I reached over to squeeze her hand. "You found one of those magical sometimes and I'm so happy for you. But that has not been my experience."

"Is this about Rob?" *Ugh. Gut shot.* Lina had a potent blend of insightfulness and directness—one I found annoying at this very moment. She called it like she saw it…and she saw a lot.

"Who's Rob?"

"A guy she dated our senior year of college that I'd still like to murder, given the chance."

"He was a bad relationship and a bad breakup. And yes, it is about him. But it's not only about him." I tipped my chin, head falling back to the chair. "I have enough to deal with. With everything it takes to manage my body, in addition to work and having a life, I'm full up. I don't have the bandwidth for dating. Spending time and energy sifting through guys like Rob, hoping to find that 'special someone' just… doesn't appeal." I looked back to Jamie. "Even with someone like your brother—who I'm sure is lovely—it doesn't make sense for me to spend so much energy pursuing something that might not work out. I'd rather gain a new friend."

None of that was a lie.

It also wasn't the whole truth. But the whole truth was not something they'd understand. How did you explain to people with functioning bodies what it's like to be a drain on a relationship? That being someone who needs care puts things constantly out of balance? That even people who love you eventually run out of patience? It was impossible.

They would tell me that it wasn't true, but they weren't living it. Ask someone who had—Rob, my parents—and they would give a different answer.

Bottom line? I was not cut out for a relationship. And that was fine. It had taken me a while to get here, to let go of some of the ideas I had about what I wanted. But I'd finally made it. *Moving on.*

I lifted my glass for a much-needed drink and locked eyes with Lina over the rim. Her wheels were turning. Maybe she could sense I wasn't saying everything, or maybe she was discontent with my answer.

Either way, I could tell she was about to pounce when I was miraculously saved by the guys' approach.

"Ladies. Future wife." Nico nodded toward Lina and me then hauled Jamie off her lounger and into his body. He was Mexican-American and had the whole tall, dark, and handsome thing going for him. He deployed it like a weapon at his fiancée, holding her with a wide, charming smile until she threw her arms around his neck and kissed him soundly.

Evan gave me a hand up and lowered his voice. "You good?"

"Yep. Feeling good." And a little like I'd dodged a bullet.

Lifting to her tiptoes, Jamie whispered something in Nico's ear. His eyes widened. "And that's my cue to call it a night."

"And mine. You kids have fun." Remy put his hands up and turned to leave, but Lina shot up from her seat.

"Nobody's going anywhere. We're still hanging out."

"Oh, I am very much going somewhere." Nico threaded his fingers through Jamie's. "As is she."

"It's only like nine o'clock. When did you get old and boring? No offense, Jamie."

"None taken." She shrugged with a good-natured grin.

"I'm sorry. Boring?" Nico's grin was more sinister. Releasing Jamie's hand, he stepped toward Lina, who instinctively edged backward. "Well, we can't have that. You'll help me get back on track, right, Lina?"

He stalked forward, but she kept distance between them. Until she backed into a lounger. She was out of space.

"Oh shit." She spun and planted a foot on the lounger in an attempt to vault herself to safety, but she didn't get far. Dragging her back, Nico hefted her over his broad shoulder like a sack of potatoes and headed for the pool.

Her fists pounded into his back as she shrieked. "Nicolas Gael Castillo, don't you even think about it. I'm wearing real clothes now, you asshole!"

She kicked and flailed, but he didn't miss a step as he dumped her into the pool, cackling when she surfaced on a torrent of profanity.

Catching Jamie's hand on his way by, he hustled her toward the door as she called back over her shoulder. "See you tomorrow, Lina."

"A good friend wouldn't sleep with him now."

"Then I'm probably about to be a really bad friend. Love you!" Jamie blew a kiss as he dragged her over the threshold.

Remy helped Lina from the pool while Evan grabbed her a towel, valiantly keeping their laughter at bay.

"I'm going to murder him."

Rem's mouth twitched. "Out of curiosity, how many times have you threatened to murder Nico in the time you've known him?"

"Good point. It's probably time I start following through."

"Not actually my point."

"At least you didn't have your phone." Plucking it from her lounger, I handed it to her.

Wringing out her hair, she worked the dry towel through it. "Silver linings, I guess. I'm going to go dry my hair again and plot a way to poison Nico's breakfast tamale. Y'all have a good night."

I kissed her cheek. Part farewell, part olive branch. I didn't want her to feel like I was shutting her out. When she squeezed my hand, I knew we were good.

With a shallow tip of his chin toward us, Remy headed inside behind Lina.

Evan and I stood side by side, turning to look over the lake. It was too cloudy tonight to see many stars, but the moon was peeking out enough to cast its faint glow across the water.

"I'm not mad about turning in early tonight. I probably would've done it anyway. Though not with as much flair as the Wonder Twins." Nico and Lina's relationship had a very sibling-like dynamic from the very beginning. They loved and annoyed each other in equal measure.

"She wouldn't know what to do with herself if he stopped giving her shit." Evan chuckled.

"Neither would he."

"So true." He shook his head in amusement.

Tucking my hands into my pockets, I rocked on my heels. "I think I may try to get a little writing done before bed. I'm making good progress."

"That's great." He grinned, draping an arm around my shoulders and tilting his head to rest on top of mine. "I'm really proud of you, ya know."

I turned into his side and wrapped my arms around his waist, grateful the tension between us from earlier seemed to have dissipated. He smelled like cigars and sunscreen and Evan. He smelled like home. "Yeah. I know."

CHAPTER 6

EVAN

I stepped out on the back patio and took the lay of the land. Lake Travis had great running trails, and I always tried to hit at least one when we were out here. I'd spent the morning on a long jog, and by the time I returned, the rest of the group was scattered across the back.

Nico and Remy were playing horseshoes, Lina was on a lounger flipping through a magazine, and Violet was in the pool getting thrown around by...

Who the fuck is this guy?

I had never seen him before in my life, but there he was with his giant arm wrapped around her waist, swinging her through the water while she splashed and flailed. My irritation was immediate and intense and for some reason, hearing her peals of laughter only made it worse. I was at the edge of the pool before I'd made the conscious decision to move.

"Violet." It was more clipped than I intended, and she looked a little stunned as her eyes met mine. I hated that look, hated that I put it there, but that didn't seem to cool the searing itch under my skin or stop the overwhelming urge to get her out of there. "How long have you been in the water? It's full sun out there."

"Oh…Uh…Only a little while, and I'm sunscreened." She was clearly confused by my mood. Well, she could join the damn club. "But yeah…it's probably time for me to find some shade for a while and reapply."

She made her way to the edge, and I pulled her from the water, snagging a towel from her lounger and pushing it into her hands. She searched my eyes and kept her voice low. "What's wrong?"

"Nothing. Just trying to make sure you don't hurt yourself." My tone was only slightly less caustic, and she was not buying my dismissal. Her eyes filled up with a slew of questions I had no answers for, but I was saved from them by Jamie's voice calling my name from the pool.

Has she been in there the whole time?

She waved me over to make introductions. Mr. Pool Fun was her brother, John-but-goes-by-Jack, and he was going to hang out with us for the day.

Jack and Jamie. Cute.

He was a big guy. Tall and muscled. And, yeah, I guess he could be considered attractive, if you were into the professional-athlete-slash-underwear-model look. But he was clearly not Vi's type. I mean, had this guy ever picked up a book? I bet he couldn't even eat ramen. Too many carbs.

He was friendly and smiling, giving me a wave and a "Good to meet ya, man." I gave him a barely there nod and hated him for no discernible reason. I needed a drink.

Confirming that Vi "could totally go for a drink" as well, I got the hell out of there. By the time I made it to the kitchen, it was a little easier to breathe, and by the time I got drink ingredients together, my irritation was receding and coherent thought was making a comeback.

God, I'm an asshole.

This infatuation with Violet was getting out of hand. I mean, obviously "Jack" needed to take three giant steps back. *He barely knows her. Who manhandles someone they barely know?* But that was probably no reason for me to be rude to him, which I was pretty sure I had been. And it was definitely no reason to be a dick to Vi, which I was completely sure I had been.

I couldn't understand why this was getting under my skin so badly. All I knew for sure was that as soon as I saw her body touching his, I lost my damn mind. Everything inside of me was shouting *MINE,* and I couldn't access a single thought beyond that.

I dropped my knife on the cutting board, letting the lime I was about to slice roll away, and braced my hands on the edge of the countertop. I had to get this under control. Ideally, I'd *stop fucking thinking about her that way,* but even I knew that was a lost cause. I'd already been trying to push those thoughts away, and if fighting yet another inappropriate stiffy while I was helping her with sunscreen yesterday and the jealous scene I'd made outside just now were anything to go by, it was getting worse. This was not going to go away, and I didn't know how to handle it, but I needed to quit taking my frustration out on her at the very least.

Doable.

And I should probably be nice to Jamie's stupid brother as well.

Yeah. We'll see how that one goes.

I finished making our drinks and gave myself one final pep talk as I made my way outside. Violet was now situated on her lounger in full sun-avoidance mode. Umbrella. Coverup. Hat. Glasses. As badly as I'd handled it before, my concern for her was real. I'd seen sun exposure cause flares for her, and I was always a little uneasy when she made expeditions out of her shade cave. She was normally good about keeping them short, but sometimes she got frustrated and pushed the limits. I couldn't blame her, and normally I was good about helping her stay safe without breathing down her neck. Just not today, apparently.

"Moscow mule, as requested." I did my best to sound normal, but Vi was skeptical as she took the copper mug from my hand.

"Are you sure you're okay?"

"Absolutely. I think the heat got to me on my jog." *The heat was getting to me all right.* "I just needed to cool down. All good now. Sorry I was weird before."

And that was all it took. She smiled as if I'd given her diamonds instead of a drink, perfectly ready to forgive me and move on like everything was normal. She forgave so easily—too easily if you asked me—and it had gotten her hurt over the years. I never wanted to take advantage of that generosity. Every time she offered that forgiveness to me, it made me want to do better, and today was no exception. I'd figure this out. I'd do better.

The rest of the morning was uneventful. We lounged. We played games. We swam. I found myself sticking close to Violet, but at this point, that couldn't be helped. At least I wasn't acting like a lunatic around her. I was even nice to Mr. Abs who, as it turned out, had a Masters in English Literature, and seriously *why is this guy here again?* Maybe nice was overstating it. But I hadn't told him to fuck off even when he was blatantly flirting with her, so I'd call it a win.

The plan was to have a light lunch and then head out to spend the afternoon on the water. Lina's family had a boat (with ample shade), wakeboards, jet skis, the whole nine. As everyone was rounding up coolers and bags, I found Vi on the couch with a book and crouched in front of her. "Hey. We've gotta get going. Do you need help carrying your stuff?"

"No. I think I'm going to pass on the boat trip today. I'm feeling a little low energy. I think I need to stay here and rest. Maybe catch a nap before dinner."

It wasn't a surprise. This kind of weekend was always a spoons juggling act. Between the travel and the sun and the drinks and lots of engagement, it was energy expenditures and triggers stacked one on top of the other. Even with an earlier night last night, she had to prioritize rest.

I didn't love the idea of leaving her here alone. She didn't say she was feeling bad, but she was not above downplaying to keep from being a problem. If she needed help, I'd ditch the boat in a heartbeat.

"Gotcha. Do you want me to stay too? I can stick around and help you. I don't mind."

"No, no. You go on. I know you've been looking forward to wake-boarding all weekend, and I'm just going to relax. Go and have a great time. I'm good here."

She really did seem okay. So with a little reluctance, I said goodbye and started toward the back to meet the others. Almost out the door, I caught sight of Jack (*no catty nicknames or mental air quotes this time—progress*) in the kitchen. "Hey, man, aren't you coming? Boat's pulling out soon."

"Nope. Gonna stick around here and start prep for dinner."

Vi radiated delighted from her perch on the couch. "Jack offered to take dinner duty from Nico and Jamie and cook for everyone. Isn't that nice?"

Well, I wouldn't have to worry about her being alone. *Fuck.*

"Yeah. That sounds…fantastic."

———

It was the longest five hours of my life. I'd been a goddamn mess on the lake. I could barely stay up on the wakeboard because I saw visions of Violet and "Jack" (*the air quotes were back, and I wasn't sorry*) flash through my mind every thirty seconds. I stalled the motor on the boat twice because I got distracted wondering if he'd asked her out yet. I even sat motionless on a jet ski for five whole minutes thinking about what they'd name their children before Remy came to guide me back in.

My friends, to their credit, gave me space. I think they could sense me unraveling and were worried one wrong word might push me over the edge. They would not have been wrong.

The good news was that with all this time to think, one thing had become crystal clear to me—this was way more than a passing crush. I had feelings for Violet. Whole-ass feelings. How long they had been there waiting for me to recognize them I had no idea, but I sure as shit was recognizing them now.

1. She was my favorite person. She had been for my entire adult life, and she always would be. How could I fall in love with some other woman when I only ever wanted to hang out with her?

2. I wanted to see her naked—fully naked, not bee-removal naked—more than I'd ever wanted anything in my life. Ever.

3. I missed her this afternoon. We were gone for five hours, and I *missed* her. I missed her smile and her laugh and her wrinkled nose. I leaned over to tell her something no less than a dozen times only to realize she wasn't beside me. The lack of Vi made everything worse, which was not just true on the boat but in all of life.

4. I couldn't stop imagining what it would be like if we were together, and I literally felt sick to my stomach imagining her with anyone else.

This wasn't about Jack. Sure, he might have lit a fire under my ass, opened my eyes to some things, but this was not about territory or jealousy. I mean, obviously, I was insanely jealous, but it wasn't *about* that. This was about my very real and very overwhelming feelings for Violet, and they could stand all on their own.

I swear to God, if they became a thing while I was on that stupid lake...

What? What would I do if they'd become a thing while I was on the lake? And maybe more importantly, what would I do if they hadn't? This is where all my revelations came to a screeching halt, because even if I now knew what I was dealing with, I didn't know what the hell to do about it. Realizing you have feelings for your best friend and actually deciding to pursue something with her are very different propositions. I needed more time to figure this out, and ideally, she wouldn't be involved with someone else before I could.

Miraculously, I kept a calm façade as we all poured in the back door. I scanned the living room and kitchen for her, coming up empty. I was less controlled when I broke into a jog down the hallway toward our rooms, nearly running her over as she stepped out her door. She stopped short, stumbling backward, and I grabbed her shoulders to keep her steady.

"Hey. Sorry." My eyes darted past her to her empty room. She was alone. *Thank fuck.* Like she was going to jump into bed with the guy the day she met him? My relief was irrational, but I couldn't help it.

"I heard everyone coming in. Did you have a good time?"

"Yeah. Great. How was your afternoon? Did you get any sleep?"

"I did. Quite a bit, actually. I ended up reading for a few minutes and helping Jack with dinner. Then I came in here and napped."

That wasn't the worst possible answer. I wasn't excited about team cooking, but she wasn't talking like anything happened between them. And the nap was good news. More than anything, I wanted her to be okay. "Sounds like a great afternoon for you too, then. I'm gonna go get cleaned up. Wash the lake off of me."

"Sure. See you in a few?" I nodded, and she floated down the hall to join our friends. For a whole minute, I stood there, listening to her voice carry from the other room. Then I went to take the coldest shower I could stand.

———

Dinner had been delicious—*so disappointing.* It was a full Italian feast. A charcuterie for starters (*but really, is that anything more than a glorified Lunchable?*) followed by a fresh salad and pasta dish with homemade marinara. The guy even made his own gnocchi, for god's sake. They were like fluffy little potato pillows and they were incredible and I hated them. He was clearly compensating for something.

With full stomachs (*I said I hated it, not that I didn't eat it*), we settled into the Adirondack chairs around the fire pit. It was a last-night-at-the-lake-house tradition. We would drink, roast marshmallows, listen to music, and talk late into the night. I had a pile of great memories over the years sitting right here. Tonight would not be making that list.

I sat next to Violet who, of course, sat next to Jack. Jamie was on his other side, curled into Nico's lap. Next was Lina, then Remy, then back to me. There were only six chairs. If he was considerate, Jack would have gone on home rather than taking his sister's seat. To be fair, she didn't seem put out by sharing with her fiancé, but it was the principle of the thing. He didn't give her much of a choice, did he? *Selfish.*

Jack and I were currently engaged in a silent game of Who Can Feed Violet The Most Marshmallows. I'd roasted three for her to his two, but I was pretty certain it was going to end in a draw because he was working on one now and six was usually her limit. He was regaling us with stories of being a high school English teacher—out there doing the good work for little appreciation and even less pay.

What would happen if I jumped in this fire?

"He won Teacher of the Year in his district last year and was voted favorite teacher by his students." Jamie was beaming with pride.

"Not surprising. I mean I'm sure you're good at your job, but have you seen you?" Lina's expression was just short of lascivious. "You've got *hot for teacher* written all over you."

He had the decency to look embarrassed as Jamie leapt to his defense. "Ew! Lina, gross. That is not why he was chosen favorite."

"What? I'm just saying he's hot and charming and I doubt he can turn it off when he's out there shaping young minds. What do you think, Vi?" The question may have been directed at Violet, but Lina was looking directly at me, never even blinking as she poked the hornet's nest. She totally had my number. She wasn't the type to spill my secrets, but she wasn't above stirring the pot.

"I'm sure that's not why he was chosen. I mean, not that he's not crush-worthy!" *Kill me.* "But they probably picked him because he's a great teacher." The perfectly diplomatic answer. So Violet.

"And you're single, right?" Fucking Lina. Change of plans. I was going to kill *her*.

"Yea. Definitely single." Jack cleared his throat as his eyes flickered toward Vi.

Not gonna happen, guy.

Thankfully, Jamie was on the ball with a subject change. "Oh! I meant to tell y'all earlier. Wedding updates. Ladies, we have a dress fitting in two weeks. I'll send you calendar invites. Guys, send Nico your measurements ASAP so we can get the tux order ready. I can give you the name of a tailor to go to if you don't already know them."

Conversation continued around me as the night rolled on. I tried to calm down. I really did. But every time he'd make her laugh, it gutted me. I was spiraling and primed to make bad life choices.

"Damn. I didn't realize how late it was." Mr. Star Teacher checked the time on his phone. "Would you guys mind if I crashed on the couch? I'm getting pretty tired and don't feel great about driving home."

Lina led a chorus of yeses, and dammit, I was not prepared to see this guy again in the morning. As I was about to be carried away on another wave of irritation, inspiration struck.

"Dude. You're huge. That couch would kill you. You need to take a bed." Six heads swiveled my way in unison, as if my expressing concern for him was the biggest shock of their lives. *Come on. I haven't been that bad. I'm a nice guy. Watch.* "You can have mine. I'll just bunk in with Vi."

Jack's eyebrows hit his hairline. He stumbled over words as he looked between Vi and me. But Vi was unfazed. "Oh, that's a great idea! You'll be so much more comfortable in a room."

"Are you sure? I don't want to put anyone out."

"It's no problem. Ev and I do it all the time."

"Ev and I do it all the time." My smugness knew no bounds.

CHAPTER 7

EVAN

I'd made bad life choices.

I was lying in bed next to Violet, something I'd done countless times before, but this time everything was different. I was hyperaware of her body next to me—as intensely as if we were touching. Every soft puff of breath pushing past her parted lips drew me in while the honey scent of her skin, sweet and smooth with a hint of spice, closed around me. I was drowning, my skin crawling with the need to touch her.

How had I not realized I was signing up for a night of unmitigated torture? What had possessed me to think I'd come in here and sleep next to her without my brain launching into a thousand fantasies?

I'm an idiot.

The only positive I could find was that she couldn't hear her skeezy best friend's thoughts while he shared her bed.

I'm an idiot and *an asshole.*

I watched her sleeping peacefully. What would it be like to pull her close to me? To hold her while she dreamed? Muscles tightened at the base of my spine. *That one wasn't even about sex!* Jesus. I was losing it.

I briefly considered getting out of bed, but as torturous as this was, I couldn't bring myself to give it up.

Swallowing a groan, I ground my palms into my eyes. This had to stop. I couldn't remember the last time I felt this out of control. It wasn't sustainable. I needed to figure this out tonight and then move forward tomorrow like a stable human being.

Tonight was all I would give myself to work this out—god knows I wasn't going to be getting any sleep. I had a chunk of quiet, uninterrupted hours ahead of me, and I would use them to get my shit together and make a plan.

Start with what you know.

I had feelings for my best friend. It was unclear to me when those feelings developed. The truth was they didn't feel particularly new. I'd recognized them over the last couple of weeks, but it felt less like starting something new and more like finally paying attention to something that had been there all along.

Memories flashed through my mind.

Getting drunk on cheap champagne and celebrating the start of our careers. Feeling like I had the whole world in front of me and everything I needed to succeed because she was beside me.

Her talking me off a ledge when my dad tore into town and nearly wrecked my sister's wedding. The way her hand on my arm steadied me when I was spiraling in anger and guilt.

Winning that award and realizing her pride in me was the only thing that actually mattered.

The wave of happiness that washed over me every time she walked into a room. Wrapping her in hugs I was never ready to let go of.

Ramen noodles and park days and marshmallows around a fire pit and every single time I was perfectly content in my whole adult life.

It was her. It was *always* her.

How had I missed this? Apparently it took a green dress, a rogue insect, and an annoyingly muscly English teacher for me to finally connect the dots. *Not real proud of that.*

And why now? It's not like I'd never seen her dressed up. To be fair, I'd never partially *undressed* her. But I'd seen her with other guys. We'd slept in the same bed before. Why was it suddenly different?

That, I still had no idea about. But regardless of when or why my feelings changed or how long I'd been oblivious to them, they were here now, and that oblivion wasn't coming back, so the operative question was what to do about it. For better or worse, I wasn't working with a lot of options. It was a binary choice:

1. Stuff the feelings. Proceed as normal.

2. Pursue the possibility of a romantic relationship.

Option 1 was…unappealing. First, there was the fact that I obviously wasn't great at managing these feelings. I was sure that could improve with time, but it was a factor to consider. Then there was the fact that it sounded like a hell of a lot less fun. Not to mention the very thought of burying this made me so sad I was sick to my stomach.

If Option 1 was unappealing, Option 2 was terrifying. This would change everything—my whole life—my whole life that I was pretty happy with. My friendship with Vi was everything to me, and I wasn't sure I was ready to exchange it for a completely new future.

And that was the real issue. Because this wasn't some sort of "our friendship is so important I don't know if I could risk it not working out" situation. If we got together, it would absolutely work out. There wouldn't be a breakup. There was no universe in which we'd go our separate ways. I wouldn't be signing up to date her. I'd be signing up to spend my life with her—marriage, kids, getting old together—the whole damn thing. If Violet and I started something, it would be forever.

My heart rate picked up. In excitement? Fear? *Definitely not fear.*

Contemplating the arc of my entire future was overwhelming, but the thought of a future with Vi was the opposite of scary. It gave me a sense of rightness deep in my gut. I wanted it.

She'd still be my best friend. I'd just get more of her. Get to do every-thing with her as my partner. It sounded incredible, actually. Suddenly, Paul's words from the banquet were echoing in my ears. *"Nothing better in the world than being married to your best friend."* And I knew the bastard was right. There would be nothing better.

If Violet agrees.

My lofty thoughts fell back to Earth. I wasn't the only one in this thing. Where was she on this? Could she possibly have these feelings, too? I'd always had the impression that Vi's feelings for me were strictly platonic. If she didn't have them, could she develop them? If I made a move, what would she do? Jump into my arms and kiss me? Feel blindsided and betrayed, like I broke the rules we'd agreed on years ago? Attempt to let me down gently with a "you're like a brother to me" and a kiss on the cheek? Pull away feeling like we couldn't be close anymore if I had these feelings and she didn't?

This was where all the risk was. Making a move with Violet was like dropping a bomb into our relationship. Maybe when the dust settled, everything would be great, and we could live happily ever after. But maybe I'd kill us. I was pretty sure we'd survive it if her answer was no, but it wasn't a certainty. If I pushed for more, I risked driving her away. The fear of that was paralyzing.

I was no stranger to being left. My dad made sure of that. He was my hero until he decided he didn't want us. I was ten when he walked away, and it crushed me, but I recovered. If Violet walked away? It would make my dad look like a cakewalk. I wasn't sure I'd ever recover.

She's leaving already. You're already losing her.

I was so wrapped up in messy feelings, I'd conveniently forgotten that part. If she went to Boston, it would be over. No way would we still have a chance with her halfway across the country. And there was no way to know where things would stand when she got back. Six months was a long time. She could meet someone while she was gone or decide she wasn't coming home. My window, if I even had one, was closing.

I told her I'd do everything I could to support her dreams, and I meant it. It wasn't like I would try to keep her here against her will. But maybe if we were already together, we could make it long-distance for a while.

The thought sent a wave of dread through me. It would be awful. And even more complicated if things worked out for me with this project and promotion. Six months across the country, especially when we were just getting started…

No. It would be fine. If we were together, we could do it. And she may not even go.

I was getting way ahead of myself. Maybe I should focus on what we both wanted now and cross those bridges when and if we came to them.

Or maybe I should take what she gave me instead of asking for more like a greedy bastard.

I tossed and turned for hours, running the whole thing over and over in my mind, waiting for that lightbulb moment when I'd know exactly what to do.

When morning came, I was no closer to an answer.

I turned on my side to face Violet and my breath caught in my chest. The morning light slanting in from the window made her glow. She was turned toward me with her hands tucked under her chin, her red curls a riot around her face. I took in every detail—eyelashes brushing her cheeks, the faint dusting of freckles across her skin, the way her parted lips formed that sweet little O.

Fucking beautiful.

Her sleepy eyes fluttered open. I could see the moment they brought me into focus because the most contented smile spread across her face.

My chest ached—like she'd reached directly into it and plucked my heart out for herself. With that single smile, I was done. Decision made.

I have to try.

————

I found Nico sitting on the end of the dock, mug in hand, feet dangling in the water, and took up my spot beside him. It was early. There was a breeze blowing in and the sun hadn't yet heated everything to within an inch of its life. The water was still calm, the volume of the world still low. Long minutes passed as we took leisurely sips of our coffee.

"So. You wanna talk about it?" He was the one to finally break the silence.

"About what, exactly?"

He sat down his mug and leaned back, bracing himself on his palms. "Oh, I don't know. What about how you've been a low-key dick to my future brother-in-law? Or maybe how you basically pissed circles around Vi all day yesterday?"

I grimaced and leaned forward, resting my elbows on my knees, and dropping my head into my hands. "Not my best work."

He laughed and clapped his hand on my shoulder. "Tell me what's going on."

Nico was my best friend outside of Violet. We'd seen a lot of shit together, and I was about to be his best man while he married the love of his life. I'd sought him out this morning to have exactly this conversation. His was the advice I needed.

Saying this out loud for the first time had a shot of nerves running through me, but I took a breath and gave him the CliffsNotes. "I have feelings for Violet. I want to be with her. I have no idea if she feels the same way or if she ever could. But I think I have to try to go for it, and I need to you tell me if that's a terrible idea."

I couldn't bring myself to look at him, to see shock or pity or whatever might be on his face.

"Well, it's about damn time."

I reared back, the shock reserved for me, apparently.

"Seriously, man. You've been gone for that girl since we were nineteen."

"And you knew? Why didn't you ever say anything to me?"

"To what end? I've heard you 'we're just friends' that situation a million times over the years. Nothing I said would have shaken that loose for you. No way. You had to figure this one out all on your own, buddy. Though I'll admit it took you longer than I thought it would. If Lina had her way, we'd have staged an intervention years ago."

My head was spinning, trying to process. "You and Lina both? What about Violet? Do you think she feels…"

"Honestly? I think she did at the beginning. Since then? Now? I won't even pretend to know. And I'm not sure I'd tell you if I did. What is or is not between you and Violet is something you two have to figure out."

That made sense. I wasn't trying to hop into some grade school game of telephone with our friends.

"So what finally did it?"

I'd circled back to that question more than once last night with no luck finding an answer, but sitting here with Nico, the puzzle piece finally slid into place. "I think it was you, actually."

That was obviously not the answer he was expecting, but it was the right one. It was the reason I came to talk to him about this. The reason Liz and I broke up shortly after he got engaged. And the reason I was finally seeing things clearly with Vi. I wanted what he had.

"When you and Jamie got engaged, I was so happy for you. But I also started to feel…restless, I guess? Ready to do what you were doing.

Not with just anyone, and not in a getting-older-so-I'd better-settle-down way. I wanted my person the way you have yours."

"So you started looking."

"And realized she was right fucking there." I felt it like a physical blow—the full weight of what I'd overlooked and the fear that I may have missed my chance, if I'd ever had one.

"Damn."

Yeah. Damn.

It was sobering. But I was about to do everything I could to fix it.

"Any thoughts on how you're gonna do it?"

"A million." Truly. Since the moment I'd decided I had to take the chance, I'd been thinking through every possible approach. "I don't think it's a good idea to blindside her—drop this proposition on her lap out of nowhere. I think I need to…woo her."

"*Woo* her?" His eyebrows rose, mocking me, breaking the tension and earning him a swift punch in the arm.

"Yes. Woo her. Romance her. Show her what I want—what it could be. Maybe help her see me that way. Then when I make a move, maybe she's feeling it too—or at the very least doesn't feel like it's out of left field."

"Makes sense."

"It also gives me the chance to feel things out before I take them too far." I massaged the tension collecting in my neck. "Honestly, my biggest fear is she won't want the same things and she'll pull away. That I'll overreach and kill what we have now. I figure this way, I can take baby steps and see how she responds. If I get weird vibes, I'll back off. No need to bet the farm right off."

"For a guy who just pulled his head out of his ass, this sounds like a relatively cogent plan."

"Your confidence is overwhelming."

His smirk fell away, replaced by sincerity as he clasped me on the shoulder once again. "I really do think it's a good approach. And I'm glad you're going for it. She's always been it for you. And I don't know where she's at, but you owe it to yourself to at least see what happens."

My thoughts had been so loud and chaotic for the last twenty-four hours, but finally they were getting quieter, calmer, clearer. I was starting to feel good about this.

"The worst she can do is shoot you down and crush your dreams, right?"

"Really?" We shared a laugh at my expense, and that was fine with me. He'd given me all the help I was hoping for. "I'm sorry about Jack, by the way. I promise I'll fix it."

"No worries, man. I get it. And don't worry about him. He's a chill guy. Not one to hold grudges. Jamie, on the other hand…"

I cringed. "Yeah. I'll apologize to Jamie."

———

This was the official Woo Violet planning session. I'd made it back from the lake house, dropped Vi at home, unpacked, showered, and gotten things ready for the week ahead. Now it was time to get down to business.

I pulled out my chair and took a seat at my desk. I'd made lots of plans of the building and strategic varieties here, but none as monumental as this one. Soft light from my desk lamp illuminated my workspace as I took my moleskin notebook from the drawer, turned to a blank page, and put pen to paper.

Step 1: Text Game. We already texted. And not infrequently. But those conversations were usually short and in service of sharing important information or making plans to see each other. The first step of this whole process was to change that. *Up the frequency. Change the tone. Create more connection.*

Step 2: Pseudo Date. I needed to spark the idea of dating me in her mind. I'd take her somewhere she'd love. Separate it, somehow, from our normal outings. Do low-key date things. But I wouldn't cross lines. *Give her a preview. Don't push too far. Just open the door.*

Step 3: Physical Affection. I was physically affectionate already—with everyone, but especially with Vi—so it's not like that would be a change. What I needed to do was shift those interactions from platonic to romantic. *Let her feel the difference. Don't be creepy.*

Step 4: Little Things. I wanted to do little things to let her know that I saw her, that I was thinking of her, that I want to take care of her. And let's face it, I was basically a Violet Encyclopedia, so I had plenty of material to work with. *Her favorite tea. Something to help her write. Spoil her.*

Step 5: Couple Behavior. If we made it to this point, I'd take her on a real date and stop holding back. Short of kissing or professions of love, I'd do everything I could to show her how I hoped things could be. *No more hiding. Be the couple you wish to see in the world.*

Step 6: Make the Damn Move. And pray she doesn't laugh me out of the room.

I rested my elbows on my desk and tugged on my hair to relieve the tension building in my head. Too bad I didn't have an equivalent for the tension building in my gut. Seeing this plan written down made it more real, and the risks felt more real right along with it. As did the potential pitfalls.

Leading that list was the fact that steps one through four were all strikingly similar to things I already did with her. More evidence that I'd been an idiot, but also a real problem. Making those distinctions would be difficult. But there wasn't another choice—not one where I was happy anyway. Whatever the challenges, whatever the risks, whatever the outcome, I'd be miserable if I didn't at least try.

I flipped my notebook closed and stood. It was the best I could do. I had a plan. Tomorrow, I'd put it into action.

CHAPTER 8
VIOLET

Delete. Delete. Delete. Delete. I held down the key, watching words and paragraphs disappear.

The submission deadline was a week from tomorrow. I'd finished my first draft yesterday and was starting my first editing pass, which came with a predictable deterioration in my outlook. When I drafted, all of my words felt brilliant. When I edited, they suddenly morphed into a pile of steaming, irredeemable garbage. *It's called a creative process, and I'm nailing it.*

I stretched my neck and attempted to release the tension in my chest. This was fine. It's not like it was a work deadline. If I finished, and if I liked what I wrote, I would submit. And if I didn't, it wasn't meant to be. No harm done.

My email pinged and I clicked over to my inbox. Another dressing-down from Gemma. Lovely.

That tension in my chest turned to fire as I read. She was tearing into me about a client who had been perfectly happy with my work but had complaints about her handling of the billing. It fell squarely in her realm of responsibility but was still somehow completely my fault.

Nothing like simmering indignation for fueling motivation.

I flipped back to my draft with renewed determination. I would finish. And it would be good. And I would submit this application. Because I wanted to, but also because staying where I was was becoming untenable. A perfect off-ramp was presenting itself, and I would not let it pass me by.

My phone buzzed on the table, my mom's name illuminating the screen. The predictable chain reaction of emotion followed—subtle dread topped off with pronounced guilt for the dread portion. I loved my mother. And I knew she loved me. But our relationship was so filled to the brim with expectation and obligation and trepidation that it didn't leave room for much else.

I wasn't keen on wading into those waters at the moment, but I'd been avoiding her for a week, and I couldn't put it off any longer without causing bigger problems.

Taking a sip of tea for fortification, I accepted the call.

"Hey, Mom."

"Violet. I haven't heard from you in days. You've had me worried sick."

"I'm fine. I've just been busy. We were at the lake last weekend, remember? And I've been trying to catch up on things since I've been home."

"Oh. Well, all right. But are you sure you're feeling okay? You're not overextending, are you?"

This was a constant refrain. She meant well. She wanted to protect me. But she hovered relentlessly even from six hours away. Truly, it was expert-level stuff. She was certain I couldn't take care of myself, so she was constantly on alert, a level of diligence that was exhausting for us both. I know it pushed her to a breaking point when I was a young teen. I overheard more than one late-night conversation that confirmed it. But even now that I was approaching thirty and lived hours away, she couldn't seem to let go of the burden.

"I'm not overextending. In fact, I've had time for an exciting project." I needed to tell her about the fellowship eventually, and it seemed best to give her as much time as possible with the news so she could adjust. Now was as good a time as any. "I've been doing some writing…"

It landed with a thud, causing a blanket of uncomfortable silence to unfurl over us. I knew that when she found words, they would not be encouraging.

"That sounds like overextending."

"Mom. It's not. I love it, and it's good for me. And actually—"

"Fine. Fine. As long as it's not getting in the way of your work. You're lucky to have Gemma and that job. She gives you so much flexibility. Lord knows what you'd do without it. You've gotta protect it. Piddle with the writing if you must, but don't let your hobby put your job at risk."

I pinched the bridge of my nose. I wanted to push back, tell her she was wrong. But it wouldn't matter. She saw this job as my lifeline. And I couldn't blame her. I'd told myself much the same countless times. A little part of me still wondered if she was right, but I was drowning that little part out bit by bit, choosing to believe that I could have more. But it was enough work to drum that belief up for myself. I didn't have it in me to drag her along. At least not yet.

Telling her about the fellowship was going to be an even bigger fight than the mention of a writing project. And if I didn't get selected, it would be a fight for nothing. Maybe it would be better to wait and see if anything materialized before opening that can of worms, adjustment period be damned.

"Speaking of work, I have a deadline, so I should probably get back to it." Whose deadline and for what project would remain undisclosed.

"Oh well, I won't keep you, then. Take care of yourself, honey. I love you."

I said goodbye and disconnected the blessedly short call to find a notification waiting.

EVAN

> Hey. How was your day?

I smiled at his mother-hen tendencies. His fretting felt distinctly different from my mother's, and it helped my mood considerably.

He'd texted to check on me every day this week. I could understand his concern given the taxing weekend—I'd been a little concerned about it myself—but, thankfully, it was unnecessary.

> I'm feeling good! I promise. You can stop worrying. 😉

> I'm not worried. I assume you'd tell me if I needed to be. I just want to talk to you.

> That ok?

Oh. A single pesky lightning bug flickered in my belly. I mentally batted it away. *You're his best friend. Him wanting to talk to you is normal.*

> Of course!

> And my day was good. I sent notes to a client and got some writing done. Now I've got a bowl of cereal calling my name.

> Dinner of champions.

> I've got a sandwich queued up myself.

> Ohhh. Fancy sandwich or sad sandwich?

> Just because a sandwich doesn't meet "fancy sandwich" standards doesn't make it sad.

> Awwww. Your sandwich is sad.

> My sandwich is solidly medium thank you.

Fine. It's sad. And I'm eating it with Funyuns and a beer over the sink. Happy?

Delighted, actually.

I live to serve.

I stood and stretched, padding into the kitchen and collecting a bowl and spoon. Between the Gemma, Mom, and now Evan diversions, I was far out of the editing flow. I might as well eat before diving back in.

I just heard another refrain of "you could never live without your job and the generosity of your boss who has deigned to give it to you" from my mother. So…that was fun.

His typing bubble popped up immediately. Then disappeared. Then flashed on and off again. I could feel his frustration in those blinking dots. He would try to be diplomatic about it, but he hated it when she did this stuff. I had to admit, it was nice to have someone who could be counted on to be outraged on your behalf. I poured my cereal and milk while I watched the bubble cycle three more times before a message finally came through.

She's wrong. You know that right? Gemma is lucky to have YOU not the other way around.

I wanted to curl up in those words. When he said them, it made them easier to believe.

Yeah. I do. Or I'm starting to.

You don't need that job. You can do anything. You already are.

If my mom could make me feel small from miles away, Evan could do the opposite. He didn't even have to be in the same room to make me feel like the biggest me.

> Thank you.

> But now I have to go because my cereal is getting soggy.

> Sad cereal. Can't have that.

> Hang out Saturday?

> Sounds great.

———

We were playing twenty questions. Only instead of twenty questions, I'd asked about a million.

We'd gone downtown for brunch, but Evan wouldn't tell me where we were heading next. I was trying to suss out the location via this game, but instead of answering the questions, he smiled and said "no comment" to each and every one. It wasn't going well.

Over migas and micheladas, my queries had gotten more and more outlandish—*Are we leaving the country? Are we committing a crime?*—and by the time we were walking toward our mystery destination, they'd veered into truly preposterous.

"Are lions involved in any way?"

"I…don't think so?"

"Of all of the questions I've asked, *that* was the one you chose to answer? Also, you don't *think* lions are involved? Which means they might be?"

His mouth hitched. "No comment."

Despite his evasions, or more likely because of them, this little outing was getting more and more exciting. He'd never done this kind of thing. Hangouts, obviously yes, but mysterious adventures, definitely not. It was fun. And I was already considering what kind of secret field trip I could plan for him.

As we made our way over a bridge, I was grateful I'd chosen a flowing sundress for today. July was coming on strong, and while we wouldn't hit the height of the Texas summer heat for another month yet, it was already plenty toasty for my liking. A sheen of sweat made my skin feel sticky, a few curls escaping to cling to the back of my neck.

"You should know that if you plan on walking me too much further, I'll dissolve into a puddle before we arrive, and you'll have only yourself to blame."

"Well then, it's a good thing we're here."

Evan veered us toward a large stone and glass building—one I was very familiar with. Evan loved it because of the interesting architecture. I loved it because it was full of books.

"We're going to the library?"

"We're going to the library." He opened the door and nodded for me to step inside. "Come on."

The blast of AC as we entered was a relief. "I'm always here for a library day, but I think you may have been overselling things with the secrecy."

"Maybe." But he looked smug. He had to have something more up his sleeve. He led us further inside, a One Dimple Smile peeking out as he glanced at me over his shoulder.

Light poured into the six-story atrium as a giant red grackle clock swayed silently on the wall. The scent of books and coffee mingled in the air. I started toward the stairs, our usual direction, but Evan kept us moving to the other end of the lobby, bringing us to a stop outside the public gallery area. He pointed toward a sign.

The Great American Author: early editions and artifacts from the authors that shaped the nation.

My smile bloomed as I read, stretching far beyond the reasonable bounds of my face. I turned toward Evan who was watching for my reaction. "Not overselling it."

"Yeah?" He looked supremely pleased with himself and it was well deserved.

"This is unbelievably cool."

"I thought you'd like it. It starts here, but there's more spread throughout the library."

I bit my lip and bounced on my toes, earning an indulgent laugh.

"Let's get going before you burst." He extended his hand, which I took without hesitation, and led me into the gallery. The large white room with wood floors and picture windows was flooded with natural light. Donning the walls and cocooned in plexiglass cases throughout the room were dozens of treasures I itched to investigate.

My excitement pulled me toward every display at once and I stalled, so overwhelmed I didn't even know where to begin. Coming to a stop beside me, Evan waited for me to choose a direction, but he must have gathered that I was stuck because he chuckled under his breath and guided me toward a starting point.

We landed in front of a collection of sketches by Harper Lee, a series of Shakespearian caricatures she drew in her younger days, along with clippings from the column she wrote for her college newspaper.

It was surreal to see her in this light. Harper Lee, Pulitzer Prize-winning author, a young woman who doodled and wrote cutting essays. Legendary—and thoroughly human.

I moved to the next piece and the next, methodically making my way through the room. I couldn't bear the idea of missing a single thing. Evan let me set the pace, happy to tag along while I geeked out on repeat.

I ogled first editions of The Great Gatsby and Little Women, Toni Morrison's day planners with outlines of Song of Solomon scribbled in the margins. I tried to memorize a recipe handwritten by Emily Dickinson that was displayed with a collection of her manuscripts. It wasn't until I was standing in front of Ernest Hemingway's typewriter that I realized Evan had never released my hand.

My heart thudded once in my chest, and I felt my cheeks heat.

Damn redhead blush. And damn this stupid crush while I'm at it.

I pulled my hand away, pointing to the next case over as a cover, and he released me easily, completely unfazed. I was sure he didn't even notice we were linked, much less that I'd severed the connection. I was the only one obsessing about contact type and duration here, and I very much needed to get over myself.

I threw myself into the exhibit. We finished perusing the items in the gallery and moved on to those scattered through the rest of the library.

The significance of this collection was staggering, and it made me feel insignificant by comparison. With their words, these authors had changed the world. The rest of us were scribbling.

But as I moved from Langston Hughes's letters to Mark Twain's pen, I recognized something else here as well. Scrawled notes. Early drafts. Paper and pens and keyboards. Writing debris, familiar and benign. I recognized the tools and trash, because I worked on the same craft. Not that I would ever be in an exhibit like this one, nor was I trying to be. But what I did was the same more than it was different. Suddenly, in this of all places, I felt a little less like an imposter.

A warm hand pressed into my lower back as I blinked back unexpected tears. "You okay over here?"

"Yeah. I'm just really happy you brought me."

He turned me toward him, searching my eyes. "I'm happy it made you happy."

His touch was so gentle, his voice so tender. Without my permission, my body swayed into his. Something flared behind his eyes as they held mine for a long second. A breath got trapped in my lungs, my heart taking off at a sprint.

This felt like *something* to me. And with his gaze locked on mine, it was so tempting to believe that he felt that something too.

I closed my eyes for a moment, an attempt to ground myself to reality, and when I opened them, he was gone, moving forward and talking about the item nestled in the next case. Unbothered as ever.

Lightning bugs are not contagious, Violet. It's still just you.

CHAPTER 9

EVAN

I sifted through my pile of notes after the project briefing with Lucia. If I wasn't already excited about this project, that meeting would have done it. It was better than I'd even imagined.

The city wanted to do something special. Create not only a functional space, but a landmark. It was a dream. The kind of building you got into the business to design but most never got the chance to. From specs alone, it would have been significant enough for me to feel some pressure. Add to that the career-making level of visibility, the department-head stakes, and the fact that my family's home depended on it, and it was still a dream, but it was also approaching terrifying.

Nothing I couldn't handle. I'd always worked well under pressure. And I'd damn well need to if I was going to nail this pitch.

I pushed aside the pinch of anxiety and tried to focus on my excitement. It would be a better motivator, and fortunately, I had plenty. My head was already flooded with ideas.

I pulled up the worksheet I used to organize myself at the start of each design. It's where I'd combine the details from the dossier I'd been given, the notes I'd taken in the briefing, and my initial thoughts into what would become my bible for the project.

I loved the creative side of my job, but I may have loved this side even more. Architecture required meticulous planning, and for as long as I could remember, planning had made me feel settled and in control.

I lost myself in the work, and the remaining tension in my shoulders eased as I pieced together a plan.

My phone buzzing on my desk broke me out of my tunnel vision. Lauren. The fact that it was a phone call and not a text meant it was a safe bet there was a problem. I swiped at the bottom of the screen to answer.

"Hey. Everything okay?"

"Oh, thank god you answered. No. Not really. I'm stuck at the hospital. Tabitha needs to be picked up from daycare in thirty minutes and Mom is in one of her volunteer meetings and I can't get in touch with her. Is there any way you could get her?"

I looked at the clock—5:30. I still had a lot to get done on this before tomorrow, but I could work on it from home later.

"Of course. I'll leave right now."

"She'll need dinner."

"I'll feed her."

"I may be late. I could try to get Mom to come by—"

"Don't worry about it. I'll lay her down, and you can get her whenever you get off." I wouldn't likely get any work done while she was still up. Five-year-olds weren't great for productivity. But I could get back to it once I put her down. It would be a stretch to prepare for my meetings tomorrow, but there was nothing more important than showing up for my people. It was a no-brainer.

"Thank you. I'll text you later. I'm getting a page—"

"You go. Love you."

———

A small human with a bouncing ponytail and two missing teeth barreled toward me.

"Uncle Evan!"

I scooped her up into a spinning hug. She smelled like crayons.

Damn, I loved this kid.

I had three nieces and nephews. Two, Mia and Dylan, belonged to my oldest sister Taylor and her husband Adam. They lived in Dallas. I saw them a few times a year, and of course, I loved them like crazy, too. But it wasn't the same as my relationship with Tabbie.

Lauren had been single-momming it from the start with her. The guy wanted nothing to do with them—talk about history repeating. I hated that for my sister, but she wanted the pregnancy and had the best single mom role model and support system you could ask for, so she decided to do it without him.

With no dad and no grandpa around, I was the only man in Tabbie's life, and I took that job very seriously. I'd make sure she could always count on me.

I kissed her head. "How was your day, kiddo?"

"Good. I drew three pictures of horses and made friendship bracelets." She still had that little kid lisp. I never wanted her to grow out of it.

"Sounds awesome. Mom's stuck at work, so you're spending the evening with me. Cool?"

"Yeah. Let's blow this popsicle stand."

She was a trip.

We got loaded up in the car. I'd already pulled her booster seat from my trunk, so it was just a matter of strapping her in, making sure all of her bags made it into the vehicle, and buckling up myself.

I adjusted the rearview mirror to see her. "What are you feeling for dinner? Happy meal? Pizza?"

"Steak."

"Steak?" What five-year-old requests a steak dinner?

"Yeah. Grammy made it last week, and it was the best thing I ever ate."

I turned and looked over my shoulder at her. "Challenge accepted." My mom was an excellent cook. I was less competent, but I could out-grill her. Not that my niece's palate should be the defining metric, but she'd get a kick out of playing judge.

"Yay!"

"But I don't have any steaks at home, so we have to run by the store to grab them. Okay?"

"Let's pick out a good one."

With a nod, I started the car.

————

I didn't know if she'd become a connoisseur in the past week or if she was going by the price tags, but Tabitha managed to pick out a decent cut.

"We've gotta have a side, too. I can't just sit you down with a steak the size of your head."

"Scallop potatoes."

Scalloped potatoes were well beyond my capacity. "How about Kraft mac and cheese?"

"Deal."

I turned the cart down the boxed foods aisle. "Okay. Your turn."

She put her pointer finger to her chin and furrowed her little brow. "Hmm. Got one! If you could only have one dessert ever again for your whole life, what would you pick?"

"Ooh. Tough one." I put on an exaggerated show of considering my answer. "I would have to say...Grammy's chocolate cake." Her favorite.

"Yes!" She threw out her arms, head tipped back and eyes closed like she was ready for that cake to fall right out of the sky and onto her lap.

I put the boxed macaroni in the cart. "Here's a good one. If you found a genie lamp, and he gave you three wishes, what would they be?"

"Easy."

"You can't ask for more wishes. That's against the rules."

"I don't need more wishes. I'll wish for a genie potion to make more genies."

I laughed. I didn't often have to do fake laughs for her benefit. She got me for real more than enough. "Very clever."

She smiled proudly, showing off those missing teeth.

My phone buzzed in my pocket.

VI

This. Fucking. Day. It's going to kill me, I just know it. Remember me. Tell my story.

"Hey, hold up, Tabbie." I pulled us out of the way to respond.

You can count on me. What's going on?

Work is a mess. I still have more to do. And I have a pile of editing to get done on my story before the submission deadline tomorrow. I'm going to be up all night.

This was a flashing neon sign for Step 4.

Step One was solid. The texts had been flowing almost constantly between us. They were fun, and they made me feel closer to her. I hoped the effect was the same on her end.

Step Two had been a resounding success. She loved the author exhibit and it obviously meant something to her. The whole day together was great.

I was less sure about Step Three. I'd always suspected it would be tricky, and that was proving to be true. I'd been able to sprinkle some of that physical contact in during the Step Two Outing, but I didn't want to move too fast, so I tried to keep it subtle. Maybe I kept it too subtle. I'm not sure she even noticed. At any rate, that step was still evolving.

Step Four was all about doing things to show her I was thinking of her, and this was a perfect opportunity. Not to mention that getting to be the one to take care of her on a bad day pushed all my buttons—in the best way.

I looked down at Tabitha, who was playing with the beads on her bracelet and humming something unintelligible.

Ideally, the opportunity would have come on a night I didn't have uncle duty and a stack of work to get to myself, but beggars couldn't be choosers. I'd figure it out.

As I took a quick scan of the store, inspiration struck. I took Tabitha's hand and led her toward the aisle I needed.

"My friend Violet is having a bad day. Would you help me pick out a few supplies to help her feel better?"

Tabbie hated it when people felt sad, so this was the kind of assignment she took very seriously. Her somber nod showed as much. "I'm on it."

———

I was getting restless. It was after eleven, and my sister still wasn't here. Not that I wanted to rush her. I meant what I said about keeping Tabitha as late as she needed, but I hoped I'd be able to get to Vi tonight before she turned in, and that was looking less and less possible.

Tabitha and I had eaten our steak dinner together. After she declared me the winner of both steaks and mac and cheese—I'd gloat about that one to my mom later—she watched Frozen, commissioned me to build her an ice castle of her own, devoured two cookies, and passed out on the couch. Now she was snoring adorable little snores while I got a couple of hours of work in.

You still up?

VI

Forever…

I'm actually getting closer, but I have probably another hour.

I still had time. I'd rather she was asleep already. But if that couldn't be the case, at least I was going to get the chance to help. My sister should be here any minute. I'd squeeze everything in tonight after all.

Have you eaten?

No. I'll get something after I finish. If I stop now, I'll never make it.

Lauren tapped gently on the front door as she opened it. She looked like me. Like our mom. Brown eyes and hair, wide mouth. Taylor had Dad's coloring. They were both beautiful, but I knew Lauren and I both were grateful to fall on the mom side of that spectrum from a purely psychological perspective.

She looked exhausted in her scrubs and messy ponytail. Her job as an ER nurse was demanding, but she was such a badass. Nobody did it better.

"How was she?"

I sat my computer on the coffee table and got up to hug her. "Awesome as always."

"I'm sorry for the last-minute call-in."

"Don't be. You know I love Tabbie time. And I'm always happy to help you."

She nodded. But she bit her lip, and I thought I saw a sheen of wetness in her eyes.

"Hey. What's going on?"

She wiped her nose with the back of her hand. "It's just days like today…I feel like I'm not there for her like I should be. Like maybe I'm not doing right by her with the career I chose."

"Lo." I grabbed the back of her neck and pulled her into a hug. "No way. First of all, she was with her uncle tonight. Even if you had all of the time in the world to devote to her, it would still be good for her to get that time in with her family that loves her. Second, you are an awesome mom. She never feels abandoned by you. And when she sees you go to work? All she thinks is how awesome her mom is, helping people who get hurt. She's proud of you. And so am I."

I kissed the top of her head as she cried into my chest for a few minutes. Then she stepped away and wiped at her eyes. "You're my favorite sibling. Don't tell Taylor."

I pantomimed zipping my lips.

Gathering Tabitha up in a cocoon of blankets, I loaded her into the car. She didn't open her eyes, but she did whisper an "I love you, Uncle Evan" as I buckled her in, which almost had me joining Lauren with the waterworks.

After waving them off, I hustled up the stairs and gathered my bag of supplies, gave myself a quick once-over in the mirror, and locked up behind me.

Step 4, here we come.

CHAPTER 10
VIOLET

This was the longest day ever. Notes due for one client. Another who needed to be talked off a ledge. More bad behavior from Gemma. I didn't even get to editing on my story submission until evening, and with tomorrow's deadline looming, it was a real Sword of Damocles situation.

I'd been locked in an all-day staring contest with my computer. We were closing in on midnight, and I was going to win, but it came at a cost. Subsisting on crackers and grapes, I was up way past my bedtime, and my eyes felt like sandpaper. I blinked in an attempt to clear the grit.

So close to the finish line.

I was tired but also hungry and wired, so falling straight into bed after this marathon workday was a pipe dream. I'd be lucky if I could eat and wind down before the wee hours of the morning.

My body is going to hate me for this.

My phone buzzed.

EVAN

Didn't want to give you a heart attack by opening your door at midnight so here's your warning. I'm about to open your door.

I heard his key in the lock as I finished reading. What could have possessed him to be awake at midnight on a Tuesday, much less appearing barely announced at a friend's house, was beyond me. Granted, not everyone had a preferred bedtime of 8:30 p.m., but this was hardly party time, even for him.

"I said 'I'm still up,' not 'rager at my place.'"

He stepped inside with a wide smile that instantly made this hellish day feel less bleak. Whatever his reason for being here, I was glad he came. "Damn. I must have misread that one. What should I do with my turntables?"

I waved him off. "You can just leave them in the hall."

He sat a grocery sack on the kitchen island and a bag of takeout on the table in front of me. "I come bearing gifts."

"I can actually hire a service to deliver me food, you know."

"Ah, yes. But can you hire them to remind you to order it when you're hungry?"

"Unfortunately not. I guess I'll have to keep you around." It was big talk, and he knew it. I was so tired, the smell of the food alone almost had me dissolving into a puddle of tears. How did he do this? Show up out of nowhere with exactly what I needed?

Affection squeezed my heart, but I stopped it short of swooning. It was, admittedly, a close call. This was the kind of thing that made it easy to let my imagination run away with me, to start reading in meaning that wasn't there. From an outsider, that might even seem like the obvious assumption—late-night meal delivery as a romantic over-ture. But this was Evan. I had to look no further than the way he took care of his family and our friends to remind myself that this was just him doing his thing. And the reminder was sorely needed. If I ever hoped to get my feelings back under control, I had to shut out those tempting fantasies.

I opened the bag to find a container of vegetable soup and a bit of crusty bread. He was even thoughtful about the food itself. This would be filling but not too heavy. I popped open the lid and took a big sniff. What was it about exhaustion that made comfort food that much more comforting? "This smells incredible."

He sat in the chair next to me, elbows resting on his knees. "So what's the plan from here? How much do you have left?"

"I need to finish my final editing pass so I can put everything together and submit it tomorrow. I'm almost there. Ten or fifteen minutes maybe? Then I'm going to eat this—" I took another long sniff. "—intoxicating soup. Then I guess try to relax and turn my brain off so I can get some sleep."

"Excellent." He took my free hand. "Why don't you finish up and eat, and I'll get to work on the relaxation part?"

"Seriously?"

"It's what I'm here for."

I wasn't sure exactly what his plan was but… "You don't have to—"

"I want to. Let me?"

Pulling my bottom lip through my teeth, I nodded.

"Then I'm on it." He stood, grabbing the grocery bag from the island. Whatever plan he was working on, he came prepared. He disappeared, bustling around my apartment while I worked on editing.

Finally, I made it to the end, and a surge of pride and excitement swelled in my chest as I exported the finished manuscript. It was good. I didn't know what would happen with my application, but I'd written something I was proud of, and whatever came next, that accomplishment was success enough.

My stomach gurgled, and I promptly filled it with soup. I was so tired, so happy, so hungry, so taken with this bread and soup that I wasn't paying a bit of attention to what Evan was up to. Only when I'd had my fill and tossed my trash did I go looking for him, finding him as he stepped out of the bathroom and closed the door behind him.

"You're all set in there. I'll get out of here and leave you to it." He slipped his arms around my waist and pulled me into a hug. A sigh deflated my chest, and he held me tighter. This was what I needed for relaxation. If I curled up into Evan, the sleep would come in no time.

He dropped a kiss on my head. "Get some rest and text me tomorrow, okay?"

"Of course."

He released me, and I felt the loss of him in every cell. Exhaustion did not help my self-control efforts. He was almost gone before I got my bearings enough to call his name.

"Evan."

He turned back, hand gripping the edge of the open front door.

I wrapped my arms around my middle, suddenly feeling like I needed them there to hold myself together. "Thank you. For all of this."

The corner of his mouth lifted, a One Dimple Smile creasing his cheek. "Goodnight, Violet."

And he was gone.

Once I heard the lock click behind him, I turned the handle and stepped through the bathroom door. My hand flew to my mouth as I stifled a gasp.

Light from a dozen candles flickered across the room. The scent of lavender hung in the air. Steam drifted up from the water in slow, lazy curls. And next to the tub, on a tiny stool, sat a cup of tea on a saucer.

Wow.

This…was not what I expected. He'd left my portable speaker on the counter, ready to connect for music. He'd heated my towel in the dryer. He'd used bath salts, for Pete's sake!

I wasted no time closing the bathroom door, shedding my clothes, setting music to play, and settling into the hot, aromatic water.

I brought the teacup to my lips for a sip and closed my eyes, tension uncoiling throughout my body.

Evan had swooped in and changed my whole night in half an hour. I had been stressed out, underfed, overtired, and anxious about finding rest, but I blinked and ended up here—in a luxury bath experience with a cup of tea and a full stomach, feeling my stress drift away with the steam.

He's the best.

And would you look at that—I was acknowledging how great he was without pining. No lightning bugs. No wondering if it could mean something more. Just loving my friend for the very great person he was. *Progress!*

Feeling more pleased with myself than I should for such a small success, I settled further into the water. I nursed my tea as my muscles slowly relaxed, and by the time I'd finished my cup and the water was beginning to lose its heat, I felt sure I could pour my loose-limbed body straight into bed and sleep.

I picked up my phone, determined to say thank you and also to show him (or maybe myself) that I knew exactly where we stood.

Nobody is getting ideas over here at all. Everything is very normal.

> Relaxation success. Thanks for being the best friend ever.

Perfect.

———

I'd slept in and woken feeling refreshed. This was going to be a good day.

I made myself a cup of tea then sat at my table to complete my fellowship application, filling out the forms with my personal information and background and composing the email to the submissions panel.

This was it.

My heart was beating a little too fast and my hands felt clammy, but it was an excited kind of nervous. I'd told myself over the last three weeks this was no big deal, that it would be fine either way. But staring it down like this, I couldn't hide from the truth any longer. I wanted this desperately. I couldn't keep going like I had been. I needed a new path. And this fellowship could give it to me.

The buzzer interrupted my thoughts. I rushed to the speaker at the front door, unwilling to be away from my computer for a second longer than necessary.

The voice on the other end crackled. "Cookie Delivery for Violet Ward."

Cookies? I buzzed the delivery up and tapped my foot, eyeing my computer. I was ready to send that email. Though if anything was going to pull me away from it, cookies would be that thing.

I returned to my seat, small box in hand, and flipped open the lid. Nestled inside were half a dozen cookies—chocolate chip, oatmeal raisin, and snickerdoodle—all fresh out of the oven and smelling like heaven, plus a small white card with handwriting I knew as well as my own.

> *You're amazing. You've got this.*
> *And cookies have to be a good start, right?*
> *Can't wait to see you tomorrow to celebrate.*
> *-Ev*

A disco of lightning bugs flared in my belly.

Shit.

CHAPTER 11

EVAN

I couldn't take my eyes off Violet as she walked ahead of me toward our table. She looked gorgeous tonight. So gorgeous I'd almost blown up my entire plan and kissed her when I picked her up. I was still fighting the urge.

Her curls were pinned back on one side, exposing the line of her neck and shoulder. I might have traced that line with my eyes all night if that yellow sundress wasn't so damn distracting. Another one that fit tight across her breasts and stomach then flowed loose around her hips. This one was held up by tiny straps my fingers itched to slide down her shoulders.

I shoved my hands into my pockets. I was going to have to pace myself if I had any hope of surviving this evening.

We arrived at our table, right up against the railing of one of the decks. Late afternoon light glinted off of Lake Travis as it stretched out in front of us, a gentle breeze blowing across the water to cool the heat of the day.

The Oasis was a gem—multiple dining decks and two live music venues perched on the side of a bluff overlooking the lake. It was a casual place, and the food and drinks were good, but there was no better place to watch a sunset.

"This is incredible." Her smile stretched and her eyes glowed, and I wanted to mainline that awed expression.

Step Four, the late-night meal and bath, hadn't gone great—not that I regretted it. It helped her, so I'd do it again in a heartbeat. But that "best friend ever" text was a kick in the gut. Maybe I'd missed the mark communicating more-than-friends feelings. Although I didn't understand how. The candles alone seemed like a flashing neon sign to me.

Maybe you communicated perfectly, and she was giving you an answer.

The gut-kick feeling intensified.

I was having a hard time reading her, which was new territory with us, and more than a little unnerving. So many times over the past couple of weeks, I was convinced she was feeling something, only to start second-guessing it the next minute. I was too in my own head, too close to the situation, and too tangled in years of history to interpret her platonic versus romantic signals. I was hoping tonight would help me get some clarity.

This was Step Five. A real date, at least as far as I was concerned. I didn't plan to spill my guts, and I didn't plan to kiss her—god help me —but everything else was fair game.

I didn't want her to have any doubt what my intentions were by the end of the night. Then I'd give her some time to figure out how she felt about that before I fully went for it and made a move. And since this was my last chance to pull the plug, I was also hoping to leave the night with a better read on what her feelings might be.

She ran her fingers across a few small padlocks attached to the railing beside our table.

"Lover's locks?"

I hummed in agreement. "Though I think they call them memory locks here. It's not just couples that do them, it's whoever—friends, families, and of course couples too. Anyone who wants to remember their time here."

"That's lovely." Her eyes were still roaming, trying to take everything in. "I can't believe I've never been here."

"I can't either with as long as you've lived here. It's unbelievable that no date has brought you." Her nose twitched, not a full scrunch, but definitely a reaction. Was she uncomfortable with the idea of being here with a date? Or being here with a date other than me? I fished a little more. "But at least we're fixing that tonight, right?"

"Right." She blinked then ducked her head to scan her drink menu, giving me basically nothing. *Damn, this inability to read her was getting annoying.* "And maybe just in time too."

Just in time…because she might be leaving.

The thought sank in my chest like a stone. It was not what I wanted to be thinking about at the moment. My feelings about this fellowship were all over the map. I was so proud of her. So excited for her. Hell, I'd been the one pushing her to take a leap and make a change, consider writing again. But this was not what I had in mind when I made that suggestion. The thought of her leaving, even temporarily, made me feel sick.

But I couldn't dwell on that now. It was a problem for Future Evan. For now, I needed to be supportive and stay focused on my plan.

"How are you feeling after submitting yesterday?"

"Good. Relieved. I didn't think there was any way I'd get it finished. But I did. And I'm actually really happy with my finished story."

"Will you let me read it?"

A smile pulled at the corners of her mouth. "You want to?"

"Of course I do." *Everything you write. Everything you think. Sign me up.*

"Okay. I'll send it to you tomorrow."

"Then I'll read it tomorrow."

She rolled her eyes, but delight leaked out through her smile. I fucking loved putting it there.

"When will you know the results?"

"An actual eternity." She was racked by a whole-body sigh, and my attempt not to laugh failed.

"An eternity, huh?"

"Fine. A few weeks."

"Basically the same thing."

"It might as well be. And I'm trying not to spiral with angst, and I don't want to be disappointed if it doesn't work out…but god, I really want it…probably too much."

Her expression was wide open, unflinchingly vulnerable, as she handed me those tender desires. However the rest worked out, being the person she shared this stuff with was everything to me. Suddenly, it didn't matter one bit how those dreams of hers might affect me. I wanted nothing more than to be there for her.

"Then I'll want it too much with you."

Her eyes were fathomless as my words hung in the air, pulling me under, dragging me deeper, till I felt like I'd never come up for air. But I didn't need it. I only needed more of her.

"Tell me."

She didn't speak right away, and I didn't push, just watched and waited as she gathered her thoughts.

"Writing again. Taking control of my life again…it's like waking up. I feel more alive—more like myself—than I have in a really long time."

I'd seen the change in her myself, recognized that light back in her eyes.

"And that's exciting, but it also feels like if I don't get into this program, all of that will get sucked away from me again. Letting myself get too attached to it seems foolish."

I reached over the table and took her hand. When she turned her palm up toward mine, a current raced up my arm like she'd completed a circuit. "It's scary. I get it." More than she knew. "But what you're doing is amazing. And you should let yourself want it. It's hard to open yourself up to disappointment, but the alternative is staying closed off completely. What kind of life is that? We have to put ourselves out there, right? Reach for what we want. Maybe it doesn't work out and we have to try something else, but maybe it does work out. And either way…" I ran my thumb across the fluttering pulse point on her wrist. "I really believe it's worth it to take the leap."

I was talking about her. But I wasn't *only* talking about her, and I think she knew it. Or suspected it? Her chest rose and fell on a breath as ragged as my own.

"Take the leap," she repeated.

"Welcome to the Oasis." Our server appeared from nowhere, snapping the thread of tension running between us. Violet pulled her hand back, and I followed suit, probably for the best. That escalated quickly, and there was a lot of night left.

Ashley Who Would Be Taking Care Of Us Tonight introduced herself. "Are we here celebrating anything special?"

I jumped to respond first. "Yes. Her."

"Awww. How sweet. How long have y'all been together?"

A blush climbed Violet's neck and stained her cheeks. "Oh we're not—"

"Almost ten years now."

Vi's eyes sprung wide.

"And you're still crazy about her."

She had no idea. I could only hope it was as obvious to the woman in question. I let my full attention settle on Vi, deliberately holding her shocked gaze for a full beat before I spoke. "Yes, I am."

Ashely was thrilled. Violet was rattled—though I was uncertain if she wanted to chide me or kiss me. Either way, I'd take it. At least I knew I was getting through.

"So. Sweet. Anyway, what can I get y'all to drink?"

We placed our orders, and as soon as we were alone again, Vi was whisper-shouting at me. "Why did you say that? That we'd been together for ten years?"

Still frustratingly unable to tell what she was thinking, I decided on playing dumb until I had a better feel for her reaction. "That's when we met."

"I don't think that's what she meant." She was still shaken up, but amusement was starting to creep in. Baffled amusement, but amusement nonetheless.

Relieved, I smiled and shrugged. "Seemed like the right answer at the time."

"You're deranged."

My heart tripped over her laugh. I'd have preferred the kiss, but this was almost as good.

Finally, she sighed. "So, how's the project coming? Is Brad going to be your boss?"

I loved the teasing grin pulling at her lips. Not surprising, since I loved all of her grins. Teasing. Sly. Contented. Excited. Give me any one, and I'd do my level best to keep it on her face.

"Fucking hell. He's going to institute a uniform, isn't he? Make us all wear belt buckles to signify our rank in the department like some kind of Rodeo ROTC."

"Yours will be smallest."

"I won't survive the humiliation."

"Please. You know that will never happen."

"You're right. I am resilient."

More musical laughter. More heart tripping. "No. I mean he'll never get the job over you."

"He might. He's infuriatingly competent." As much as I was her person to talk to, she was mine, and even on a night like tonight, it would be unbelievably nice to unload all the things that had been cycling in my head these past few weeks—things I'd only tell her. *Yet another way in which she's perfect for me.* I took a deep breath and leaned in, resting my arms on the edge of the table. "Jokes aside? I'm feeling good about the project. It's a beast, don't get me wrong, but the proposal is coming together. I just don't know if it'll be enough. And there's a lot riding on it."

"Of course there is. Building a dream building. Running the department. A huge pay raise. Avoiding belt buckle humiliation."

"All true. And all big. But not the biggest."

Our drinks arrived in a display of perfect timing. I took a giant gulp of mine while her brows knit in question. I hadn't told her this part. I hadn't told her anything about the house. I'd been holding this one all to myself, like maybe if I didn't say it out loud it would stay small and manageable. But it was only growing bigger and heavier.

We ordered food, and I took one more fortifying swig before unloading the whole stressful mess.

"There's a list of things wrong with my mom's house—a growing list. She can't afford to get it repaired, and they can't stay there and let it fall apart. She may have to sell, which would crush all three of them. Not to mention the fact that she'd take a huge financial hit since she wouldn't get a great price with all the work that needs to be done. It would make getting into a new place hard, especially since they want to stay in the same area. Tabitha is starting school in the fall, and they want her to be able to stay with her preschool friends."

Concern warred with confusion on her face. She cared about my family's problems, obviously, but she didn't quite see how this fit with my job opportunity.

"The promotion comes with a big bonus up front."

Understanding dawned. "And if you get it, you can pay for the repairs."

"Keep Mom and Lauren and Tabbie in their home. The rest of it is great but…"

"That's what matters most to you."

I nodded. And now it was her turn to reach across the table.

"It's wonderful that you want to do that for them. And I hope you get to. Just…don't put that responsibility all on yourself, okay? It's not all yours to fix."

She read me like a book. Half a dozen words and a nod was all she needed to understand exactly how I felt about the situation. But she was wrong. It *was* mine to fix. I knew what she meant, but they were my family. It was my job to take care of them. And I would.

I shook off the weight of that. This could easily veer into heavy territory, and I had other priorities. Nodding again, I flipped my hand over, tugged her knuckles to my lips, and brushed a kiss over them before releasing her. That was not something I'd ever done before. Kisses to her head or her cheek, sure, but never to her hand. It felt different, maybe less intimate, but somehow more romantic. As another round of shock flitted across her face, I knew she felt a difference too. But this was still about pace, so I reached for a subject change.

"Any new entries for Weird Shit?"

"A guy in assless chaps on the street yesterday."

I scoffed. "Amateur."

"Right? It's been done, guy. And by superior buns."

"Three for creativity."

"And minus two for disturbingly hairy cheeks."

My own laugh leapt out of my chest. She looked truly shaken recalling the traumatic memory, her nose crinkling in delayed embarrassment. And damn if it wasn't adorable. My fly started feeling tight under the table.

From reading my mind to making me laugh to turning me on in less than two minutes.

This is why you're in love with her.

It didn't even feel like a revelation.

———

The sunset bell rang, and people gathered on the decks to watch the sky light up with pinks and oranges. I knew the view across the water would be outstanding, but I couldn't pull my eyes away from the view across the table.

The breeze ruffled her curls, the warm light painting streaks of copper through the strands. The freckles across her cheeks lit like flecks of gold scattered over her skin. Serene green eyes took in every second of the display while her full lips parted in wonder.

She was so fucking beautiful. I never wanted to look away. Not tonight. Not ever.

So I didn't. She watched the horizon, and I watched her, grateful for every damn second.

"I don't ever want to forget it." Her thoughts echoed my own, her eyes still trained on the fading sunset.

Heart pounding, I reached into my pocket and closed my hand around a small silver lock. Metal bit into my palm as I squeezed it tight. I had no idea how this would land, but it felt pivotal. If she didn't like it, I could write off anything more right now.

Pulling it free, I passed it to her across the table and willed myself not to speak as she studied it, running the tip of her finger over the "E + V" I'd written in black sharpie.

"You brought this with you?"

I could see her trying to work out what it meant. The answer to which was: whatever the hell she wanted it to.

"In case we wanted to lock the memory."

Her mouth tipped as she hooked the lock onto the railing and snapped it closed. "Yeah. I think it's a keeper."

I felt the click in my chest. Maybe someday we'd put a real lover's lock on this rail. But this one represented us, exactly as we were right now. And it was pretty great all on its own.

I pushed our dessert plate toward her. "You want more of this?"

"I'm more than full." She fell back into her chair and laid a hand across her stomach.

"We're all paid up, so we can take off if you're ready."

She reached for her purse. "Sure. Let me send you money before I forget. How much is my half?"

"Tonight is my treat." Before she could argue, I stood, pushing back my chair and offering her my hand. "Come on. Let's get out of here."

———

Cafe lights created a canopy above us, and music from one of the venues drifted down as we strolled through the sculpture garden.

It was a strategic detour.

There were some encouraging signs over the course of dinner, pink cheeks and a quick pulse and uneven breaths and sweet smiles. Hell, she put a lock with our initials on the rail when given the chance, the click of which was still reverberating behind my sternum. But even with the evidence in front of me, I still wasn't confident in my ability to read her reactions. I was sure I could safely rule out repulsed. But was she attracted and interested or nervous and confused?

I needed more—more time, more information. So instead of walking us to the car, I led us here.

I stayed close to her, my hand resting on her lower back, the fabric of that yellow dress burning against my palm.

We took our time. Meandered. And aside from a few stray comments about the sculptures, we let peaceful silence settle around us.

The song changed, the first notes of *To Make You Feel My Love* reaching us and inspiring her to hum.

"My mom loves this song. I remember her playing it when I was a kid."

I took a step back and offered her my hand. "Dance with me?"

Her eyes darted to the few people milling around. It wasn't as crowded as it would be on a weekend, but we weren't alone, and she was clearly unsure about the prospect of dancing with an audience. But then her gaze locked on mine, and I watched as everyone else disappeared from her world. It was no longer a matter of whether she would dance in front of people, but whether she would dance with me.

The moment pulled taut, filled to bursting with everything that had passed between us over the last few hours, the weight of the entire evening packed into one invitation.

I held my hand steady despite the tremors running through my body.

"Please."

Reaching up, she placed her hand in mine. Satisfaction rushed through me. With one hand cradling hers in the air and one hand splayed across her back, I pulled her forward until her torso met mine. Her ribcage expanded as her breath hitched. The scent of honey closed around me.

Goddamn.

It was like a hit from a wrecking ball. Cracks fissured through me, and I threatened to collapse completely at the world-shattering feeling of having her in my arms. We hugged all the time. We'd cuddled. Hell, I was sure we'd even danced. But this felt completely new, and unbelievably good. Settling my cheek against her temple, I closed my eyes and let myself fall.

We swayed to the music, too far away to hear the lyrics, but I knew them. Fuck, I was drowning in them.

Did she know them too? I hoped like hell she did because I couldn't bear the thought of being in them alone. I needed her to know the words that were threatening to beat out of my chest.

Just a little longer. You're showing her. Give her a little longer to feel it. Then you can tell her. And maybe...

As if in response to my unspoken hope, her body softened against mine.

Hell yeah.

CHAPTER 12

VIOLET

Light from streetlamps flickered through the car window, catching the edges of his hair and lighting it up like a halo…or a cologne ad. He drummed his fingers on the steering wheel then looked over at me and smiled—a full Two Dimple Smile—and *god, he's killing me tonight.* How was I ever going to be able to get over my feelings when he smiled at me that way, when he made jokes about us being together, when he DANCED with me in the middle of sculpture gardens?

Every time I thought I was getting it together, he'd go and do something that sent the lightning bugs swarming and my imagination running wild.

Case in point: literally all of tonight.

It felt like a date. Which was delusional.

Evidently I could no longer be trusted to have a simple dinner with him. All of my attempts to get myself back on track had failed. I couldn't keep going like this, and I didn't know how to fix it, and I was starting to feel a creeping panic that the situation was about to spiral completely out of control and threaten my most important relationship.

I adjusted the AC vent to blow directly at my face.

We were only about halfway home. With that much driving time left, I was going to need a distraction. I scrambled for a workable subject, something happy and benign.

"So you had Tabbie this week?"

"Yeah. Tuesday before I saw you. I got her from daycare." Affection shone in his eyes as he shook his head, his adoration of her obvious. "The little tyrant had me making her steak."

"I respect it."

"Right? If you can get that kind of service…" Lifting a shoulder, he checked his blind spot. "I know when it's my own kid, I won't be such a pushover, but as the cool uncle? It's fun to give her what she wants."

"Who are you kidding? You'll be a pushover as a dad too."

"Okay, maybe. But tell me you won't be tempted to give your kids some crazy thing just because they're so damn cute. They'll get to you at least sometimes."

His words pushed a throbbing ache into my chest, like pressing on a bruise. So much for a benign subject. "I…" I cleared my throat. "I don't think I'm going to have any."

He reared back, his brow furrowed. We hadn't talked about having families in a while. In truth, I was avoiding the subject with him. My plans on that front had changed considerably, and I wasn't sure he would understand why.

Reaching for the dial, he turned down the music. It wasn't loud, but apparently it was too much for the conversation he was about to launch into—a conversation I was not prepared for given how frayed I was feeling by the events of the evening. I needed my wits about me for this talk, but like it or not, it was coming for me at a time when my wits were decidedly scattered.

"What do you mean, you don't think you're gonna have any? You've always wanted kids. *Really* wanted them. Why wouldn't you have any?"

I blew out a long breath through pursed lips. *Here we go.* "I've given it a lot of thought over the last few years, and I don't think I'm cut out for the wife and mother thing. The lupus stuff is a lot. Marriage and kids are a lot. I just…don't think I have all of that to give, and I probably wouldn't be very good at it even if I did." Thinking about this always made me feel heavy, but I attempted to keep my voice light. "And let's be honest, who would want to have kids with this hot mess, right?"

He was not amused. His knuckles drained of color where they wrapped around the steering wheel. "I would."

The throb in my chest quadrupled. That was exactly the kind of statement that would be so easy to misinterpret, to let myself twist into something it wasn't. I rolled my eyes to cover a wince. "That's sweet of you to say, but not everyone is like you, Evan. *Most* people aren't like you. Somebody isn't going to want all this baggage. I'm too much."

His jaw flexed. "Who told you that?"

"I… They didn't have to tell me for me to know—"

"But someone did, didn't they?"

At times like this, I hated how well he could read me. He wasn't going to let me get away with that evasion, and it was useless trying to dodge him further but, *oof*, he was not going to like the answer. "Rob."

"Rob? That dick you dated senior year?" Outrage punctuated each word.

"Yes. And I concede that he was a dick. But even a broken clock, you know?"

As painful as it was to acknowledge, that was the truth. Rob was there through some very bad, very weird body times. He was sympathetic at first, sweet even, but when I didn't get better like he expected me to, it became harder and harder for him to find patience and compassion. And when my health got even worse, making me unavailable for sex for a few weeks, it was the last straw. Not only was I a drain, I wasn't even taking care of his needs anymore.

He'd let me know, frequently and in no uncertain terms, how difficult it was dealing with me, working plans around me, taking care of me. I recognized that he was not kind about it (hence the dick moniker) but his frustrations themselves were valid. I *was* difficult. Could I blame him for acknowledging that?

"He was right about some things."

Evan did not agree with that assessment. Anger rolled off him in waves. "Like hell. What did he say to you?"

"You take and take, Violet. It's constant trouble, constant drama. And I tried to stay with you in spite of that, but you make it impossible. Who wants to be in a relationship where they're always taking care of someone and getting nothing in return? It's selfish to expect me to."

I remembered every word, and they still stung. Less, I think, because of Rob specifically, and more because I knew those sentiments would be shared by others. How could they not be? That night he left was the moment my plans started to feel shaky.

I wanted to tell Evan the truth, but I couldn't bring myself to use the actual words Rob had. They were still too sharp, too bitter.

So I summarized. "Basically that I was a lot to deal with. That all of my physical stuff meant that anyone who was with me would end up having to take care of me all the time and that I wouldn't be able to take care of him in return. It's unbalanced, and nobody wants that." Silence. "Obviously he didn't say it that eloquently, but that's the gist. It was an ongoing problem with us and, ultimately, why he broke up with me."

While I spoke, his rage melted, replaced with an expression that could only be described as pained. His anger on my behalf was easier to handle. My sadness over this was hard enough to try to control without adding his. I willed myself not to cry.

His voice softened. "You never told me he said that."

"We were about to graduate. He was about to move. It seemed...irrelevant."

He covered his mouth with his hand, leaning his elbow into the door. Minutes crawled by, thick silence hanging in the air. When I thought he might leave the conversation there, he dropped his hand. "You have to know he was wrong, Violet. So, so wrong. That guy is a moron, and that isn't how relationships work. There are guys out there…" His eyes flicked to me before returning to the road. "Guys who would kill to have a family with you."

"Sure. Maybe."

I wasn't convinced. He knew I wasn't convinced. But he also knew that I was done talking about it. I reached for the dial to turn the music back up.

The thing was, even if he was right about someone being willing to sign up for all this, *getting* into a relationship with someone like me was a lot different than *staying* in a relationship with someone like me.

People only had so much to give, and chronic illness had a way of draining those wells fast. How could I get married knowing that I would always be taking, never able to give enough to catch up? That it was just a matter of time before I tapped him completely. That if this unfortunate imaginary partner wanted kids, it would be even worse since they'd be stuck caring for me and our children with little in the way of help.

Not to mention the disappointment I'd be to the kids themselves— unable to keep up, missing baseball games and ballet recitals, building their lives around my limitations. I'd drain them too, when it was supposed to be a mother's job to fill those little wells.

I couldn't do it. I *wouldn't* do it.

We pulled up to the curb in front of my apartment building and Evan shut off the car. It seemed this would not be curbside service, and I was relieved. It had been such a lovely night. I didn't want it to end this way.

Circling the hood, he came to walk beside me, hands tucked into his pockets, but close enough that I could feel the heat of his body, even on this warm night.

When we reached the top step, he turned and drew me close, his hands gently encircling my upper arms. Everything in me wanted to melt into his chest.

"Let me just say this, and I'll shut up about it, okay?" He waited for my nod to continue. "Anyone lucky enough to have you in their life would be better for it—family, friends, kids, a partner…me. You're the best there is. Don't let anyone make you believe different."

Tears made my eyes glassy.

He pressed a hard kiss to my forehead and stepped back. "Come over Saturday? I'll make dinner."

"Sounds good." The words were only slightly strangled.

With a tiny hook at the corner of his mouth, he walked backward a few paces before turning fully toward the street. Even after all of this, it was impossible not to watch his retreating form with ill-advised longing.

He waved over the hood of the car, making sure I was inside with the door shut safely behind me before getting in and pulling away.

I struggled to sort through the hurricane of emotions that battered me as I climbed the stairs. The effort proved unfruitful. All I could say for sure was that with every step away from Evan, the urge to go back to him grew more intense.

As soon as I'd locked my front door, I pulled out my phone.

> Thanks again for dinner.

EVAN

> My pleasure. Can't wait for Saturday.
> Goodnight sweetheart.

It feels like a date.

I stared at his message for five whole minutes while I stood in the middle of my hallway. Then I kept staring at it…while I brushed my teeth, while I changed my clothes, while I crawled into bed, and far into the wee hours of the morning.

———

The bell above the door tinkled as we entered the cafe, and it took Lina approximately four seconds to identify a table being vacated by the window and steal it right out from under the noses of people who were already present and table-searching. She was cutthroat.

She seated herself there triumphantly, and Jamie and I wove our way through tables to join her. She was flagging down a waitress before I even made it into my seat. "I'm starving. We're doing truffle fries, right? I don't even care what you say. The answer is yes. I'll eat them all myself if I have to."

"Hell yes." Jamie inspected the menu with lust in her eyes. "I've been running all day, and the muffin I had for breakfast was gone hours ago. I'm ready to eat this whole restaurant."

The waitress made it to us. "Please feed us immediately…" Lina checked her name tag. "Chelsea. We've been dress-fitted within an inch of our lives. Do you have booze?"

"Uhhhh. Yes? We have wine."

"Then bring that, too."

Poor Chelsea stared at her notepad, visibly unsure how to translate Lina's instructions into an order, but Jamie jumped in to interpret. "Don't worry. She has this effect on people. We'll each have a glass of house red and truffle fries for the table, please."

Chelsea gratefully took the lifeline, scribbling down the order and scurrying back toward the kitchen.

"Really, Lina? Within an inch of your life? We were trying on dresses, not going to war."

"Everything is war when you're hangry."

"Touché." Jamie nodded. "On the bright side, your boobs looked great in the dress."

"Damn, they did, didn't they? But we all looked amazing. You, especially, were a total smoke show. Nico's going to lose his mind." Jamie glowed at Lina's praise. "Don't you think, Vi?"

"Oh." I'd been struggling to keep up all afternoon. I tried to stay engaged, but my mind kept drifting to Evan, my brain multitasking him into every event and conversation, leaving me extremely distracted. Lina's prompt reminded me, once again, that I needed to participate. "Yes. She looked gorgeous. Most beautiful bride ever." Lina narrowed her eyes at me. "And your boobs did look great?"

"Obviously." She crossed her arms on the table and leaned in. "What's up with you today?"

"You have seemed really distracted, Vi. Is everything okay?"

Maybe I needed to talk it out. Surely my friends could help me find some sanity.

The prospect made me nervous. I had no idea what their reactions would be. I'd locked my feelings up so tight inside, like giving them any bit of oxygen would make them uncontrollable. Lina hadn't heard me talk about Evan like this since we were in school, and Jamie never had at all. I was sure it would seem completely out of the blue to them both but desperate enough to lay it out there and see what they had to say.

"I may need an intervention. I think I'm losing it over Evan."

Lina muttered something under her breath but looked amused more than anything.

Jamie almost came out of her seat. "Oh, yes! This is something I very much want to talk about. I've asked Nico about it, but he's given me nothing. And I wanted to ask the rest of you, but nobody ever talks about it. Why does nobody ever talk about it?"

"Why does nobody talk about what?"

"You and Evan! Whatever is going on between you. Whatever has gone on between you. The scandal. The intrigue. The romance."

"What? No. There is no me and Evan—past or present—at least not that way. Nothing has ever happened between us. It's just me and an unrequited crush. A crush that I thought I got under control a decade ago but is now causing me hallucinations."

"Hold on. Hold on. You're telling me that between *you and Evan*, *nothing* has ever happened? Not even almost?"

"No!"

"That's not true." Lina sang it like a taunt while I scowled at her, and I hurried to set the record straight.

"There was *one* drunken almost-kiss right after graduation, and he backpedaled very quickly when he realized it was me on the other end of it. It wasn't real, and it doesn't count. It was *nothing*."

Lina hummed, but Jamie was back on task. "I'm not convinced there's not more to that than you're saying. But let's get back to you losing it. I need more backstory."

"I…liked him…our first year of college, not long after we met. It got kind of intense, but I knew he didn't reciprocate, so I put it to bed. Not that I…un-liked him…per se, but I moved on. Everything has been completely fine and normal for years. But I guess my likes have made a return because I'm feeling all…something…around him, and I'm imagining these moments between us—they feel like they could be real sometimes. And I know he could never have those kinds of feelings for me, so I'm right back at the beginning."

"And the hallucinations?"

"Last night, I hallucinated an entire date."

Jamie's eyes were wide. "You hallucinated him taking you out?"

"No. He actually took me out. Last night. But I imagined it meaning more. Like when he brought me flowers when he picked me up or when he paid for the meal…or danced with me when a song I love came on."

"Oh my god." Lina threw her hands up and looked to Jamie as she explained. "Nico is going to kill me. He told me years ago that I couldn't do this—that whatever was between them, they had to figure it out for themselves. But I mean, fuck Nico, right? He doesn't know everything." Jamie snorted a laugh as Lina gathered my hands in hers and softened her voice. "Babe. I adore you. And you are so, so wrong."

"About what?" I'd simply recounted the facts. I wasn't even sure what there was to be wrong about.

"Everything. First, you did *not* move on. Maybe you don't think about it much? Maybe it doesn't torment you? Fine. But there has not been a single day over the last ten years that you were not in love with him."

In love with him? I was not in love with him.

"And then the whole 'he could never have those feelings' thing? Ridiculous. I don't know if your crush was 'unrequited' at the very beginning. Who can know the minds of nineteen-year-old boys? Jesus, who wants to? But I do know that he is as crazy about you as you are about him and he has been since we were still in school."

That's…no… That's not possible.

"And finally, of fucking course you're having moments. That was a real date, and the sexual tension between you two—"

"Sexual tension?" I squeaked, my building shock threatening to topple.

"Sexual. Tension. You see, when a man and a woman love each other very much…"

"Carolina!" I grasped for the words to convince her that she was completely off base and came up empty, my thoughts flying by so fast I couldn't seem to catch them.

I had no idea how long we sat that way, but eventually Jamie leaned in to Lina, both of their eyes trained on me. "I think you broke her."

Lina shrugged, completely unperturbed. "Had to be done."

———

I curled up on my couch with a bowl of ice cream. My body needed rest, but it was pandemonium inside my brain.

This week was officially off the rails. A long day and late night pushing to meet the application deadline. Submitting. Errant feelings and positively-not-a-date with Evan, followed by that fraught kids conversation. Dress fitting. Lina's conspiracy theories.

This ice cream was doing A Lot of work.

The details surrounding the end of my relationship with Rob were not something I'd ever intended to discuss with Evan. He didn't need to know. It was pointless, especially now that it was ancient history. I'd never be able to convince him that, jerk though he may be, Rob actually made some good points. Ev was too consumed with his defense of me to see their validity.

Now I was going to his place for dinner tomorrow night, which should have been completely fine and normal, but was going to be complicated by his sweet but misplaced need to tell me that *a guy like him* could give me the things I always wanted and that I shouldn't give them up. All of this on the heels of me letting the lightning bugs run amok to invent a date that couldn't have happened. And Lina losing every one of her marbles and telling me that the date was not invented and, unbeknownst to either of us, Evan and I were in love.

Fine and normal were out the window while awkward and hopelessly pining were charging right through the front door.

What was she even thinking? Evan could not, in one million years, in one million multiverses, be crazy about me. I had a *decade* of proof to support that. In the ten years we'd been best friends, he had never looked my way. And why would he? I was just…Vi. He saw me as a friend, maybe even as a sister (*blech*) but as a love interest? It was laughable.

Sexual tension my ass.

From my end, maybe. And yes, sometimes—occasionally—it felt like it could be mutual, but that was wishful thinking, my old crush sneaking back up to sow chaos. And Lina was trying to feed the beast.

But she also said that I was in love with Evan, which was patently untrue. I had kept that crush in check for ten years, thankyouvery-much, and just because I was having a little hiccup with it now did not mean I was in love with him.

Lina was clearly an unreliable reporter, and her judgment in these matters could not be trusted.

I nodded resolutely as I dropped my spoon into my empty bowl. There. That was settled. Everything was fine, and I could go right to sleep.

I peered at the puddle of melt that had collected in the spoon. The bowl of sugar may have been a mistake.

Nothing for it now. The spoon rattled as I deposited the bowl on the coffee table and grabbed the remote.

Binge-watch it is. No regrets.

CHAPTER 13
EVAN

"Special delivery." I stepped through the front door of my mom's house and heard an answering shriek followed by the thunder of small, running feet.

Tabitha flew around the corner and into my open arms.

"Uncle—" She gasped as she noticed the stuffed rabbit in my hand. "Mr. Bigglesworth!" She snatched it from my hand and squeezed it tight to her chest before pulling it back to give it the stern talking to it clearly deserved. "Gilbert Reginald Bigglesworth. Where have you been? I been worried sick."

"Not sure it was his fault, Tabbie. Seems he got left at my house the other night."

She pursed her lips. "Hmm. So it was *your* fault."

"Or yours for not putting him back in your bag before you laid down?"

"Nope. Yours. But I forgive you." She gave me a smacking kiss on the cheek and tore off toward the kitchen. "Mom! Uncle Evan brought Mr. Bigglesworth back 'cause he stole him."

"Whoa. I *stole* him? These charges are escalating." I followed her through the dining room to the kitchen, where Lauren was pulling chicken nuggets from the oven.

"Be glad it's theft and not kidnapping. Those were the charges her other stuffies were facing. There was a trial. Nobody came clean, and I think things were about to take a dark turn." I chuckled as she set down the tray, and I pulled her in for a hug. "Thanks for bringing him back."

"Can't have the stuffies going away for a crime they didn't commit."

I found a seat at the island while Lauren dished nuggets and green beans onto a plate for Tabitha.

"Uncle Evan, is your friend feeling better?"

"She is. We helped a lot, and I couldn't have done it without you." She beamed, and I put my hand up for a high five. "Mission accomplished." She slapped my hand.

"Dinner, kiddo." Lauren handed Tabbie the plate, which she accepted with a wrinkled nose before turning back to me.

"It's not steak."

I leaned forward to inspect her plate. "What's wrong with chicken nuggets? They're awesome."

She stage-whispered like she was divulging a scandalous secret. "They're from the freezer."

Lauren cut in. "All right, ma'am. Go to the table and eat your dinner."

"There's not even sauce!"

Lauren opened the refrigerator and added a generous squeeze of ranch dressing to the plate. Deeming it adequate, Tabbie trotted off to the dining room, rabbit tucked under one arm.

"What's with the new food critic?"

"She started watching The Food Network with Mom, and now her palate is *refined*." She picked a chicken nugget off the tray. "So…who is this *friend* my daughter is helping you take care of?"

"Vi. She was having a rough day Tuesday, so I had Tabbie help me put together kind of a care package at the store. She's good now."

How was that only three days ago? I felt like I'd lived years with Violet since then, and they'd been a helluva rollercoaster. Last night, though…last night had gone well. Really well. I couldn't definitively label our interactions as green lights, but they certainly weren't red. I had a real chance, and that was all I could hope for coming into tomorrow.

"Of course it was Violet." Her smile was wry.

"What's that supposed to mean? Should I not help my friend when she's having a bad day?" I snagged a nugget for myself.

"You should. I just… Never mind." Shaking her head, she spun toward the refrigerator, retrieving a bottle of ketchup and squirting a helping onto the tray between us.

"No. Tell me. What were you going to say?" I had a strong feeling I knew.

"I don't get why you two aren't together is all. I know, I know—you're 'just friends.' But I have 'just friends,' and you and Violet have always seemed like…I don't know…not that." She raised her hands in deference, but her smirk didn't look very deferential. "It's none of my business. Ignore me. Or, you know, date her already."

I scratched the back of my neck, bracing for the shit she was about to give me. "I'm trying."

"To ignore me?"

"To date her."

"Wait. Seriously? After all the years of friend talk?"

"Yep. You're right. I realized my feelings weren't as exclusively friendly as I've been telling myself, and I want to be with her so…I'm trying."

"Okay, one, of course I'm right. And two, oh my god, that's huge!"

That wasn't so bad. It looked like her excitement outweighed her desire to gloat.

"Potentially huge. She has to agree." Which was still uncomfortably uncertain. I loaded up a chicken nugget with ketchup and popped it into my mouth.

"You have a plan, though, right? How many steps?"

I swallowed. "Six."

Her grin spread like the damn Cheshire Cat. "And you're on step…?"

"Last night was five. I took her to The Oasis. Tomorrow night is six. I'm making her dinner at my house."

She slammed her hands down on the counter. "You're getting together tomorrow night."

"Lo…"

"You're in love with her."

"Yes." Damn, it felt good to say that out loud.

"And she's in love with you."

"Remains to be seen." Though I was starting to have hopes that she could be.

"She is. Trust me. The biggest miracle is that nothing has happened between you before now." She leaned in on her elbows. "Have you seriously never even had a close call?"

Images pulled at my memory. *Her packed boxes stacked around us. A haze of alcohol. Her upturned face and parted lips.*

I shifted uncomfortably in my seat. "Maybe one."

Tucking a curl behind her ear. A bolt of electricity down my spine.

"Details, please."

Leaning in. Feeling her breath across my lips. And then a crack in my chest as she stepped away.

Damn, I hadn't thought about that night in a long time.

"There's not much to tell. I almost kissed her once, but she stepped away, so I backed off." All the way off. That's when I knew she wasn't interested in me that way, that we were in a strictly platonic situation. "Before that, I thought maybe…But I got the message loud and clear."

"Wait. She stepped away, and that was it? You didn't talk to her about it?"

"Of course not. I'm not an asshole. I can take an answer when it's given."

"Right, but *did* she answer you? I mean, I'm all for respecting nonverbal communication. But it sounds like maybe you jumped to a pretty big conclusion without stopping to get more information."

"I…" *Well, damn.* I was so shaken at even the hint of rejection from her, the person that already mattered most to me, that I turned tail and ran. (I'd be spending some time unpacking the reasons for that later.) But Lauren was right. I could have respected her boundaries while having an actual conversation about it, but I didn't. I didn't ask questions. I didn't try to understand what she was actually feeling. I made some quick apologies and promises that I got it and that we were friends, and I shut my shit down.

That night was the last time I can remember being aware of her romantically until recently. It's like my brain got the no-go and convinced itself that if she didn't have feelings for me, I didn't have them for her either. I built those walls high and never looked back.

"Fuck. I'm pretty sure I Jedi Mind Tricked myself into believing I wasn't in love with Violet for the last six years."

She cackled. *Cackled.*

"How is that funny?"

"I'm sorry. It's not." She tried and failed to compose herself.

"You're a jerk. Taylor's my favorite now."

"No. Really, I'm sorry." She finally settled down. "So six years, huh? Your senior year?"

"Right after graduation. I was helping her pack. We were both freshly single—" The thought hit me like a train, nearly knocking me out of my seat. "Holy shit." She had just broken up with Rob. Rob, who was apparently feeding her garbage about not being worthy. I'd bet every dollar I had that was a factor that night. How could it not be? She was hurting. And I missed it completely. Instead of being there for her like she needed me to be, I got drunk and hit on her. "Shit." I dropped my head into my hands. "She was going through a bad breakup at the time that I didn't even know about until…well, until last night, actually."

"So what does that mean?"

"I…have no idea. Probably nothing." Nothing to build conclusions off of anyway. Even with this new information, I didn't know if she wanted me then and I didn't know if she wanted me now. But I was sure as hell going to find out. This time I would approach her in a way that was worthy of her. And I'd be damn sure about the answer. "I've gotta go."

"Where are my babies?" My mom's voice rang from the direction of the front door.

"You will call me later to finish this conversation." Lauren hissed at me before Mom entered the room.

"There they are." She wrapped me in a hug and kissed my cheek. "What you doing around here tonight?"

"Returning a Mr. Bigglesworth."

"Thank god. It's been like an episode of Law and Order around here. I don't know where she gets this stuff."

Lauren cocked an eyebrow. "Really? No idea?" Mom placated her with a kiss to the cheek.

"All right. I've gotta go."

Mom's face contorted in exaggerated outrage—half teasing, half guilt trip—a Donna Marshall classic. "So soon? I just walked in the door."

There wasn't a lot I'd skip out on my mom for, but prep for tomorrow couldn't wait any longer. "I know. But I have a big project I'm working on."

"It's the weekend. What kind of project are you working on over the weekend?"

"Yeah, Evan. Tell us about your project." Lauren was a menace. I grabbed her in a too-tight hug and whispered *Taylor* in her ear as she tried to contain her laughter.

———

I stirred the pot of sauce and replaced the lid. Ramen was well beyond my skill set, but since Vi had never met a noodle that she didn't like, spaghetti was a solid runner-up and a strong choice for tonight's meal.

Step Six. I'd spent almost two weeks in Woo Violet mode, telling her in every way but with my words how I felt about her, what I wanted. I'd done what I could to lay the groundwork and spark anything for her that was going to spark.

Now I was about to change everything. Up till now, there had been plausible deniability. But by the end of the night, there would be no going back. If I was tipping my hand before, now I was putting my cards on the table.

I had reason to believe it would go well, but not nearly as much certainty as I'd like. Despite scouring her every reaction for clues for the past couple of weeks, I couldn't be sure. Though the memory of her softening against me while we danced was a real fucking confidence booster.

Still, there was nothing concrete enough to be positive that this would go well, and fear that I was risking my best friend tightened my throat. But my best friend was also the woman I loved, and if there was even a chance I could have it all with her, I wouldn't let it pass because I was too chickenshit to take the risk. I gave myself a nod of approval as I heard the front door open.

"Hey! I'm in the kitchen," I called out to her over my shoulder as I turned the burner on under the pot of water I had ready and waiting.

In Vi's apartment, you could see the entire living space from the front door—hell, you could practically touch the entire living space from the front door—but my townhouse was a little bigger, and while she wouldn't exactly need to stage an expedition to find me, I was too eager to keep quiet.

A moment later she was turning the corner.

"Hey. So am I." She smiled. She always smiled when she saw me, like I was the person she wanted to see most in the whole world. That had to be a point in my favor.

I wiped my hands on a dish towel and dropped it on the counter as I closed the distance between us. My hands skated across the bare skin of her arms as I stepped close—closer than I normally would—so that there was practically no space between us. I leaned in to place a soft kiss on her cheek and felt her breath hitch.

It was subtle, but it was a start.

CHAPTER 14
VIOLET

Evan's lips brushed across my cheek and my body went on high alert. He stood closer, lingered longer. His entire demeanor felt charged and at the same time softer somehow.

Goosebumps lifted on my arms, and I slid out of his hold, hoping he'd miss the telling texture.

This was going splendidly. I had been in his presence for forty seconds, and already the armor I'd built to bolster me through this evening was disintegrating. I had to stay focused. Tonight was about getting back to normal. My attraction had been spiraling out of control, and if my performance on Thursday was any indication, my chances to right this thing before it careened into disaster were dwindling. Now was the time to get a grip.

I pulled my crumbling pieces of armor close and cleared the lump building in my throat, willing my voice to come out even. "It smells delicious." It was a barely passable effort, but if he noticed, he didn't comment, just turned and circled back around the island.

It was *riveting*.

A black T-shirt clung to the lean muscles of his arms and back. Worn denim hugged his truly spectacular backside. It was an incredible, if ill-advised, feast for the eyes. My gaze ticked lower to his bare feet as they padded across the kitchen floor. Heat flooded my cheeks, a truly ridiculous reaction. They were just feet! Feet I'd seen a million times. But right now, the sight of them felt so domestic, so intimate, it was like walking in on him in the shower.

And now I'm thinking about him in the shower.

My cheeks grew hotter as I fought the urge to clamp my hand over my eyes. It wouldn't save me from this mental image anyway.

"It does, doesn't it? You can go ahead and bow to my cooking prowess."

He shot a sly smile over his shoulder, and I had to make a very concerted effort not to pair the image with my deviant shower thoughts. Instead, I focused on his words, and my tension eased by a degree as I latched on to our typical banter. "Please. You can make like five things."

"Quality over quantity, Violet. I'm a craftsman, an artist. Would you criticize Michelangelo for not painting enough chapels?" He slid a tray of bread into the oven. "Wine?"

"Yes, please." *Immediately, if possible.*

"Stir the sauce while I pour?" He nodded toward the pot on the stove, and I stepped up to it while he retrieved the wine and glasses.

"So just to be clear, you're Michelangelo in this scenario? Creating epic masterpieces with every meal you produce using recipes you stole from your mother?"

One side of his mouth hitched, punctuated by that damned roguish dimple as he worked the cork from the bottle. "I also got one off the internet."

"Ah, yes. Just like the true masters." A puff of heat and the scent of tomato and herbs wafted out as I lifted the lid off of the pot. Donna's recipes would never steer him wrong.

I grabbed the spoon and opened my mouth to speak again but stopped short.

He was behind me, crowding into my space, hand gripping my waist. He barely touched me, but I felt his presence pressing against every inch of my back. His jeans brushed against my bare legs beneath the hem of my shorts, his body heat radiating through the cotton of our T-shirts. His breath fell across my neck. With a squeeze of his hand, he sent pulses fanning out to every illicit part of my body, and they clenched in response.

His other arm loosely encircled my body, holding something in front of me. I had to blink twice to bring it into focus.

"Your wine." His voice sounded like sex. Or maybe my ears heard sex. Which made a lot of sense—with Evan wrapped around me like some kind of hot, human Snuggie, my brain was screaming *SEX!*

"Oh! Yes! Thank you!" I sounded deranged.

I took the glass from his hand, and he was gone, busying himself salting water and dropping pasta and leaving me feeling like I'd plunged into an icy lake.

"I see the problem."

My god, I hope not.

"You're overcome with jealousy. My culinary skill intimidates you."

Cooking. He was teasing me about cooking while I was fantasizing about sex and Snuggies.

Clearly a new low.

I forced a playful scoff. "Why would I be intimidated? I'm every bit as good a cook as you."

He tsked, shaking his head in mock sympathy. "Violet, Violet, Violet. Don't make me remind you of the Great Grilled Cheese Fire."

My mouth fell open as I gasped, his peal of laughter echoing through the kitchen.

"We were never to speak of that again."

"Hmm. I've conveniently forgotten that ban."

"Evan!" I reached out to slap his chest, but he caught my wrist, using it to spin me to face him and haul me into his body, arm pinned firmly behind my back. My chin tipped. His soft brown eyes may as well have been quicksand because I was sucked right under. I didn't even try to squirm free. My brain was screaming that I should get some distance, but my body saw no reason it shouldn't be pressed against his solid chest, letting his sandalwood and citrus scent tempt me like no sauce ever could.

"Violence is never the answer." His face was lit with amusement and mischief, and I couldn't have looked away if my life depended on it. "If I let go, can I trust you to be good?"

"Probably not." There was no hope for me.

His gaze flared with something new I couldn't identify, and my heart pounded in response. "Promises, promises."

A sexy grin curled the corner of his painfully perfect lips. The bottom one was fuller while the top one flared out ever so slightly, cresting in a flawless cupid's bow. They grazed the shell of my ear as he bent closer. Tingles pricked at the back of my neck.

"Stir, Violet." His voice was low and smooth, and it took me a couple of seconds to realize he was waiting on me for a response.

"I...what?"

"You were supposed to be stirring." He nodded to the spoon still clutched uselessly in my unpinned hand. I blinked at it, surprised to see it there even though I'd been holding it for...minutes? Hours?

He loosened his grip and slowly, torturously increased the distance between us until we were fully disconnected, his eyes last to release me, that unidentified something still simmering behind them.

Metal scraped as he pulled the tray of bread from the oven, grating against my raw nerves. He took it to a waiting cutting board and began slicing while I stepped up to the stove, mindlessly stirring the sauce and attempting to gain control of my heart rate. I located the wine I'd abandoned at some point and guzzled half the glass without taking a breath. I would not get drunk—*that would be a disaster*—but maybe getting a glass on board would help dial me down a notch.

"Dinner's ready. Let's go eat." He reached around me to switch off burners and pressed a kiss into my temple. My heart squeezed.

He drained pasta at the sink, and I watched his back as he worked, his movements relaxed and efficient. Beautiful. Even in this mundane task, I was captivated by him, pining over the tiniest of things.

And it will always be this way because I love him.

No more denial. No more minimizing. No matter how hard I tried to will it away, it wouldn't change the truth. Even if there would never be anything other than friendship between us, it wouldn't stop my heart from tripping and falling for him over and over again.

This should have been a major revelation, but it felt…obvious, a little ridiculous that I was only just now acknowledging it.

I wasn't the only one who thought so. Lina had been right, at least about my part—*only* about my part. *Right?*

The image of Evan's eyes lit with that thing I couldn't name flashed in my mind.

Surely not…

"Hey. Where did you go?"

I blinked at Evan taking his seat beside me. "Uh. Just…thinking about something Lina said." That was at least a partial truth. I laid my napkin across my lap. "This really does smell delicious. Thank you."

"My pleasure."

The words were benign, but the way he said them had desire coiling low in my belly. I shoveled an enormous bite of spaghetti into my mouth as my mind poured over the last twenty minutes. It *all* felt like innuendo. The touches. The smiles. The lingering looks. The texture of his voice. I swallowed hard around the too-big bite.

That was impossible. Nonsensical. Ten years, and now he's suddenly coming on to me?

Is it sudden? Or have you been ignoring signs?

I...I had no idea. It still seemed absurd to imagine he had romantic feelings for me, but it was getting harder and harder to believe that this was all a figment of my overwrought imagination.

"You have something..." His fingers grazed the line of my jaw, his thumb coming to rest at the corner of my mouth and dragging across my lower lip, collecting a smear of sauce. His eyes bored into mine. Without so much as a blink, he pulled his hand away, slipped his thumb between his own lips, and sucked it clean. One of his eyebrows lifted while a slow, seductive smile spread across his mouth. "You were right. Delicious."

Oh. My. God.

My stomach swooped. Heat pooled between my legs. Desire was crashing through me, carrying me away, and Evan was looking utterly pleased with himself.

Any armor I'd walked in here with seemed like an optimistic joke. I was without defense and too disoriented to make sense of any of this. I needed to get out of here, have a meltdown in the privacy of my own home, and attempt to rethink my entire belief system.

You'll make it. Just finish up and get out.

I blinked down at my full plate of spaghetti.

I am in so much trouble.

———

Water swept the last of the suds off the colander and carried them down the drain.

He'd flirted all through dinner. And I tried desperately, uselessly not to love it.

I couldn't even begin to unpack this, not while I was still smack in the middle of the mayhem upending everything I thought I knew. I needed time, distance, and six tubs of ice cream. Then maybe I'd let myself crack the lid. I'd pull each fact out one by one and ~~obsess~~ *analyze* this properly.

In the meantime, I needed to survive the night. But with my armor a distant memory, every look, every touch, every sweet comment or suggestive joke penetrated my skin, pulling at long-buried desires, coaxing them into the light.

My grip on this situation—on myself—was slipping. My body vibrated with anxiety, but there was a sweet ache bubbling in my chest that threatened to melt it all away.

"I think it's clean." His chuckle raked over me as he reached around me to shut off the water. He pulled the colander from my hands and settled it on the drying rack, and I took the opportunity to create distance. Every inch was a necessity. I plucked a kitchen towel off the island and dried my hands, my back to him.

"I'm going to have to take out a loan to pay the water bill. I'm not sure the dishwashing help was worth it."

"At least I'm pretty." I snapped my mouth closed, but there was no pulling it back. It was a stupid, throwaway joke, but in light of tonight...god, I was hopeless. My eyes screwed shut on a wince.

"Beautiful."

I sucked in a breath, shocked by the word and his unexpected proximity. He was right there, turning me to face him, tugging the towel out of my hands and tossing it back toward the island. His hand slid around my waist, palm pressed against my spine as he pulled me closer.

I was frozen. Scared to move or speak or breathe—scared that something might happen, scared that it wouldn't. Only my heart didn't get the memo as it raced in my chest.

His other hand found my face, fingers wrapping around my neck, thumb grazing over my cheek. "You are so beautiful."

Electricity arced from every place he touched me. My heart pounded harder. My breath was a shaky rasp. "Evan…what are we doing?"

"I think you know exactly what I'm doing."

A wave of longing surged through me, the temptation to let go, to let myself be carried away by it, threatening to overwhelm me. I was grasping for straws, for the last shreds of my control. I found his eyes again. "This is…we need to think about this."

"Sweetheart." The endearment made my belly flip. His eyes held mine, vulnerability edging into his expression. "This is all I can think about."

A perfect confession. One that mirrored the truth I could no longer deny in myself. The last of my resolve slipped away, and I felt myself soften in his arms.

"I've been trying to show you for weeks how I feel, what it could be like between us." He dropped his forehead, nose nuzzling against mine, mouth hovering so close I could feel his breath across my lips.

"Let me show you, Vi. Please." His voice was soft, his plea aching in my chest.

And there was only one answer I could possibly give. It was a whisper, barely audible, but it rang through the room as if I'd shouted.

"Yes."

CHAPTER 15

VIOLET

His smile unfurled slowly as he cradled my face in his hands. We were sharing the air between us, his lips skimming mine in brushes so light, I could almost doubt they were there—except that I felt them *everywhere*. This was not a few lightning bugs. It was a million of them, filling my entire body and lighting me up from the inside. They flickered down my spine, in my belly, at my fingertips. They caught in my lungs and halted my breath.

Evan was about to kiss me.

Oh. I want this. I'd wanted it so much for so long—more than I'd let myself admit. And now it was about to happen. So close I could literally taste him. Desire and excitement and fear coursed through me. Tears pricked the backs of my eyes.

His voice was rough and quiet as he said my name. Just once. And then his lips were pressing into mine. The lightning bugs exploded in bursts of light. A strangled whimper escaped me. He threaded his fingers into the back of my hair, tipping my chin as he parted my lips with his, tongue sweeping in to taste me while I clutched at the fabric of his shirt.

This. Was. *Heaven.* Could you die from too many lightning bugs? If so, I might perish right here on this spot. Because the way Evan was kissing me, like my mouth was the center of his universe, was painfully perfect. He moved with such intention, like he knew every step to this dance we'd never done before—sipping, nibbling, stoking the heat building between us with sure, deliberate strokes.

We kissed for endless minutes—slow, drugging kisses. Until the world around us blurred and fell away. There was nothing else. Nobody else. Just the press of his lips, the glide of his tongue, the grip of his hands.

I didn't know what any of this meant, where it was going or what he intended. I didn't know what tomorrow would bring. But I knew he was here with me right now, and if I only ever got one encounter with Evan this way, I was not stopping with a kiss. I would take everything he was willing to give me and leave the aftermath for Future Violet to worry about.

I lifted the hem of his T-shirt, running my fingers along the soft skin above his waistband, the feel of his bare skin enough to pull a moan from my throat. His muscles clenched in response.

It was like the first bite of a rich dessert—profoundly satisfying, but in no way enough. I gripped his waistband.

"Hey. Hey. There's no rush. We don't have to—" I slipped his button free, but he caught my wrists before I could make it further. "Violet." It was half groan.

We stood in silence, chests heaving. His eyes searched mine with questions he didn't even need to speak aloud. I willed him to see the answers, poured every ounce of my need and desire into that look. Recognition glinted back. Of course he would see. He always saw me.

His hold on my wrists loosened. I brought my hands to his chest, felt it rise and fall on one shuddering breath, and the room ignited.

Our mouths fused as his hands found me. They were everywhere— grasping at my hips, my waist, sliding up the sides of my breasts, my shoulders, my neck, down my back—as if they needed to touch me everywhere at once and were determined to find a way.

They skated up the backs of my thighs, gripping below my ass and lifting me onto my tiptoes. I looped my arms around his neck, arching closer as he pulled me against him, his hard length pressing into my belly. He groaned into my mouth. The sound sent heat flooding down my spine and pooling between my legs.

He trailed kisses up my neck. "Bedroom?"

I nodded vigorously and felt his grin against the sensitive skin behind my ear.

We stumbled up the stairs and down the hall to his room, a tangle of desperate kisses and searching hands. I lost my shoes along the way. Evan knocked a picture askew. He pushed me against his closed bedroom door, and we tumbled inside when I twisted the handle.

We were here. In his room. In front of his bed. Getting ready to blur every line I'd thought was so firmly drawn between us. And despite all the confusion and uncertainty that got me here, despite the fresh surge of nerves tumbling through me, I didn't have a single doubt this was what I wanted. I turned to face him, his unfathomable gaze pinning me in place.

As the weight of the moment settled around us, we were no longer hurried, as if by some silent agreement, we decided to savor instead of rush. Desire swirled between us, but instead of being carried away by it, we stilled and let it close in, unwilling to lose a single second of this to a blur of action.

He stepped forward, hands slipping under my T-shirt, sliding up the hot skin of my sides as he tugged it up and over my head. Nothing had ever felt as good as his hands on me. I craved them the moment they left my skin.

He dragged a line down my front with the backs of his knuckles, leaving tingles in his wake. Stopping at my shorts, he unhooked the button before slowly opening the zipper, the sound of each tooth releasing echoing in the silence. He pushed them over my hips, and they slipped down my legs, pooling at my feet.

His hands were back at my face, his touch aching with tenderness, his voice laced with reverence. "You are the most beautiful thing I've ever seen."

How was this even real? It was like my most secret fantasies come to life—the ones I held so close and never dared to look at.

One. Two. Three featherlight kisses fell over my lips. Pressing his thumb to the base of my spine, he swept upward until he reached my bra. He unhooked it, toying with the straps before letting it drop, his eyes raking over my exposed skin.

This was where I was supposed to feel self-conscious, at least it had been with other partners. But this was Evan. And standing in front of him like this, I'd never felt more confident. He told me I was beautiful. Touched me like I was beautiful. And now he was looking at me with hunger that fed my own.

He cupped my breasts, running his thumbs along the sensitive skin underneath, then rising further to tease circles around my nipples. I arched into his hands as they pebbled.

Walking me back toward the bed, he reached up, grabbing a fistful of his shirt at the back of his collar and dragging it over his head. *Wow.* I'd seen him shirtless a thousand times, but this was a brave new world. He was lean and well-defined. Broad shoulders tapering down to a trim waist. A light dusting of dark hair started just under his belly button and dipped below the waistband of his unbuttoned jeans.

"You wanna let me know when you're done or…?" I blinked up at him as he waggled his eyebrows. Caught gawking. *Very smooth, Violet.*

He placed a gentle kiss on the bridge of my nose where it scrunched. "It's a miracle my eyes aren't popping out of my head like that cartoon wolf. You're not the only one affected here." His voice went a little husky. "And I'll be honest, it feels pretty damn good to have you looking at me."

Of course he let me off the hook. Would he enjoy my defenselessness? Absolutely. Would he tease me about it? Likely. But he would never,

ever leave me in it alone. He wouldn't hide his own vulnerability. He'd lay it at my feet.

I lifted onto my tiptoes to kiss his generous mouth, unzipping his jeans and cupping him over his boxer briefs. I loved feeling his reaction to me, the stiffness and weight of him in my hand, the shudder that racked through his body as I gripped his shaft. Muttering a curse under his breath, he wasted no time pulling a condom from his wallet, dropping it on the nightstand, and divesting himself of his pants.

He eased me back onto the bed and followed me down, never breaking contact until I was pinned beneath him. Our gaze held for a long moment. I'd never seen him this way—naked, mussed, panting, his eyes dark with lust but something else as well, a new kind of tenderness I could easily get lost in if I let myself.

His hand cradled one side of my jaw as his lips and teeth scraped up the other. He brushed a kiss to the sensitive spot under my ear then nipped my lobe, sending a tingle down my spine and eliciting a squeaking whimper. I felt his chuckle more than heard it.

"I want to know every sound you make in bed." He dragged his mouth down my neck. "Every. Single. One." Kisses fell between each word as he continued his descent, placing more kisses on the hollow of my throat and down my sternum then over the swells of each breast. He licked my nipple, a long, slow lap with the flat of his tongue, then sucked it into his mouth with a demanding pull that I felt all the way to my core. I arched, seeking more.

He gave it to me. He nipped and sucked while he caught my other nipple between his thumb and forefinger, rolling and tugging it in coordination with the work of his mouth, coaxing me higher, then pulling away to start the process all over again on the other side. It was incredible torture, and the ache between my legs was becoming unbearable.

Sensing my need, he slipped a hand between us, grazing me over the cotton of my underwear, where my arousal was unmistakable. His forehead dropped to rest against the center of my chest, his groan sounding pained. "You're so wet, baby." He kept stroking, rubbing the damp fabric, increasing my need. My hips rolled mindlessly, seeking the relief he kept just out of reach.

His eyes flicked to mine. "Let me taste you?"

Those words from his mouth were surreal and wonderful in equal measure, sparking desire in me—desperate and sharp and focused. I needed it, needed *him. My Evan.* The thought was dangerous, and I felt certain I would pay for it later, but I was far beyond restraint.

"Yes. Please. Yes."

I squirmed in anticipation as he laved open-mouthed kisses down my stomach, dipped his tongue into my belly button, nipped at my hip bones, each touch sending sparks skittering across my skin. He caught the elastic of my panties and dragged them down my legs, tossing them carelessly aside, then ran his hands up the insides of my legs, spreading me wide and settling himself between them.

He kissed the inside of my thigh. The pad of his thumb grazed my seam, followed by his tongue. I gasped as he groaned, returning for another taste.

He explored me with his mouth—meandering licks, indulgent sips, lingering kisses. He teased and tasted. His tongue found my clit, flicking it gently before circling it twice, then sucking it between his lips.

"Oh, god." My back bowed off the bed as I threaded my fingers through his hair, spreading my legs wider. Evidently this was a response that he liked because he redoubled his efforts.

He slid his hands under my ass, grabbing my hips and tilting them up to give himself better access. His mouth found me again, this time with none of the teasing restraint. It was the most erotic sight of my life—his head between my legs, his shoulders straining, his hair mussed by my hands, his mouth devouring me like a man starved. My breath turned to pants as the threads of my orgasm began to tighten in my core.

He delved deep, using lips and tongue to build pleasure in my body until it threatened to break me apart. My fingers tightened in his hair.

"Evan…." I was so close. Standing at the edge of the cliff, begging him to push me over.

He slid two fingers into me, filling me, pushing me higher, crooking them forward to find that sensitive spot that made me cry out. I was desperate. Unraveling. Just a little more…

His mouth moved to my clit again, sucking hard. And I fell.

EVAN

She was coming. In my bed. On my tongue. Moaning and rocking, her fist twisted in my hair, and I was fucking destroyed.

Her pussy clenched around my fingers, and I eased my pace but stayed with her, working her down from her high.

When her body finally relaxed, I slipped my fingers from her and pressed one more kiss to her opening. *Honey.* Of course she tasted like honey. But earthier here than the sweet notes I was constantly smelling on her skin. I was already addicted.

Pulling myself away, I trailed kisses up her naked body. Licked her damp, salty skin while she wiggled and writhed beneath me. I nipped at her breasts, small but full with perfect, pink little tips better than any of my pasty fueled fantasies.

I kissed her deeply, licking into her soft mouth and earning a whimper that made my dick pulse. *God, her sounds were going to kill me.* Her greedy hands grasped at the elastic of my underwear, trying to push them down.

"Now. Please." Her voice was thready, a little desperate. She didn't need to beg. Anything she wanted. Any time she wanted it. I'd be the one begging to give it to her.

"Absolutely, sweetheart." I rolled to my back, shoving my boxer briefs down and kicking them off as I reached for the condom packet on the nightstand. I had myself sheathed and settled between her thighs in seconds. Bracing on one elbow, I hovered above her, my other hand cradling her jaw and pulling her mouth up to meet mine.

I rocked my hips, sliding myself through her slick folds, teasing her clit. Relief and torture. Grunting, I ground down into her. Another rock, another slide. Her eyes screwed shut as she arched into me, lips parted, panting.

I notched myself at her entrance. Her hands clutched at my sides, trying to encourage my movement, but I needed her eyes, needed that connection as I slid into her for the first time.

"Violet. Look at me."

Her eyes fluttered open, muted green and hazy with desire. Beautiful. And, I hoped, all mine. I sure as hell was hers.

Slowly, I pushed in, giving her time to adjust and savoring every hot inch of her until she softened and I seated myself completely. We both released shuddering breaths. *Fucking incredible.*

I drew myself out and pressed back in, taking my time. I refused to rush. The need for release was raging in my body, but the need to appreciate every second of this with her was stronger. Being with her like this was everything I could have imagined and more. I wanted to live in it, stretch it out into forever.

Our mouths brushed, not kissing—we were too far gone for that—but sharing breath. I moved again, rolling my hips in a way that made her moan. I set a slow, steady rhythm, dipping into her again and again. Stretching out our pleasure. Her nails scraped down the muscles of my back. Pressure built at the base of my spine.

"Perfect. You're perfect." I thrust harder, and she tightened around me. "I feel you, baby. Gripping me so tight. Are you gonna come again?"

"Yes." She was breathless, gasping.

I was so damn close. Fighting my release with every thrust. But I was determined to get her off first. Still braced over her with one arm, I spread her legs wider with mine, coming up on my knees. I snaked my other arm under her hips, lifting her into me, tilting her up to take me deeper—*fuck, so much deeper.*

She was keening, the sound pushing me to the very edge.

"Evan. I need…"

"I know. I've got you, baby. Come with me."

I ground against her clit, and she released on a sob.

"Evan."

My name. My name was on her lips while she came around me.

It broke me. Pleasure seared through my veins as I detonated, her name the only word I could manage to say in return.

We clutched each other tight as we rode out our orgasms, jerky movement and messy grinding until our breathing calmed and our heart rates slowed. Finally, I slipped out of her and collapsed, falling to the bed beside her and pulling her with me. We faced each other as I gathered her into my arms, fingers tangling in her curls, my mouth finding hers once again.

If I was destroyed before, this moment was putting me back together. Reshaping every part of me around loving this woman.

I held her close, unwilling to break our connection, and replayed every second of what had just happened, willing it to embed itself in my memory. Her eyes drifted closed, her body growing soft and heavy as her breathing slowed.

I nudged her nose with mine. "I'm going to go clean up. You wanna go after me?"

She hummed. I brushed one more kiss over her lips and got up to take care of the condom. By the time I got back, sweet little snores were drifting from where she lay curled up in my bed.

The sight almost brought me to my knees. She said yes. We were together. She was asleep in my bed, and I got to go sleep beside her.

Trying not to wake her, I eased under the covers and pulled her body into mine, her back to my front. Soft skin. Tangled hair. I pressed a kiss to the freckles dotting her shoulder and counted her breaths until I fell asleep.

CHAPTER 16

VIOLET

It wasn't the first time I'd woken up next to Evan. But it was most definitely the first time I'd woken up next to Evan naked. *Naked!* Naked and wrapped around me like the ultimate sex Snuggie.

Oh my god.

I was going to hyperventilate.

Deep breath, Violet. You will figure this out.

Holding that deep breath and trying to suppress my rising panic, I freed myself from his hold and then from the sheets tangled around my legs, narrowly missing a tumbling-out-of-bed-and-onto-my-face disaster.

I tiptoed around the room, collecting clothes to cover my (*yep, also very naked!*) body, and slipped out the door with Evan still snoring softly.

Success! The hard part is truly over. Now I just have to FIGURE OUT WHAT MY LIFE IS.

I had the overwhelming urge to flee before he woke up, but this was Evan, not some shameful one-night stand, and I could not bring myself to treat him like one. Not that I'd ever bolted on someone, but I sure wasn't gonna start now. I had to stay and make this right...somehow.

Stiffness in my hips turned my journey down the stairs into a hobble. I hadn't even realized they were sore, which I would have if I'd bothered with my morning check, but I guess there was nothing like a full-scale freakout to disrupt routine.

Tea. Make a cup of tea. Tea can fix anything.

Fortunately, I had a full complement of supplies here, and I fell into the ritual—filling the kettle, portioning my favorite loose-leaf blend into an infuser, collecting a mug, and pulling the honey from the cupboard. I even had the presence of mind to start a pot of coffee for Evan, successfully holding thoughts of last night at bay until I landed on an island stool, mug clutched tightly in my shaking hands.

With three deep breaths to center myself, I calmly approached the most pressing question: *What in the fuckity fuck have I done?*

Images of last night streamed through my memory. Evan's arms wrapped around me. Evan's breath on my neck. Evan's mouth. Evan's tongue. Evan filling me and moving in me and making me come apart and—*oh my god, STOP. You will not sit here and relive it.*

What was I thinking? It was reckless. Foolish. And I didn't even get up to pee! I had probably wrecked my relationship with my best friend and given myself a UTI in one fell swoop.

I let my head fall to the counter. *What a disaster.*

I didn't exactly have a robust sex life, not partnered sex anyway. Try as I might, casual sex was not for me, and since relationships were also not for me, I'd been in an epic dry spell. I'd love to blame my lack of self-control on that, but it would have been a lie. No, this was all Evan-based indiscretion. The weight of my feelings for him had been intensifying for weeks, my ability to contain them faltering. By the time he lit the match, I was primed like a room full of methane, ready to ignite.

The thing was…he *did* light the match.

What was this to him? I'd been so convinced that he would never, could never feel anything more for me than platonic affection. But obviously he felt…attraction? Was that all this was? Having a bit of fun, letting physical urges run wild?

"You are so beautiful."

"This is all I can think about."

"I've been trying to show you for weeks."

Those were not *having some fun* words, and last night felt anything but casual. Thursday, these last few weeks, all the times I thought it could be more but talked myself out of it—they didn't feel so casual either.

He wanted me. Not only as his friend. And not for a night in his bed. He was asking for more. Showing me, like he said.

The joy of it tore through me. My heart squeezed. My vision blurred behind a well of tears.

He. Wanted. Me.

But he shouldn't.

I had been so focused on dealing with my feelings for him, so sure that he'd never reciprocate those feelings, and then so shocked that he actually might, that I had never considered what it would mean if he did. Now with that reality staring me down, it was heartbreakingly clear that, mutual feelings or not, this could never happen. He needed a partner, someone he could marry, build a life with, have children with.

"And let's be honest, who would want to have kids with this hot mess, right?"
"I would."

No. No no no. I swore I would never do that to anyone. To do it to Evan, of all people? Absolutely not.

He didn't understand what he'd actually be signing up for. I couldn't give him the life he wanted. My illness and limitations would be a constant burden. I'd drain him—of energy, of patience, of happiness— until eventually, he ran out.

What then? Would he walk away like Rob? Stay out of obligation even though he was miserable like my parents? I didn't know what would be worse. Either would crush me. And either way, I would know that I was the one who crushed him.

I had to shut this down. I could feel my heart breaking at the very thought, but there was no other choice. I couldn't bring myself to regret last night. One night with Evan was more than I could have hoped for, a greedy dream I never imagined I'd get to make real.

But I had to let him go. I could only hope to do it without hurting him too badly, that we could keep our friendship intact. I was under no illusion that it wouldn't sustain damage, but maybe it could survive. It had to. Because the other option was unthinkable.

I had a lot of experience putting away my feelings for Evan, and I could do it again…for him.

———

"Morning."

Evan stood at the entrance to the kitchen, sweatpants hanging low on his hips, a dull orange T-shirt with a faded longhorn stretched across his chest. His scratchy morning voice sent a shiver down my spine. For a moment, I let myself imagine abandoning my plan and dragging him back to his room for round two.

"Morning," Even I could hear the tremor in my voice, so I cleared my throat and tried again. "I made you coffee."

"Thanks." He moved further into the kitchen, making himself a cup and watching me from the corner of his eye, like I was a wild animal he was trying not to spook.

I needed to be first to address the elephant in the room, so in my best upbeat voice, I dove into the script I'd spent the last half hour crafting. "So…last night was fun. Guess we got a little carried away." I forced a laugh as his eyebrows descended. "It was bound to happen at some point, I guess. It's out of the way now though, right? Haha!"

That second forced laugh may have been too much.

"Violet."

"You don't have to say anything. Believe me. We're on the same page. One night only. Fun and done. No worries here!"

Setting down his mug, he leaned back against the counter opposite me, face screwed up like he had swallowed something bitter. "What are you talking about? That was not a one-night stand. We both know it wasn't."

"Oh, well, I just assumed—"

"I don't think you did."

Damn. It's okay. You've got alternates locked and loaded.

"Evan, don't you think it's a bad idea for us to mess around longer-term? I know friends with benefits works for some—"

"Friends with benefits?" An edge had crept into his voice. "I don't want to be your friend with fucking benefits, Violet, and I think you know that, too."

On to Plan C.

"You were thinking something more serious. Doesn't that seem risky? I mean, what if it didn't work out? Our friendship means so much—"

Again, he didn't let me finish my sentence before his clipped words flew at me. "If it didn't work out? We've been in a relationship for ten years, Violet. We've been through more shit than most married couples I know. We work it out. We've always worked it out. We'd keep working it out, together or not. And if I thought even for a second that's what you were actually worried about, this conversation would be going a helluva lot differently, but something tells me that's not really the issue."

Shit.

This was going about as badly as it could. He'd burned through my scripts so quickly, and I only had one left. A last resort. I knew it would hurt him, but it had to be done. I clutched my tea tighter. "Ev, you know I love you, but last night was a big mistake." His eyebrows shot up and I could feel his ire climbing with them, but I pressed on. "You'll always be my best friend, but I just don't feel—"

"Stop." It was a strained whisper, a quiet hammer dropping to silence the room. "Why are you lying to me?" His hurt and anger built around him like a storm as he spoke. "You don't want to change our relationship? That's fine. I knew going in you may not want the same things I do. But I know you too damn well not to see when you're bullshitting." His volume steadily increased, each terse word drawing blood. "You've sat there feeding me one excuse after the next, but not a single thing you've said since 'I made you coffee' has been true. You can still say no to this, always, but goddammit, at least be honest with me while you break my heart."

———

EVAN

She looked stricken and my anger drained immediately. *Fuck.* That wasn't okay. "I'm sorry. That wasn't fair. My heart…that's not something you're responsible for."

I dropped my head and pushed a thumb at the knot of tension between my eyes. I needed to regroup. My frustration was not helping me here.

It was the lies that I couldn't stand. She'd lobbed them at me, one after another, as soon as I walked in the room. I was ready for a no—didn't want it, but I was ready for it. I'd never push her, never assume I knew what she wanted better than she did. I just wanted the truth.

After last night—being with her, thinking we were starting something, feeling like she was right there with me, falling asleep with her in my arms—I needed to know what she was thinking, what she was feeling. Maybe that was asking too much, but I didn't think so, and it was the only way I was ever going to make sense of this for myself.

With a deep breath, I met her terrified eyes and softened my voice. "I did mean the part about wanting you to be honest. That's all I'm asking for here."

She was clearly in distress. Keeping my distance, not touching her, not comforting her—it felt wrong on every level, but I didn't know how welcome I'd be in her space at the moment. I took a hesitant step toward her, and she didn't shy away, so I took another and then another until I was beside her, only the corner of the island separating us. I sat one hand over hers where she was wringing them on the countertop. It wasn't as close as I wanted to be, but it was safe for now.

"Please, Vi. Talk to me."

"You're right. I'm sorry." It sounded like the words were choking her, a lump forming in my own throat in response, but I watched her gather her resolve. "The truth…the truth is, of course I want you that way. I have for a really long time."

She wants me. They were the sweetest words I'd ever heard. Hope flared in my chest.

"The fact that, somehow, you feel the same right now is…elating. But it can't work."

As quickly as the hope arrived, she was trying to extinguish it, but it wouldn't go that easily. We were perfect together. If she wanted me like I wanted her, I couldn't imagine what else we needed that we didn't already have. "Why can't it work?"

Her voice was pained. "Evan. I'm not going to have the life you want. I'm not going to have kids."

Her hesitation came into focus. This is what was stopping her. She thought we wanted different things, but she didn't understand. What I wanted was her.

I had my doubts about her change of heart around kids, but if that's truly what she wanted, then so be it. I'd love to have them, but there was a lot that could get in the way of that, and none of those things would change how I felt about her. If she'd wanted them and we couldn't have them, I wouldn't stop loving her, wouldn't stop wanting her. This was the same. "That's okay with me."

She looked skeptical.

"Look, I know those are things I've talked about. And I'll be honest, they're things I want. But they aren't things I need."

"They are things you need! I know—"

I squeezed her hand. "You trust me, right?"

"Of course I do."

"Then trust me to know what I need. And trust me to tell you the truth. Those aren't dealbreakers for me. Not if everything else is with you."

Her eyes went glassy. Her chin trembled. "What about Boston?"

I had plenty of complicated feelings about Boston, but if kids weren't a dealbreaker, it sure as hell wouldn't be. "We'll be okay. We can manage long-distance for a few months."

There was something more, something she wasn't saying that was holding her back.

Her eyes fell to the table, like she couldn't bring herself to look at me. "You said you tried to show me how it could be, but what you're imagining, that's not the whole picture. It's…I'm too much in all the wrong ways, and not enough in the right ones. You don't realize what you'd be signing up for."

The thought was almost comical. "How could that possibly be true? I know you better than anyone, just like you know me. I've been in it with you for years already. Day in, day out. I know exactly what it is, because I'm already your person." I chanced a smile, a tease. "How can there be surprises when I already know all your secrets?"

The corner of her mouth tugged, just a little, but it felt like a huge victory. But then she sobered, her brows knitting, her voice barely audible. "What if you get into this and you're disappointed? What if I can't be what you want?"

To hell with distance. I stepped around the corner of the island and turned her stool, stepping between her knees and taking her beautiful face in my hands.

"You already are. I don't want some person I hope you'll become. I want you."

The hope in her eyes was all I needed to lay myself bare. I pulled her hands to my chest, willing her to feel the truth beating hard against my ribs, willing her to trust me.

"I love you, Violet. And any life we make together is the one I want."

She had my whole damn life in those hands as I waited for her answer, and when she finally gave it, it blew my chest wide open.

"I love you, too."

CHAPTER 17

EVAN

I was floating through the office like a damn fool, and I couldn't even bring myself to be embarrassed. It was the unavoidable side effect of a perfect weekend. I refused to do anything less than revel in it. And if that drew a few stares…well…they could go right ahead and look.

Flipping on the light, I stepped into my office. Like most of the offices here, it was on the larger side (big enough for my desk and a drafting table off to the side) and well-appointed, traditional in a way that still felt fresh, flooded with natural light. Nancy was a big believer that environment impacted work, and they'd invested in making this an environment that generated great work. I loved it here. But today, I didn't see any of it.

I went through my morning routine, and she infiltrated every thought. Put down travel mug. *Violet.* Unpack bag. *Violet.* Dock laptop and boot up. *Violet.* Arrange notepad and pens.

Violet. Loves. Me. Back.

The memory of her saying those words still made my heart feel like it was going to explode out of my chest.

Saturday night had been such a high—being with her for the first time, feeling like we were starting something. And then yesterday morning came and pulled the rug right out from under me. Waiting for her response after I told her I loved her was the most scared I've ever been.

But then she said it back. And she stayed. And it was perfect.

After so many years of friendship, I honestly thought the transition to a new dynamic (if we got that far) might be a little bumpy, that there might be a learning curve to Evan and Violet 2.0. But I couldn't have been more wrong. Being together like this was as easy as breathing.

We had sex until we were spent. She wore only my T-shirt while we gorged ourselves on ramen and watched TV curled up on the couch. I fell asleep with her body tucked into mine and her wild curls spread over my pillows.

She was still in my bed when I left for work this morning, and forcing myself out the door had been a fucking feat. Not only because I wanted to crawl back under the covers and bury myself between her legs. I wanted to hang out with her, play hooky, and spend another day in our bubble. Or at least go back to her when I left here. Eat dinner with her. Sleep beside her. Wake up next to her. Every day. For the rest of my life.

I probably needed to dial that back. It was way too early to ask her to move in with me—not that I wouldn't have a new house and rings picked out in a heartbeat if I thought she'd say yes—but maybe we could have a little bit longer.

> You should stay at my house today. I'll bring home dinner. You can spend the night again.

VI

> I have no clean clothes!

> Great news. Clothes are not a requirement.

> Very tempting. 😊

> But I don't have toiletries or any of my work stuff either and those actually are requirements, unfortunately.

I understood that being without her stuff wasn't tenable—I couldn't expect her to put her life on hold to wait around at my house for me—but damn, I hated the idea of being without her tonight. We'd spent two nights together and already being apart felt wrong. It was a small consolation that she didn't seem excited about leaving either.

Understood.

Although if neither of us wanted to be apart…

Hey can I come over tonight?

Hahahaha.

Yes.

Or I could go pack a bag and come back?

Thank god. My relief was probably overblown, but following the theme of the morning, I did not give a shit.

Perfect. Just so we're clear the bag is only toiletries and work stuff right? The no clothes requirement stands.

My already dopey grin grew even bigger in response to that little kiss.

"You're looking mighty pleased with yourself." Nothing to bring you back to reality like a sudden pain in the ass. He was leaning casually against my door, arms and ankles crossed, a manila folder in his hand and a bolo tie around his neck begging to become a murder weapon.

"Morning, Brad. It's going to be a good day."

"Right, right. Reviewing your city proposal in staff this morning, aren't we?"

Shit. We were. And I needed to get my head in the game for it. I'd been floating through my Violet haze and had all but forgotten about outlining my RFP response in our department staff meeting today. Fortunately, I had my materials prepped and ready last week, but I needed to review them and get my mind right, or I'd be looking like a fool in front of Lucia, Paul, and the rest of the architecture team.

That would not fly. This proposal was too big. It didn't matter how much they believed in me, they couldn't afford to let me take this pitch if it looked like I wasn't prepared. I would make sure that wasn't an issue. I'd prove their faith in me wasn't misplaced.

But it was a little concerning how quickly Violet had replaced thoughts about this project. I'd need to get that under control.

The more pressing concern at the moment, though, was how the hell Brad knew I had a proposal to review. As my peer, that's not information he'd typically have beforehand. Not that it was a secret. We just didn't have much reason to track each other's projects outside of being briefed and providing minor input during staff meetings. So maybe the most important question wasn't *how* he knew, but *why*.

"I'm looking forward to weighing in." He tapped his folder twice on my door and strutted away.

My internal alarms were blaring. Those words may have had the appearance of being benign, but they very much weren't. He was up to something, and he was putting me on notice.

———

"This looks good, Evan." Lucia sat at the head of the large oak table, flicking her pen as she gave my proposal a final scan.

Relief rolled through me. It seemed to be generally well-received. There were only a few questions, and no pushback to speak of (not even from Brad, which was suspect) but I hadn't let myself relax until those words of approval from her.

"I see you've got Lynn listed as the designer and Carlos as the project manager. I assume you've coordinated with them already?"

"Yes. I've consulted with them both, and they're good to go."

She nodded. "Paul?"

He sat to her right. He wasn't one to pull rank. This was her department and her meeting, and he gave her space and his full support to run both as she saw fit, but on a project this big, he'd be deferred to.

"It's a solid proposal. Represents us well. I'm good to proceed if you are." Meeting my eyes across the table, he gave me a barely perceptible nod. His approval, affirmation that I was on the right track.

Luce flipped the folder shut. "Excellent. This looks ready for submission then—unless anyone else sees something we need to discuss?"

A chorus of no's and looks good's filled the room, the last of my nerves carried away with them.

"Actually, I do have one thing..." *And there it is.* Across the table from me, Brad lifted his finger, looking a little too pleased. I leaned in, forearms against the edge of the table, bracing for whatever he had coming. "The sustainability section is, no offense Evan, a little weak, I think."

I fought the urge to roll my eyes. That section came basically directly from our RFP answer library. We'd used that framework dozens of times, and this request didn't indicate anything different was needed.

Still, my gaze darted to Lucia as she flipped back to that page of her packet. "This is pretty standard. And the brief didn't include anything about a special focus here."

Well, at least we're on the same page.

"Right, right. It's fine for what the brief lays out. But I have a contact on the committee. He seems to think that a proposal that's on the cutting edge of sustainability could really sway them."

Of fucking course. Sustainability was his specialty. We weren't niche players. We were all competent in eco-friendly architecture, but it was an area of focus for him, and he was damn good at it. And now—surprise, surprise—it was exactly what was needed per a mysterious inside source. He was creating an on-ramp for himself right into my project with a need for his expertise, an advantageous connection, and insider information that he was content to sit on until it served him.

This guy was the worst. The words formed in my mouth to call him out, but I trapped them there. Getting down in the mud with him would dirty me as much as him. I could only hope that his play was as obvious to others as it was to me.

Lucia's gaze was sharp. "And you didn't think that was information you should have passed along to Evan?"

Thank you.

He leaned back and raised his hands. "I only spoke with him this weekend. I'm sharing at my first opportunity." *Unlikely.* "I'm here to support Evan on this. I'd be happy to join the project. Help him get the sustainability aspect up to snuff. And having my name on it couldn't hurt with the committee, given my connection. My plate is a little full at the moment, but I can make room to help the team."

If I bit my tongue much harder, I was going to draw blood. He was a snake, and he'd put me in a no-win situation. If I protested, I'd look arrogant and territorial, but if he got this inch, he'd take miles and miles. I wanted no part of that power struggle. But I sure as shit didn't want to roll over and hand my project to him either.

Luce straightened, both hands on the table and ready to issue a ruling. I held my breath. "Evan, I'm not sure whether sustainability will be a high priority for them given the lack of emphasis on it in the program, but it would be smart to beef that up in case Bradley's contact has the right of it. I'm sure you'll be able to adapt accordingly. Run the changes by me before we send in the final proposal." She turned to address Brad. "Bradley, I don't think we'll need to monopolize your time by adding you to the project. But please do meet with Evan after this to fill him in on any information that may help, and make yourself available to *consult* if needed."

I released my breath in what I hoped wasn't a completely obvious gust. Lucia was wrapping up the meeting, but my mind was already making a new plan.

Even though I'd dodged a bullet, I wasn't totally in the clear. Handling Brad's potential-but-not-really-verified tip could still turn into a disaster. If he was wrong or exaggerating and I changed things too much, it would look like I didn't understand the client's priorities. If he was right and I didn't take his input, I'd look territorial and stupid. I'd have to find the happy medium. Hopefully I'd be more equipped to figure out what that was after I met with him to get more details.

It would be fine. I'd kept my afternoon blocked off to work on any changes Luce or Paul wanted to make. Just because the changes were more annoying now didn't make them any less manageable.

I'd make it happen. And then I'd go home to Violet.

A smile threatened as a gathered my things, but as I stood, my gaze clashed with Brad's across the room. His expression hardened with barely contained frustration.

Honestly, same, asshole.

Still, I won this round. And it wasn't even the best thing to happen to me today.

Maybe it was petty, but I let him see the full force of that smile unfurl as I made my way out of the room.

CHAPTER 18

VIOLET

It had been forty hours since I'd last set foot in my apartment, and as I crossed the threshold, it was a little jarring to see it intact. Colorful afghan draped across the couch, computer charging on the table, the beginnings of a grocery list hanging on the fridge—exactly as I'd left it. But surely that was an impossibility given the landscape of my entire life had shifted since I was last here. Where were the cobwebs? The thick layer of dust? The crumbling ruins of my grocery list drifting away on the wind? Anything at all to account for the whole life I'd just lived outside these walls.

This familiar place where nothing at all had changed felt suddenly eerie when I was still reeling from the biggest change in my entire life.

Evan and I were officially in a relationship. Elatingly, terrifyingly in a relationship.

I had resolved not to go down this road with someone. Had been so certain that pairing up was not a feasible option. But then it was *Evan* —kissing me, touching me, telling me he loved me, asking me to trust him—and all of that resolve crumbled around my feet.

Maybe if it had only been the love part, I'd have been able to resist. Also maybe not, but at least I'd have stood a chance. My desire for him was strong, but my desire to protect us both may have been stronger.

Ultimately, it was the trust part that unraveled things. Because he was right. He did know me and my situation. And he did have the right to decide what he wanted. If I wanted the same things (which I obviously did) I had to trust him. And I did trust him. More than anyone.

Though it was a lot easier to feel confident when we were wrapped up in the little cocoon we'd constructed out of declarations of love and sex hormones. Now, with my apartment making the last forty hours feel like an illusion, doubt was attempting to worm its way in.

I wasn't going to let it. I was leaning into the trust. He would make good decisions for himself. He would be honest. He wanted me. He was happy.

But for how long?

I groaned and dropped my keys on the table. Maybe that was the voice of reason talking, but right now she sounded like an asshole.

I didn't have to listen, right? And I didn't have to continue to be disquieted by this BE (Before Evan) time capsule that felt strangely undermining.

I stomped forward into the kitchen and ripped the grocery list from the pad on the refrigerator, balling it up and flinging it into the trashcan. That was probably going to come back to bite me on my next store trip, but as ill-conceived as the move may have been, it gave me an undeniable rush. And pushed that asshole voice into the background.

I wanted more. I scanned the room on a surge of resolve.

Things have changed, apartment. Get on board.

I spun into action. I washed a bowl. I lit a brand-new candle. I switched the throw blanket in the living room with the one from the bedroom. *Transformation!*

It was a bizarre way to cope with my doubts. Even I could recognize it. But despite the oddity, it was working. My apartment had become the physical embodiment of change. Erase the nothing-has-happened vibes, erase the nothing-should-happen doubts. I was committing, dammit. Embracing this new relationship by making barely discernible changes in my home.

This really is weird.

Whatever. Trust the process, I guess.

Riding the wave of satisfaction from my bare-minimum home refresh, I made myself a bowl of cereal and folded into a seat at the table to check emails. New pages from one author. A question from another. And a brief for a project to put in my queue.

I cringed around my spoon. I might not be here to see that through. Ideally, I'd start making contingency plans now to deal with work that would be impacted if I got accepted into the program. But there was no world in which that would go well with Gemma. She did not take kindly to situations where she wasn't in complete control. If I whispered even the possibility of moving on, she'd probably fire me on the spot in a fit of pique.

I wasn't ready to lose this job. Even in the best-case scenario, I needed to feed myself for almost two more months until the program started. Plus, that best case was a long shot anyway. I likely wouldn't get in. Then where would I be? Still here, jobless and homeless.

Well, probably not homeless. Evan would take me in before I had to resort to sleeping in my car. But still, losing this job before I was ready was not a scenario I wanted any part of. I'd have to keep things under wraps and deal with the fallout later. I hated the idea that I might have to blindside some authors, but my hands were tied.

And while I was on the subject of precarious housing and impossible juggling acts, I had to figure out what to do about my lease. It was almost up, and I would have to make a decision on renewal before I knew about the fellowship. Maybe they'd let me go month-to-month.

Ugh. Planning to maybe possibly but probably not move halfway across the country on short notice was stressful. I'd been rigorous in avoiding thinking about it. I hadn't made plans to move. I hadn't even told anyone but Evan...with whom I'd just started a brand new romantic relationship that would have to go long distance if this worked out.

Of all the stressful things, that was the most stressful. He said we'd be okay.

And of course we would. He'd been supportive of this from the beginning. My biggest encourager in pursuing writing. That wouldn't change because our relationship dynamic did, right?

We'll make it work. Even in my own head, I didn't sound convinced. *Lean into the trust.*

I had the sudden urge to go flip my toilet paper on the holder.

Underside TP dispensing?? A bridge too far, Violet. A bridge too far.

My phone vibrated on the table. *Pulled back from the brink.* My spoon clattered in my empty bowl as I sat it on the table and picked up the phone.

JAMIE

Family dinner at our place Saturday night?

Likes poured through while excitement and nerves swirled together in my belly. It would be our first time with everyone as this new entity, and I didn't quite know how to feel about it. It was big. Good. But also had me feeling a little anxious for reasons I couldn't quite put my finger on.

Another text popped up. Just to me.

EVAN

I can't wait to tell them about us. I love you.

Gonna be covered up at work this afternoon.
See you at home sweetheart.

My heart warmed and my stomach settled. Time to pack that bag.

———

EVAN

My head pounded as I tossed my keys into the wooden bowl on my entry table.

It had been A Day. After that roller coaster of a meeting, I met with Brad to get his Very Important Inside Information—which basically amounted to "maybe they'd like to see some cool eco-friendly stuff included?" So in a word, nothing.

I decided against reworking my whole approach. The brief was thorough, and they were clear about their priorities. I felt confident I was on the right track with what I had, but I still needed to cover my bases just in case. Ultimately, I added mentions of a couple of cutting-edge techniques that would show them we were capable of going down that road if they wanted to but didn't steal too much focus from the rest of my proposal.

If that had been the whole afternoon, I probably wouldn't be dealing with the jackhammer between my eyes, but I was unfortunately not that lucky. In the middle of making those adjustments, a last-minute change request on one of my current projects caused a complete cluster of a fire drill. It was a scramble. Finally, after going approximately twenty rounds with the client and convincing my project manager not to light something on fire, I got everything resolved. But I was later than I wanted to be getting back to Vi, which pissed me off even more than Brad's bolo tie. So here I was, working on the tension headache of the year.

I rounded the corner into the living room and stopped short. She was there, curled up in the corner of my big leather couch under a blanket even though it was three degrees hotter than hell outside. Her hair was piled high on her head, a few curls escaping containment. She still wore one of my T-shirts even though she'd been home, a fact that made something in my chest flip over. Her brow and nose furrowed as she stared something down on her computer screen, clearly so engrossed she hadn't heard me come in.

The stress that had been squeezing me for hours loosened, and I couldn't wait another second to be close to her. Finally seeing me as I came toward her, her face lit up but quickly fell as she read my mood.

"Hey. What's wrong?" She reached forward to set her computer on the coffee table, and I dropped the takeout bag I was carrying next to it before leaning over her and pressing a long kiss to her mouth.

Nothing that had happened today could touch this. I got to come home to her, got to kiss her without hesitation. It was enough to put the whole day to rights.

"God, I'm glad you're here." I fell to the couch beside her, one hand reaching out to touch her while the other worked at the ache between my eyes. "Today was kind of a shit show. I had an issue on a project. Brad tried to take over the city proposal." Her eyes went wide. "I'm home late. And my head is killing me."

"Come here." She hooked one leg up on the couch and patted her lap where it made a cradle. "Bring me your head."

"I'm fine. Really. Nothing to worry about."

"I'm not *worried*. But I can help. Come here and let me."

She pulled me toward her, and I went reluctantly. Laying my head in her lap sounded like heaven, but I didn't want her to have to fuss over me. I was supposed to be the one taking care of her. I didn't even know how she was feeling. We'd had an…active weekend, and I'd been too caught up in my own busyness and stress to even check in on her today.

Damn. Day two and you're already slacking.

"What about you? Are you feeling okay? I don't—"

She pressed into my brow bone with both thumbs, and I cut off with a groan, my eyes falling shut.

She hummed in satisfaction. "Exactly." She swept her thumbs outward toward my temples then came back for a second pass. "I'm feeling fine."

"The food…"

"Will reheat." She bent over me and brushed an upside-down kiss across my lips. "Relax and let me take care of you."

I was out of resistance. I melted into her lap, into her touch. She massaged my brow, my temples, my scalp, my neck, slowly releasing the tension of the day, dissolving my headache with each stroke.

She tugged gently on my hair, the sensation zipping straight down my spine to my groin. I felt her light chuckle. I wasn't sure what gave me away, but she clearly knew the effect she'd had. She ran her fingers through my hair and tugged again.

Reaching up, I snagged one of her wrists, tipping my head back and peering at her through one open eye. "Ya know, I'm suddenly feeling so much better."

"Fantastic. Tell me about the Brad thing."

"Ugh. Cockblock." I screwed up my face as she cackled. If I'd had any bit of angst left over, that laugh would have banished it. Coming home to her after a hard day was a gift. I pressed a kiss to the palm of the hand I was still holding and released her. She resumed running her fingers through my hair (no tugging this time) as she waited for an answer.

"He tried to make a move when we reviewed my proposal in our staff meeting this morning. He said he had a connection on the committee and some inside information. Tried to leverage it into a spot on the project."

"Oh, shit."

"Yep. I expect him to be generally difficult to work with, but this was a slimy move. I'm guessing he knows the lay of the land on the promotion just like I do. He's got plenty to bring to the table. More experience than I do. But maybe he's not feeling so confident. This felt kinda desperate. Like he was trying to make sure I didn't have this one up on him."

The sabotage, the power play—those were obvious up front, but I was too pissed earlier to see the desperation. Now with some distance, I had the right read on the situation. I wasn't sure if that should make me feel better about my chances or worried about what else that desperation might prompt him to try.

"I'm assuming it didn't work, given you're not completely losing it."

"I think it backfired on him. Luce seemed to see right through it and shut him down pretty quickly. She's no bullshit. She won't be impressed with the maneuvering."

He could still make life hard for me, but I was confident now that leadership wouldn't be swayed by him at least.

"Good. You deserve this project. And you deserve the promotion too. Brad and his belt buckle can kick rocks."

Damn, I adore her. "Thank you. And thank you for taking care of me tonight." She ran her hands over my chest. "Though I'm surprised you're willing to part with that belt buckle so quickly. Thought you were into those cowboy types. Something about buttered biscuits?"

"Mmm. Maybe I changed my mind." She slipped my top button free.

"Oh yeah?"

"Yeah." Her nails scraped down my sternum, dropping a hot weight right into my groin, before she worked the next button open. "I'm starting to think I'm partial to hot, sweet, slightly obsessive, best friend, architect types."

"Pretty niche." A third button undone. I was already hard as steel and aching to take her right here on the couch. "But I think I have just the guy."

She grabbed two fistfuls of my shirt and pulled it free from my pants. "Show me."

Yeah. Coming home to her was a fucking dream.

CHAPTER 19
VIOLET

"Hey. What's going on?" Evan turned off the car and shifted in his seat to face me.

I'd barely registered the ride over here, inexplicably anxious about the big reveal we were about to make at this Family Dinner. I blinked away from the cute craftsman-style house on the corner. "Nothing. I'm good."

"The Vi poker face strikes again." He smirked as he ran a finger down the bridge of my nose, smoothing the crinkles that gave me away. But when his teasing did nothing to ease my tension, his gaze softened. "Tell me what's wrong. Are you nervous?"

"Yes?" He slid his palm against mine, and I grasped it like a lifeline. "That's absurd, I know. There is literally nothing to be nervous about. These are our people. And this is good news. And according to my conversation with Lina and your conversation with Nico, it won't even be terribly surprising. I just…" My head fell to the headrest as I closed my eyes on a sigh. "I'm happy. And I want this to go well."

His hand curved around my neck, fingers threading through the hair at my nape. "It will go well." His thumb stroked my jawline as I opened my eyes to meet his. "But it's not absurd to be nervous. This is important. And you want everyone to be supportive."

That was true, but I didn't think it was the source of my angst. I expected them to be supportive, excited even. We were likely in for some light needling, especially from Lina, but it would be in the spirit of fun and gloating. But if I was so sure of their reaction, why was there still a pit of unease in my stomach?

"If I had my guess, you're also probably a little unsure of how this will feel in front of the group."

That was exactly it. Before I was even able to identify the problem, he'd plucked it out and put words to it. He just knew.

We'd only been this new version of us in private. I didn't know what it would look like out in the world. And we'd be road-testing this major change where the group dynamic was already so well established. It's not that I thought it would go badly, but I didn't know what to expect or how it would feel or where to put my hands.

I leaned further into his touch.

"We'll figure it out. Everyone will be happy for us." A smile tugged at his lips. "And we can go with whatever level of PDA feels good to you. I swear I won't feel you up until you give me the go-ahead."

Huffing a laugh, I leaned across the console to press a hard, grateful kiss to his mouth. He made it look easy—identify the issue, provide support, make a disarming joke, and just like that, he'd reached in and turned my anxiety right down, easy as turning down the radio. I was still nervous, but now more excited than worried.

"That wasn't the reaction I was expecting, but I'll take it."

I nuzzled into him. "Thank you."

He nuzzled back. "Any time."

With one more quick kiss, we were out and making our way up the flower-lined walkway.

Nico and Jamie moved in here about three months ago. A small three-bedroom in an adorable neighborhood a little outside of the city and close to Jamie's school, it was the ideal place for them to start their family.

A pang of longing lanced through me. What they were building here was what I'd always wanted. And I was truly so happy for them. It just snuck up on me sometimes, the remnants of those dreams I'd mostly let go. My life would look different than I'd imagined. I wouldn't have kids. I wasn't even sure I'd get married. But that was okay. I was happy. Especially now that I had Evan.

But how long will he be happy?

I shoved the thought away. He was happy. He told me this was what he wanted. *Trust.* I was trusting him. And limiting myself to one anxiety spiral per night.

I let those worries slip away as we stepped through the front door. We could see straight into the kitchen, where everyone was already gathered. Jamie was shooing Nico away from a tray of food while Lina and Remy poured wine on the other side of the island.

As we made our way to join them, Evan caught my eye, one more discreet check-in before we fully joined the group. At my nod of assurance, his spine straightened and his shoulders rolled back. He was proud of us, excited to tell our friends. He just needed to know I was with him.

I ran my fingers along the back of his hand. A wide smile split his face and lightning bugs danced in my belly.

Lina gasped. "Oh my god. You finally banged."

The room froze.

We'd made it to the island where everyone was gathered, and apparently we hadn't quite tucked away our moony expressions before our arrival. So much for the play-it-cool-until-we-make-an-official-announcement plan.

Stepping closer to me, Evan wrapped his arm around my waist and pulled me into his side. "Vi and I have some news to share. We're together." He looked down at me, grinning like a maniac, his joy palpable, and I knew my own smile was no more restrained.

"Yes! I win. Pay up, Nico."

Lina's outburst shattered the sweet moment, and there was a beat of silence before a laugh boomed from Evan's chest, the rest of the room following.

Honestly, I wasn't shocked there was a bet, knowing this group. "So you bet on whether we'd get together?"

Nico worked his wallet from his back pocket. "No. You two were a foregone conclusion. The bet was whether or not Lina could make it without interfering."

"Which I did. Even though it took a thousand years."

"Ten." Evan corrected the record.

"That's basically the same."

Nico rested his elbow on the granite, a folded-up bill between two fingers. He extended it toward her but quickly snapped it back, narrowing his eyes. "Wait. *Did* you interfere?"

"No!" He continued his skeptical stare-down, tucking the cash into his pocket as she crossed her arms indignantly. "I didn't. I was approached for advice and answered honestly. Once. That does not count as interference."

Remy shook his head and stepped toward Evan. "What they're attempting to say is 'congratulations, we're really happy for you two.'"

Evan released me to return Rem's back-slapping hug, kicking off the receiving line.

Nico was already rummaging in cabinets by the time we'd made it through everyone. "Let's line 'em up." He passed shot glasses to Remy who set them out on the bar while he retrieved a bottle of peach schnapps from over the refrigerator.

I couldn't even remember what we were celebrating the first time we did this. The original four of us were in Nico's dorm room, needing to toast some college freshman success, and all we could find was a bottle of peach schnapps under his roommate's bed, so we toasted over shots. Now, long after that ill-advised choice was made, the tradition remained. We all kept a bottle on hand exclusively for this (since it's not like we'd be drinking it for any other reason), and we'd celebrated all manner of life victories this way.

Now our friends were celebrating us.

My earlier freakout seemed silly. Dubiously appropriate outbursts, a decade-long bet, and peach schnapps. It all felt exactly right.

Shots poured, Lina was the first to put hers in the air. "I'm so so happy for you two. Even more than I am for the fifty dollars I will definitely make Nico cough up. I won't even tell you I told you so."

Jamie chimed in helpfully. "I think you just did."

"Well, it's as close as I'm gonna get. Everybody raise a glass"—six small glasses lifted into the air—"to two of our own…finally getting their shit together."

Cheers.

The peach schnapps was disgusting as always. And better than ever.

———

"I can't get over how he's looking at you. He literally cannot take his eyes off of you."

My face heated as I glanced toward the back of the yard, where Evan stood with Nico and Remy discussing landscaping plans. Jamie was right. He was decidedly uninterested in Nico's presentation, eyes only for me.

I bit my lip, and he winked at me, earning a squeak from Jamie and a groan from Lina. "You're disgustingly cute. I should have seen this coming."

I took a sip from my glass. The wine was cool and crisp, refreshing in the heat. Even now with the sun dipping below the horizon and the cicadas humming to life, it was just shy of oppressively hot. Still, we'd chosen to post up on the cozy back deck. It was charming enough to brave the heat.

"This place really is great, Jamie."

She glowed at the compliment. "There's a lot of work left to do, but I love it. And it's a great neighborhood." She nudged my shoulder with hers. "There are some houses for sale. Maybe we can entice you and Evan to move out here. It's a great place to start a family."

My stomach took a little dip. There was so much wrong with that proposition. Starting with the fact that I might not be living here in six months, and ending with the family that I didn't intend to have. I hadn't told them any of it.

I still couldn't bring myself to crack into the family chestnut. I didn't think they'd understand, and I didn't have it in me to try to convince them.

But I wanted to tell them about the fellowship. I'd been keeping it under wraps until I got my application in, but now that it was submitted, the possibility was real, and I was getting excited. I knew I'd have their support.

I cleared my throat. "Actually, I have one other piece of good news. I applied for a writing fellowship. It's a six-month program in Boston, which is terrifying." I tucked a stray curl behind my ear. "But honestly you wouldn't believe how amazing this program is and what the alumni go on to do. I still won't know for a few weeks, and I'm trying not to get my hopes up, but I'm really excited."

"A writing fellowship? Vi, that's amazing." Lina was nearly bursting with enthusiasm.

Jamie's smile was soft. "I didn't even know you wrote. But this sounds so great, and I'm so proud of you for doing this."

"You have no idea, Jamie. She's incredible. Writing is what she's meant to do. And she's put it aside for way too long."

Warmth flooded my chest. "That's probably an exaggeration."

"It is not an exaggeration. And I will kick your ass if you say my friend isn't brilliant, so I'd leave it right there if I were you."

I rolled my lips between my teeth. Nobody could express love through subtle bullying like Lina. And Jamie was jumping to be proud of me before she even fully knew the story. I had the best people.

"So give us all the details. How did this happen? What's it going to be like when you get in?"

At Jamie's prompting, I told the whole story. My writing history for Jamie's benefit, then Gemma and rage googling and Miranda Freaking Schultz. Submitting my application and being proud of the work I sent in. We talked about the program and Boston and even started planning a girls' weekend up there.

A tiny wrinkle formed in Jamie's brow as she stared down into her nearly empty glass of wine. "So not to be a buzzkill because that's not at all my intent, but when you get this, what happens with you and Evan?"

A feeling of unease swept through my stomach. "We're going to make it work long-distance. The timing obviously isn't ideal, but he's been so supportive. I...I think we'll be okay."

I couldn't quite cover the tremor of uncertainty in my voice, and they both rushed to reassure me.

"You will be. People do long distance all the time." Jamie placed her hand over mine with a reassuring squeeze.

Lina's eyes held mine. "If anyone can make it work, it's you two. You're soulmates. And I don't even believe in that shit."

I laughed, my uneasy feeling receding.

"Of course you'll work it out."

I released a deep breath. *Of course we'd work it out.*

———

"She wasn't even very smug."

Evan glanced over his shoulder with a raised brow as we walked down the hall and into his kitchen. It had been a good night. After all of my fretting over the reveal and the new dynamic, it had felt remarkably normal. One more thing that came so easily with him.

"Okay. For Lina, she wasn't very smug."

"I'll give you that." He opened the refrigerator and slid in the leftover beers he was carrying. "Honestly? I didn't want to say anything because I didn't want to stress you out more, but I thought they'd give us more shit for sure."

"Me too." Handing him one of two leftovers containers I was carrying, I pulled my bottom lip between my teeth. "But you were right about the rest. It seemed like they were really happy for us."

"They were." Straightening, he ran a hand down my arm and brushed a chaste kiss across my lips. "We're something to be happy for."

I felt my smile in my whole body. *We are, aren't we?*

He moved to take the last container from my hands, and I snatched it back, clutching it to my chest. "I'm not ready to part with the shortcake."

A chuckle rumbled through him as he closed the refrigerator and opened the silverware drawer. He lifted two spoons out, a silent question on his face.

"Definitely."

Grasping my hips, he lifted me onto the island, taking his place between my knees. I ripped the lid from the container, tossing it toward the sink. It would no longer be needed. This shortcake wouldn't see morning.

We each took a heaping spoonful, and I groaned around the bite. "Jamie is a goddess."

"You're not wrong."

It seemed like everything she made was sprinkled with some sort of delicious magic. Even something as simple as whipped cream tasted like heaven. Dragging my finger through the fluffy white topping, I popped it into my mouth and sucked my finger clean.

Evan's gaze heated. He dropped his spoon into the container and braced his hands on the countertop, bracketing my legs. "Whipped cream, Vi?"

"What?"

"That's practically an invitation. You're playing with fire."

His eyes were molten as they peered at me from under his lowered brow. A seductive smirk curled his soft mouth. I hadn't intended it to be a tease, but with that look on his face, I was catching up quick. And I wanted to play with fire. Very, very much.

Anticipation fluttered in my belly, but I kept a mask of innocence as I dropped my spoon next to his and collected another helping of whipped cream onto my finger.

"I have no idea what you're talking about." I lifted my chin and brought a dollop toward my mouth. As I parted my lips, Evan snagged my wrist.

"Maybe I need to show you then." His voice was thick. He slipped my finger past his lips, pulling it deep into his mouth and sucking hard, running his tongue from knuckle to tip. Sparks zipped up my arm. My lower belly clenched.

Still, I wasn't quite ready to give in. It was too much fun playing with him. I struggled to keep my voice light as he released me with a pop.

"Compelling demonstration." I feigned deep thought and willed his eyes to stay on mine while I covertly reached into the container, gathering a healthy glob of cream on two fingers. "I do have one small note though."

His searing stare didn't waiver. "And that is?"

"It seems like you need a little more." I lifted my loaded fingers and painted his nose in white fluff.

He reared back, his eyes flying wide with shock then narrowing as he growled. "Oh, you're dead."

His arms were banded around my lower back in an instant, pulling me to the edge of the counter and into his strong body. I shrieked a laugh as he ran his nose up my neck, smearing the whipped cream on me as he went, but laughter quickly dissolved into a moan as he began to suck the sweet cream from my skin. Goosebumps rose in the wake of his lips and teeth and tongue.

I arched into him, turning my head to give him greater access. One strong hand splayed on my lower back while the other traveled up to grasp the back of my neck, holding me in place. He ground himself into me, his hard length pressing right where my need was growing, flooding my body with desire.

I clutched at the back of his shirt, and he stepped back, allowing me to pull it over his head, before running his hands up my body to divest me of my own. Then his mouth was back, parting my lips with deep, savoring slides of his tongue.

His hand dipped under the hem of my skirt, his thumb drawing light, swirling circles up the inside of my thigh, enticing me to open them wider. Reaching my apex, he hooked a finger through my underwear, running it up and down, grazing my center with the back of his knuckle on every pass. Teasing circuits, every one of them making me softer, wetter, more impatient, but he didn't relent. Not until I whimpered his name in frustration.

Finally, he tugged, and I lifted to help him slide the yellow cotton down my legs. His hand returned, resting at the juncture of my thigh while his thumb found my clit and applied pressure. I moaned into his mouth. He dipped his thumb lower, running it over my seam, gathering wetness then returning to that little bud with small, firm circles.

My breathing turned ragged. It felt so good, stoked my hunger, but it didn't satisfy. As if in response to my unvoiced need, he pulled me closer and pushed two fingers into my channel.

"Yes." It was a guttural sound, ripping from my throat as my head fell back.

He worked his fingers inside of me, crooking forward to rub against my sensitive front wall, that perfect place that made me feel so needy. My hips rocked, begging for more.

He grasped a handful of my hair, tipping my head as his lips skimmed the shell of my ear. "No notes now?"

A laugh bubbled out of me as I shook my head furiously, but I choked on it when he ground his palm into my clit and picked up his pace. A waterfall of pleasure poured down my spine. My legs trembled.

I tightened around his fingers, and he growled into my neck. He replaced his palm with his thumb, rubbing hard against my clit while his fingers continued to pump.

My orgasm shimmered right under the surface, straining for release.

He pulled back, looking at me in a way that sent fire licking across my skin. "You are so fucking beautiful like this. Let me watch you come."

It was that look, those words that ignited me. His eyes never left my face as my breath halted and my core tightened, ecstasy rocking through me. I writhed on his hand, gasping and shaking as he worked me through my climax.

Still trembling, I reached for his jeans, unfastening them and slipping my hand into his boxer briefs. My fingers closed around his shaft, smooth skin over hard arousal. I gripped him and tugged.

He ground out a curse. I loved seeing my effect on him. I never could have imagined this. Never dared to dream that he'd ever respond to me in this way. But here he was, teeming with desire, flushed and panting and hot in my hand, looking at me like he'd die if he didn't have me soon. I'd never felt so sexy in all of my life.

He pulled a foil packet from his pocket.

"You had that quickly accessible."

"I'm an optimist."

I trailed my fingers down his bare chest and stomach, and together we slid his pants and underwear down over his hips. When they fell to the floor, he stepped out of them and kicked them away. Taking the condom from his hand, I opened the packet, then slowly rolled it down his length as a tremor moved through him.

He pulled me to the very edge of the counter, and I spread my legs wider as he stepped close, one hand guiding his head to my opening, the other gripping my hip.

I stretched around him as he pushed into me with one firm thrust, that glorious feeling of fullness satisfying my ache and intensifying it all at once.

His head fell to my shoulder, and I ran my fingers through the short hairs at the back of his neck as he rolled his hips, sliding out and then back into me. A pained groan fell from his lips.

Unfastening my bra, he pulled it from my shoulders, tossing it away, then gathering me close, pressing bare skin against bare skin before thrusting into me with even more force. I knotted my fingers in his hair, bringing his mouth to mine and nipping at his bottom lip, feeding the frenetic energy building between us.

His hands clutched at my back, my neck, my hips as he drove in hard, setting a demanding pace that I met with every thrust, my hard nipples scraping across his bare chest, my clit grinding against him for relief.

We were a tangle of writhing bodies and grasping hands. The sounds of our pleasure were nearly drowned out by the sharp slap of his skin meeting mine over and over.

He hooked an arm under one knee and pushed me wider, rutting deeper, finding that place inside me that felt achingly hollow and deliciously full at the same time. A bead of sweat rolled down my spine. The coil in my core tightened, aching to release again. A desperate moan slipped from my lips.

His rhythm faltered, his thrusts becoming sloppy before he pushed deep one last time and held himself there, gasping my name once more as he came, his body shaking with his release. He reached in between us, thumb finding my clit once more, pushing me over the edge to join him.

The pleasure detonated low in my belly, sending a shockwave racing through my body, stealing my breath, my sanity. White bursts flashed behind my eyes.

I was barely aware of what sounds I might be making or the feeling of Evan gently laying me back on the cool granite. He dropped his forehead to my sternum as we both fought to regain our bearings.

"I'm going to have to sanitize this counter ten thousand times."

"You could always move."

He poked my side. My laugh was a fizz of happiness settling over my sensitive skin.

A shudder rocked through him. "Holy shit." I looked down, finding his eyes lit with humor and heat. "The squeezing…you gotta cool it with the laughing unless you're ready for another round."

He looked so perfect. Sex-mussed and happy. I brushed a wayward hair out of his face.

It had never been like this with another partner. Amusement flowing into arousal and back again. And still somehow that was the hottest, sweatiest, most erotic *fuck* of my life. Nothing else even came close.

"What is it?" He was studying my face, peering up at me over my naked body. And I loved it.

My smile must have looked drugged, but I let him see it all. "Sex with you is exceptionally fun."

I caught a glimpse of three dimples digging deep with his widest smile before he lifted me off the island, wrapping my legs around his waist and stomping out of the kitchen, him fully naked, me in only a skirt rucked up around my waist. I giggled as I held on.

"Where are we going?"

"To the shower for that round two."

Even carrying me, he took the stairs in record time.

CHAPTER 20

EVAN

New Weird Shit entry. Galaxy spray paint street art.

VI

…

EROTIC galaxy spray paint street art.

Like everything was boobs?

Like everything was dicks.

Noooooo. -5.

-10

Fair.

I'll miss you tonight. Have fun with the girls.

———

"So are you next?"

I sat beer bottles in front of Nico and Remy at the table they'd staked out and took my seat. "Next?"

"Next up for a bachelor party. Or are you gonna take another decade and let Rem beat you to the punch?"

We were tucked into a corner table near the dartboard. Nico wanted to keep his party low-key, and this place fit the bill. Downtown but off the beaten path, it was one step above a dive, with wood-paneled walls that could barely be seen through beer signs and license plates. It was plenty lively on a Saturday night, but wasn't so crowded that we wouldn't be able to move or hear each other talk. The three of us had come early to share a round and hold down a couple of tables before the rest of the party showed up.

Remy huffed into his bottle. "Thanks, but I'll pass."

"You say that now…"

"I say that period." Rem leaned back in his chair. Everything the guy did was at a volume of two. You had to know him well and pay attention if you wanted to get a read. His posture remained casual, but there was a faint edge of discomfort in his voice. "I'm not that guy."

"Oh, you absolutely are that guy. You're practically begging for some woman to come and knock you on your ass. Don't worry. We'll find her for you."

"You're getting married so you're a matchmaker now?" He didn't seem eager to sign up for the service, but was happy enough to indulge Nico for tonight.

"Hell yeah, I am. Gotta see my boys settled."

Rem rolled his eyes, but his mouth twitched. It was about as close to a smile as he was gonna give up. I, on the other hand, bristled.

"Hang on. Where was this matchmaker stuff for me? You kept quiet for years and let me be an idiot with Vi."

"Ah. But you already had your match. Beyond that, it's out of my hands. Can't save you from your own idiocy, my friend. Horses to water and all."

"You're an ass."

He grinned around the mouth of his bottle. "But seriously, how are things going there? It's been a couple of weeks."

"Three." I was sure I was sporting the same dopey grin that was becoming a fixture on my face these days. Every time I thought about her, I lost any hope of regulating it. Didn't even have the will to try. "It's…incredible. Perfect. Happiest I've ever been."

Everything that had made our friendship so great was thriving in this new setup, plus we'd added about six extra layers of goodness, not the least of which was the discovery that we were as compatible sexually as we were platonically. We'd been availing ourselves of that perk as often as her body was able. Add seeing her, kissing her, sleeping next to her, and I was done for.

As good as I'd hoped it would be with her, it was better.

"As far as the 'going next' question, that's really up to her. I'll be on my knee as soon as I think there's a chance she'll say yes."

"Hell yes." Nico clasped my shoulder.

"I hate to ask…" Remy leaned forward to rest his forearms on the edge of the table, his voice low. "This fellowship thing…"

It was a fair question, but not one I had a satisfying answer to. The nausea that accompanied the thought was also becoming a fixture in my life, my excitement for her getting harder and harder to hang on to when the idea of her going filled me with such complete dread.

"Sorry. I didn't mean to—"

"No. It's okay." I stared down at the beer bottle in my hands and scraped at the edge of the label with my thumbnail. "There's not a lot to say. I mean, we don't know if she's going to get in. If she doesn't, she'll stay and everything will be great. And if she does—"

"Then you'll be celibate for six months." Leave it to Nico to lighten the mood in the starkest possible terms.

"Fuck you, man." The jab was ruined by my laughter.

"But seriously, long distance can be hell on a relationship, especially at the beginning. Any chance she'll stay even if she does get in, now that you're together?"

God, I wish. But this meant a lot to her. It was about taking control of her life, getting out of a bad working situation, pursuing her dreams. There weren't options here that presented the same opportunities.

"I don't think so. Between work and my family, following her isn't really an option either. And we're sure as hell not breaking up. So assuming she gets in, long distance is kind of it."

Remy looked equal parts skeptical and concerned. "And that's something you're good with?"

Missing her every day for six months? "Not really. But as bad as it is, all the other options seem worse." They both looked at me with pity, and damn, I was acting like a sad sack. "Sorry, man. Not trying to be a downer at your bachelor party. It's good with me and Vi, really good. We'll cross the other bridges when we come to them."

"There's no need to apologize. It's what we're here for. And for the record, if it comes down to long distance, I know you'll figure it out. You two can make it work." Nico sounded confident—a helluva lot more confident than I felt—and Remy nodded his agreement. I tried to take some of their reassurance to heart.

I wanted to believe it. But it was a long separation, in both distance and time. Would we be able to hold on to what we were building? Would she even want to once she was living a whole new life up there? Would she want to come back to Austin—to me—when it was done?

What if she leaves for good?

I drained the rest of my beer, trying to shake off that sense of impending doom. Now was not the time. I was one of the best men.

My job here was not to shit on this bachelor party.

"Yeah. Of course we will." I pushed my chair back from the table and stood, trying not to look as unbalanced as I felt. "Who needs a refill? I'm gonna hit the restroom. I can grab another round on the way back."

By the time I finished in the back and made my way to the bar, I'd shaken off most of my edginess. This was gonna be a good night. We'd drink some beer, shoot some pool, celebrate Nico. Then Violet would meet me at my place, and we'd have our own fun. If that wasn't enough to make me happy, I didn't know what was.

My phone buzzed in my pocket as I ordered drinks, and without even looking, I knew it was her. Leaning back against the bar top, I pulled it free and opened our text thread.

A video opened and her face filled the frame, wide smile and wild hair. I caught glimpses of Lina and Jamie in the background. They were on a dance floor somewhere, belting out god knows what (no way to hear in here even if I turned up the volume) but it didn't matter. Just the sight of her laughter was enough to have my heart rolling over in my chest.

> Looks like you're having a good time.

VI

> THE BEST!!!!!!!!!!!

> Jamie is talking to Nico! We're gonna meet up later!!!!

She was never shy with exclamations and emojis, but this was a lot even for her. She'd obviously had a couple. Drunk Vi was cute as hell.

An unfamiliar voice called my name, pulling my attention from my phone, and I scanned the space to find Jack weaving toward me at the bar.

And here we go.

I was not looking forward to this conversation. I'd been a colossal ass to him at the lake. The poor guy had been in the wrong place at the wrong time looking at the wrong girl, which had unfortunately put him squarely in the path of my Violet meltdown. Apologies were owed.

I'd already given one to Jamie, who was surprisingly gracious, I think owing to the fact that I'd publicly declared my love for her best friend. I didn't think that would work in my favor with her brother.

Nico had assured me he'd go easy on me, but no amount of decency on his part made "Sorry I was a dick. Remember that girl you liked? I'm with her now" a blast to say. Still, we were going to run into each other, and I was banking on tonight as an opportunity to clear the air. Right up front and without an audience was actually the best-case scenario.

"Jack." I extended my hand, and he shook it without hesitation. It was more than I deserved. Nico was right about him, which made me feel even worse about my behavior. "The guys are in the back." I nodded toward our tables. "Have you been over?"

"Ah, no. You were the first one I saw."

I nodded and flagged down the bartender. "Let me buy you a beer."

"You don't have to."

"Oh, I really think I do." Amusement passed between us. Another good sign. Once I had his beer added to the order, I turned to face him and the music directly. "Listen, man. I'm sorry I was such a jerk at the lake house. I was trying to figure some things out at the time, and you kinda got caught in the crossfire."

"Yeah. Jamie filled me in on you and Violet." I ducked my head, but he was quick to let me off the hook. "Believe me, I get it. Not sure I'd have handled myself much better if the roles were reversed." The bartender passed us four beers. Jack took his and extended it toward me. "No hard feelings."

Gratefully, I completed the ritual with a clink of my bottle to his. "I appreciate it." Gesturing to the other two bottles, I pulled my phone back out of my pocket. "Hey, would you mind running these to Nico and Remy? I just need to…"

His smile was knowing. "No problem."

Damn. He really was a good guy. I was honestly a little relieved that he hadn't gotten to know Vi better before I got my shit together.

I let him get a safe distance before reopening my messages.

> Can't wait. Be safe. I love you.

She replied with a block of emojis.

———

We were coordinating a meetup with the girls during a change in venue for both groups. They were heading from one club to another, and we were moving to a cigar bar to finish out the night.

Maybe it made me ridiculous, but I missed her. We'd been together almost constantly since that first weekend—most nights at my place, some at hers, but not a single evening spent apart. Tonight with the guys had been great. But I'd be lying if I said I wasn't getting a little buzz from the anticipation of seeing her, even for a few minutes.

I caught sight of her from about a block away, and that buzz died a quick death. She wasn't okay. I could see it from here. Her body was rigid, her movements slow, and she held herself in a very slight hunch, compensating, I knew, for some unseen pain. I picked up my pace.

She was toward the edge of the group talking with someone I didn't recognize. I had no idea if this woman could see what was happening in front of her, but to me, they were giant flashing warning lights. More appeared the closer I got. Stiff smile. Uneven breath. A hard swallow.

Fuck.

I got to her, finally, and a little relief flashed in her eyes as she said my name. I kissed her cheek and gently pulled her to my side, silently offering her physical support. She took it, leaning into me, but she didn't drop her game face. "Ev, this is Claudia. She teaches with Jamie."

I did my best to follow her lead, pinning my own game face in place and fighting the urge to haul her away in a princess carry. I extended my hand. "Great to meet you." We shook. Vi tensed at the movement, and my worry ratcheted up another notch. "Sorry to cut in, but I was hoping to steal her away for a second." My smile felt as forced as Vi's looked, but Claudia didn't seem to be picking up on either. If this weren't a damn crisis, I might have teased Vi about how we deserved People's Choice Awards at least, but it *was* a crisis, and I had no more patience, much less a sense of humor.

Claudia waved us off. "Oh, of course. You two are so cute. How long have you been together?"

Goddammit, Claudia.

"Well technically, just a few weeks—"

I could feel Vi gearing up for the long explanation, so I jumped in to speed things along. "But really more like ten years."

Claudia's confused silence was exactly the off-ramp I was hoping for. I hustled Violet away from the crowd, pulling her into the niche of a nearby building and rounding on her as soon as we were out of earshot.

"Why do you keep doing that?" She looked exasperated, maybe a little amused as well, but I was too focused on making sure she was okay to pay much attention to why.

"Doing what?" I ran my hands across her shoulders and down her arms, like I'd be able to find the hurt by touch. The compulsion didn't make much sense, but I was well beyond that.

"Telling people we've been together for ten years."

"Oh." I paused and blinked. "Because it's true. In a way, at least. It's not like we were less important to each other before we started dating. Saying we've been together for a few weeks feels like discounting our relationship before this." Her eyes went soft. "And I said it just now because I needed to get you over here sooner." She shook her head as I resumed my inspection, brushing my thumbs across her cheeks. "You're getting red."

She tried to push my hands away. "I'm fine."

"You're not."

"All right. I'm medium."

"You're pushing. I should take you home." Not in the way I'd been hoping for, but making sure she was okay was a much greater concern.

Crossing her arms, she took a step back. "I said I'm fine." Her amusement was long gone, and exasperation was well on its way to anger. "I'm staying."

"That's reckless. You need to call it a night."

"That's not your call." The sharpness in her tone had me rocking back on my heels.

"I'm just trying to protect you. Apparently against your will." I wanted to reach for her, to carry her home where she'd feel better, but that would obviously not be well received, so I shoved my hand into my hair instead, gripping the ends in frustration. "I don't know why you're being so stubborn about this. I can tell you don't feel good. If it's like this now, what's it going to be like by the end of the night? What is the fallout gonna be tomorrow?"

"Right. You *don't* understand." Her voice caught and her chin trembled, but she held her ground. "I know there will likely be a price to pay, but I'm willing to pay it. Not every time—you know better than anyone that I spend my whole life counting spoons, conserving spoons, limiting, adjusting, making compromises—but tonight I don't fucking want to." She dashed away a tear, and I felt it like a punch to my gut. "Tonight is important. I don't want to miss it. So I'm going to stay. And if there's fallout, so be it."

I hated this. It was a no-win situation. Watching sadness and frustration hurt her heart crushed my own. I wanted to make it better, to change her circumstances, or at least champion anything she wanted to do within them. But the desire to support her warred with the desire to keep her safe. Weren't we supposed to look out for each other? I could understand tonight being a high priority for her, but nothing should be a higher priority than her health. Ultimately, though, my conflicted feelings didn't matter. Like she said, not my call.

Taking a deep breath, I resigned myself to a plan I did not like. "Okay. I don't like it. But I get it."

I stepped toward her, reaching out to take her cheek in my hand, and she leaned in to my touch. It was a relief. I was still upset, anxious about her being okay, a little pissed at her for being reckless with herself, sad that she had to make these decisions in the first place, but I didn't want to fight. I wouldn't leave her with shit between us.

I pressed a kiss to her forehead. "I love you. You still coming over when you're done?"

She nodded.

"Good." With one more kiss, I said goodbye for now and rejoined the guys who were peeling Nico off of a very enthusiastic Jamie. His reunion had gone better than mine. *Good for him, I guess.*

When we'd freed him and were on our way, Nico threw his arm around my shoulders. "You're looking a little tense."

"Feeling a little tense."

"Well, we can't have that. It's my bachelor party. I think this calls for some liquid relaxation. What do you say?"

Was it a great idea to go drink these feelings away? Probably not. But I also didn't want to stew in them for the rest of the night. I had an obligation as best man not to be a buzzkill, right?

"I say lead the way."

CHAPTER 21

VIOLET

I felt like I'd been hit by a truck. Predictably, my it's-worth-the-tradeoff chickens were coming home to roost.

I stood by my choice. While the inevitable result of overdrawing on spoons and overtaxing my body was decidedly not fun, sometimes living life was worth the price. A couple of days' recovery and this would be behind me, but I'd have the memories of last night forever. I'd do it again in a heartbeat.

Today, though…today was going to blow.

I pulled my basket of medication down from Evan's kitchen cabinet. Now that I was staying over so much, it didn't make sense to cart a pharmacy back and forth, so I'd set up a full drug station here. Today's cocktail: Regular Meds and good old naproxen to combat the inflammation attempting a full takeover of my body.

I wasn't reaching for Flare Meds yet. If I took steroids every time I felt bad, I'd be taking them constantly, and since that wasn't something that bodies did well with long-term, I had to be judicious with their use. Today's inflammatory response didn't rise to the level of flare, though if I didn't take care of myself, it could easily spiral that way. With any luck, a day or two of rest would be all I needed to bounce back.

I cursed under my breath as I struggled with the naproxen bottle. Swollen hands and stiff fingers did not help with dexterity. Oh, the irony of a medication bottle that was inaccessible precisely because you needed it.

I briefly considered and firmly rejected the idea of asking Evan for help. I was already asleep by the time he got home last night, and he was still snoring softly when I shambled out of bed.

Stupid, sexy, infuriating man.

We weren't fighting, per se. We'd left things in an okay place last night, but I still refused to involve him—almost definitely because I was still a little mad at him and not because I was feeling guilty about my current state.

He'd been overbearing. Infantilizing. I was perfectly capable of monitoring my own situation and making my own choices without him stepping in to manage me. Of course, he'd also been spot-on with his concerns and was trying to keep me safe, which was actually lovely. Plus my choices affected him too, which he had a right to have feelings about.

Oof. Could it be both anger and guilt simultaneously? Regardless, I was not waking him to deal with a lid crisis. That was off-limits from any angle.

I gave the lid one more frustrated push. Finally, it popped loose, but the release was too sudden and my grip was too weak. The bottle slipped from my grasp, evading my bumbling attempt at a save, and crashed to the floor, erupting in a volcano of small blue pills.

"Shit." I straightened, ramming the top of my head into the corner of the still-open cabinet. "Shit!"

Pain bloomed from the spot, enough that I checked for bleeding before slamming the offending cabinet door. Something new hurting was exactly what I needed. Plus we could now add head injury and formidable mess to the bad day tally. *Doing great.*

Rubbing at the soon-to-be bruise, I stared daggers at the offending sea of tablets and the empty pill bottle rolling lazily away from me. They did not respond to dirty looks, which was a shame because I was not in any shape to be crawling around on the floor collecting them.

With a bracing breath, I grasped the edge of the counter and gingerly lowered myself to the ground. I'd made it down when the sound of Evan's footfalls thundered down the stairs.

I winced. I hadn't wanted to call him in on a lid problem. Now he'd be walking into to a pharmacological disaster zone, a decidedly bigger pain in the ass and an even more embarrassing failure.

"What the fuck is going on?" He stumbled into the kitchen, pulling on a T-shirt, hair in disarray. Concern and confusion knotted his brow as he scanned the room at eye level before spotting me on the floor. "Jesus. What happened? Are you okay?"

Crouching beside me, he gathered me up off of the floor, my body protesting every inch. I was hurt. Weak and wobbly. But he held me close, making sure I was steady on my feet before inspecting me for injuries with gentle hands.

I hated that he was fussing over me because of something so ridiculous. All of this because I couldn't manage a pill bottle on my own. Or maybe all of this was because I'd refused to make reasonable choices for myself. Both made me want to cry.

"I'm fine. Well, mostly. I hit my head. I needed meds and…" I gestured to the mess.

He narrowed his injury search to my head, accounting for the new information. "You needed meds because you hit your head?"

"No. I hit my head when I dropped them. But it wasn't too hard." I pulled his hands away and held his scrutinizing gaze. "I'm fine."

He nodded absently, but his wheels were still turning, trying to make sense of the chaotic scene. Then it clicked. His eyes fell closed on a heavy sigh. He squeezed the bridge of his nose between his eyes.

"You needed meds because of last night?"

I didn't answer. It wasn't really a question.

He shoved a hand through his hair, sending it into further anarchy. "Of course. Who could have seen that coming?" It was half under his breath but loud enough to reignite my frustration.

My spine snapped straight, and I squared my shoulders to him, crossing my arms over my chest. "I did see it coming. I knew this would probably be a rough day, but I—"

"Fucking did it anyway."

Angry. I was definitely angry.

My back teeth clenched hard as a gritted out a response. "I made a choice."

"A reckless choice."

It didn't matter that I was thinking the same moments before. It was mine to decide. It was already hard enough figuring out what I felt about it, balancing the validity of my decisions with my guilt over their consequences, without him adding his judgment to the mix.

It was like a replay of last night, only tempers were hotter and I had even less energy to give. I couldn't do this right now.

As if reading my mind, his shoulders dropped and he gave up the fight. "Can you make it to the couch? I'll clean this shit up and bring you some."

"I can help." I was absurdly out of my depth and still couldn't bring myself to hand it over without a fight, my pride digging in its heels.

Again, he tunneled his fingers through his hair and tugged. "No. You can't. Just go sit down, okay?"

I really looked at him for the first time this morning. The tugging at his hair, the way he squinted at the light, the dark smudges under his eyes. There was more going on than being upset. He was tired, and I suspected he had a headache, maybe a full-on hangover. He'd had his own big night, and he should have been able to rest this morning, but here I was, wrecking that.

In silent agreement, I shuffled out of the kitchen and left him to it, guilt surging in to edge out the anger as I made my way into the living room and curled up in the corner of the couch.

I didn't necessarily regret my choice, but I regretted what my choice meant for him. Now that we were together, I wasn't the only one impacted by the fallout of these things. I'd done what I wanted, and in doing so, I'd made life a little bit harder for him.

I'll always be making his life harder.

Whether it was caused by a choice or a random rebellion from my body, he would always be contending with the difficulties of my condition. Already, cracks were forming in his patience. How long before he ran out completely?

He rounded the corner into the living room, hands full of supplies. A ramekin with the appropriate dose of naproxen along with the Regular Meds I hadn't gotten around to taking. A stainless steel tumbler of water to take them with. A banana to keep me from getting sick.

I choked out a thank you and blinked away the sheen of tears that blurred my vision as I accepted his offerings.

He collapsed onto the couch at the other end, head tipped back, eyes closed. He was slumped down low, fingers laced together and resting on top of his head as if he were trying to hold it together. I studied his profile as the silence stretched. He didn't exactly look peaceful, but at least he was relaxed.

I took my meds. I ate my banana. He didn't move.

Maybe he'd fallen asleep. I knew I should probably let him rest, but there was no way *I* was going to be able to rest with all of this tension lingering between us. And since rest was at the top of my priority list, I was going to have to speak up.

I opened my mouth and closed it again. What would I even say to him? *Thank you for taking care of me so relentlessly. I'm sorry I didn't listen to you, but only partially. I'm completely sorry, however, for being such a pain. We probably should never have done this. Please don't get fed up.*

That was incoherent. An exasperated sigh escaped me, and Evan's eyes flew open to meet mine. Not asleep, after all. And now I had his attention.

"I know you're mad at me, but—"

His eyebrows slammed down, his head jerking back as if I'd slapped him. "What?"

"I know that you're frustrated with having to take care of me today because of my decision to stay last night."

He was already shaking his head. "No. Sweetheart. I am not mad at you. I'm worried about you."

It was so tempting to believe, but if he wasn't mad, he was undeniably something.

"I was frustrated. With the situation. And yeah, maybe some with your decision because I was worried you were hurting yourself. I don't know if that's fair or not. But that is not the same as being mad or frustrated with *you*. I probably didn't do a great job showing you that. Especially this morning."

He extended a hand toward me, and I reached back to take it. Tugging on the connection, he hauled me onto his lap. His face was open and earnest as he looked up into mine, his hands running up and down my thighs where they bracketed his. Closing the distance felt so good, it threatened to melt all of my fears away right there.

"I'm sorry I was a grumpy ass. I'll never be mad at you for being sick. And I sure as hell won't be frustrated with taking care of you." He moved his hands up to cradle my face. "Taking care of you, Vi... I may not always get it right, but it's all I want to do forever."

My heart tripped. It was the most perfect promise. One I wanted desperately to latch on to. I could grab hold with both hands and let it carry me away into a fairy tale. I could pretend the utter conviction pouring from his gaze would never run out.

But it always ran out. Slowly that nurturing support would be replaced with resentment. If it had only happened with Rob, I could believe this would be different. But it happened with my own parents, my own self, even.

I was supposed to be trusting him, but no amount of trust could scrub away the truth. I *knew* I was a burden to others because I was a burden to me. My body had been my adversary for as long as I could remember.

"What are you thinking?" His voice was gentle, his hands resuming soothing circuits over my arms and legs, coaxing me to open up.

"That it would make sense if you were frustrated with me." A knot formed in my throat and the well of tears returned to my eyes. I knew I'd have no luck blinking them away this time. "I'm frustrated with me."

He ran a thumb down the tense muscles in my neck. "Tell me?"

I didn't even hesitate. We were still in new territory in so many ways, but these paths were well worn. Maybe he touched me differently than he used to, but when he asked the question, it was still my closest confidant on the other end. Words that had been eating away at me were suddenly pouring out.

"Sometimes it feels like I'm fighting myself, my body, just to live my life. Like I'm handcuffed to an enemy that's constantly attempting sabotage—and succeeding most of the time. Any time I give it an opening—even when I don't—it's there. Causing pain. Taking energy. Stealing things I want. Making me a burden."

I expected him to cut in and refute that, but he continued to work at the tension in my neck, silently giving me space to say every piece out loud.

"So I am frustrated. I'm frustrated that my body betrays me. I am frustrated that I can't even enjoy a night out without paying a price. I'm frustrated that I take too much from the people I love. I'm frustrated and I'm angry. Because no matter how well-managed I am, it will never go away."

I'd never said those things out loud, not even to him, and as they left me, they took what little energy I'd been working with right along with them. The full weight of my exhaustion pressed in on me. Exhaustion from my body, exhaustion from the endlessness of my situation, exhaustion from fighting with him and fighting with myself and opening tender wounds up wide.

The tears finally fell, cutting damp trails down my cheeks, Evan swiping them away, one by one, until they slowed. Only when my breaths were long and even did he finally respond. "What if it was me?"

"If what was you?"

"If I was sick, would you be frustrated with me? Even if it meant I let you down or made something harder or needed help?"

"Of course not."

"So if you wouldn't get frustrated with me about that, why would you get frustrated with yourself? Being sick is not a failing. You're not an enemy, and you're not a burden. You're doing your best. You'd be the first person to give that grace to me or anyone else in the same position. I wish you were as kind to yourself."

His brown eyes were impossibly soft, holding me and everything I'd unloaded with such tenderness and care, asking me to do the same for myself.

The idea felt so foreign. Thinking of my body as anything besides a traitor seemed impossible. But he was right about how I would treat him if the roles were reversed. There was an impulse to reject it, to insist it was different, but somewhere deeper, beyond that embattled instinct, a little truth bell was ringing.

Now though, I needed to rest. My spoons were significantly depleted, and with the adrenaline of conflict and catharsis waning, I was feeling the scarcity.

"How about a cup of tea? I need about a gallon of coffee."

My smile was a little weak, but I felt it down to my bones. "That may have some undesirable side effects."

"I have a stomach of steel."

"You tell yourself that. And tea sounds great."

Moving me back to the other end of the couch, he pulled a throw blanket from the back and tucked it tight around me, settling me emotionally as much as physically. "You relax and choose something to watch. I'll be right back with drinks and a more substantial breakfast than that banana." He bent to brush a kiss to my forehead.

I was lulled by the sounds of him moving around the kitchen. The burble of the coffee maker, the whistle of the kettle, the scrape of the toaster. They sounded like love.

Everything was okay.

He wasn't tired of this. Tired of me. At least not yet.

CHAPTER 22

EVAN

MY LIVING ROOM LOOKED LIKE A DRUG DEN BUT SMELLED LIKE A COFFEE house. With a giant bag of a brown (thankfully not mysterious) powered substance to her left and stacks of paper envelopes to her right, Violet perched on the couch, adding more of the powder to a glass measuring cup as she squinted at the food scale beneath it.

She looked good, lightyears better than she had a week ago. It had been a slow week of recovery since the bachelorette party, but she'd gotten there. And was feeling well enough for whatever this project was. It was a relief.

"Are we starting a coffee trafficking ring?"

Her head snapped up and a smile lit her face. Damn, that would never get old. Her in my place, filling it with that smile—I wanted it every day.

"Hey!"

I put my bag down by the entry table and entered the impromptu workshop. "Seriously." I waved a hand at her setup. "What is all this?"

"My share of the wedding favors." She held up one of the kraft paper envelopes with *The Perfect Blend* printed in dark blue ink across the front.

"All right. That's precious."

"Right?" She picked up the precisely measured cup of coffee and poured it into the empty envelope. "But I have about a zillion of these left to do. If you ever want your couch back, you'll have to help."

Hooking my knuckles under her chin, I lifted her lips to mine and took a long, slow taste. Another thing that would never get old.

"Put me in, coach."

She smiled against my mouth, and damn if it wasn't almost as good as the kiss. I'd do anything she wanted if she'd keep letting me taste her smile. With one more chaste peck, she pulled away and patted the spot on the couch next to her, which I dutifully took, rolling up my sleeves.

"Here's the system. We measure out two ounces of coffee, dump it in the pouch, and seal it." She picked up a strip of ribbon from a basket I hadn't noticed by her feet. "Then we tie a bow and add a sprig of baby's breath."

"Tell me I'm on measuring duty. I don't think my bow and baby's breath skills are up to snuff, and I really don't want to answer to Jamie for shoddy workmanship."

A smirk stole across her lips. "As fun as that would be to watch, I put you on that side for a reason. You fill. I'll decorate."

I rubbed my hands together and reached for the coffee scoop, but stalled when she leaned forward to grab a ribbon. Her loose-fitting tank fell away from her body, giving me a teasing peek at her bare breasts. My dick swelled and my palms itched to slip under that shirt. Lurid fantasies flashed in my mind, all of which involved us doing things on or near the wedding favors that Jamie would not appreciate.

"Oh my god!" Violet jerked upright, snapping me out of my little daydream. "You distracted me. Your interview—how did it go?"

She wasn't the only one distracted. Nothing like coming home to a sweatshop and a peepshow to throw the most important meeting of your career out of your mind.

This afternoon, I'd led our RFP interview with the city.

"Really well, I think. We won't know for a while, but they seemed excited about what we were showing. Paul and Luce seemed confident after." Finally, I grabbed the coffee scoop and measured out a serving. "We can't control what our competition may look like, but at this point, I think we have as good a shot as anyone."

I dumped the grounds into an envelope, sealed it like I'd been shown, and handed it over to Vi who was beaming at me with her bottom lip tucked into her teeth. It was the *I'm proud of you* look in full force, and it inflated my chest like a hot air balloon.

"You're gonna get it."

"Let's not get ahead of ourselves. I'm trying to stay cautiously optimistic."

"You're gonna get it. And you're gonna get that promotion. And you're gonna take care of your mom and Lauren and Tabbie. And Brad can eat glass."

"Easy, killer." I tugged on the end of her ponytail. Sweet, gentle Violet had been showing a vicious streak when it came to supporting me, and I couldn't say I hated it. She was cute when she was wishing vaguely violent fates upon my enemies.

She shrugged as if it couldn't be helped. "I'm glad it went well. I knew you'd be amazing." Finishing a bow with a flourish, she slipped a sprig of tiny white flowers into the tie. "Speaking of kind of crazy work things, I got a call from this editor I know…"

I could feel her nervous energy building and braced for whatever bullshit shenanigans Gemma was pulling now. Was she somehow sabotaging her with other editors?

"And?"

"She offered me a job."

"Holy shit. Seriously?"

"Yeah. We've interacted at events, and I guess she's familiar with my work. She wants me to come join their group."

Hell yes, they wanted my girl. "She's headhunting you. As she damn well should be." I nudged her shoulder with mine as she tried to mask her smile, but I could see the way her shoulders pulled back and her spine straightened. She was proud to have people seeking out her work, recognizing her talent.

Working with Gemma had been a beatdown for her self-esteem. I was not above wishing a bedbug infestation on that woman, so I guess Vi wasn't the only one with a vicious streak.

She was brilliant, and she deserved so much more. Maybe a fresh start with people who appreciated her was exactly that. "Would you be interested?"

"The opportunity is pretty great, actually. They're a small company that serves indie authors, so staying in my wheelhouse. The team has three other editors, and I would join as a peer, not in a junior position like I am now. Which means I'd have more control over the projects I took and my workload. And the pay would be better by a lot."

So basically tailor-made for her. "Plus, no Gemma."

"No Gemma." She grinned. "Which would likely mean a much more pleasant working environment. I mean, obviously everything is so up in the air right now with my plans…"

For the first time, the topic of her leaving didn't come with an imme-diate wave of nausea. This job was a kernel of hope. It sounded perfect for her, maybe even better than the fellowship. This could be the best of both worlds, that elusive alternative that gave her all the opportuni-ties she needed right here at home.

She could keep a steady, flexible job that worked for her needs while losing the toxic boss, making more money, and giving herself more time to pursue her writing. And most importantly, it didn't require her to move halfway across the country away from her support system. And she needed that support. Hell, we'd just dealt with the fallout from a single night out. How was she going to be able to take care of herself when help was 2,000 miles away?

This was an ideal solution. Everything she needed.

And she won't leave me.

Guilt pinched my gut at the thought. That wasn't what this was about. I wanted what was best for her, wanted to take care of her. This job would make it possible.

"…really inconvenient not knowing until the last minute whether I'm going to be moving in a month. Oh, and I heard back from the landlord. They won't let me go month-to-month. I have to let the lease go and be out by the end of the month or sign another year lease. And they want to know by Monday, so I basically have the weekend to decide if I'd rather be potentially homeless or stuck with a lease on an apartment I'm not using."

"Move in with me."

Her hand froze on the coffee package I was passing her, and my heart rate kicked up. It may have seemed abrupt to her. I had kind of blurted it out there. But I'd been thinking about it since that first weekend. I was waiting to jump at the first possible opening.

"Like stay with you until I find a new place if I need to?"

"No. Like move in. Permanently. Whether you go to Boston or not, make this your home."

A home with Violet. I wanted it so bad, I ached. Searching her eyes for a reaction, I caught a spark of excitement that fed my own. But still, she hedged.

"Are you sure? You don't think it's too fast?"

"Ten years, Vi. It is comically slow."

The smile breaking across her face felt like fucking Christmas.

And then she was lunging at me, arms thrown around my neck, tackling me to the couch. I went willingly. Her mouth fused with mine as my back hit the cushions, and a faint pop froze us in place. Violet's eyes flew open as a puff of fragrant powder shot down my back and up my neck into my hair.

Between my shoulder blades, I felt her hand flex around the exploded coffee bag while she used the other on my chest to push back and assess the damage. The plume of dust swirled around us, and the freckles over the bridge of her nose scrunched.

It was the nose wrinkle that broke me. I snorted a laugh, cracking the silence and sending Vi into a fit of giggles.

That shut me up real quick. Her body on top of mine, shaking with laughter, was providing friction in all the right ways. My fantasies from earlier came flooding back. Doing it while covered in coffee grounds wasn't exactly what I'd had in mind, but I could adapt a plan better than anyone.

My hips rocked into her, seeking more of that friction, while my hands came up to cradle her jaw. Her laughter died as I nipped at her lips.

"Move in with me." Pouncing on me had been pretty clear, but I wanted the answer again, needed to hear her say it out loud.

"Yes."

She barely got the word out before I took her mouth in a deep kiss that sent sparks shooting down my spine. She was so fucking perfect. And somehow she kept saying yes to me.

I could see our life coming together, a perfect plan taking shape. She would move in. Maybe take this new job and not have to go to Boston. She could write from here and I could take care of her while she did.

And maybe before long I'd ask her to marry me, and she'd say yes again.

CHAPTER 23

VIOLET

"I'm going to murder her." Jamie held a finger up to the makeup artist sweeping blush across her cheeks and tipped her champagne flute back, draining half the glass. "And now I'm a bridezilla."

It had been a near-perfect morning. An incredible suite at the Hotel Van Zandt had become a bridal paradise. We'd spent the morning wrapped in satin robes, grazing over a delicious brunch spread, drinking champagne, and being pampered at the temporary salon that had popped up in the middle of the room.

The only minor hiccup? The Maid of Honor was MIA.

It hadn't caused too much distress in the beginning. Jamie's cousin, Amber, was notoriously flighty, and a late arrival was to be expected, but the grace window was now long-past. The getting ready portion of the day was almost finished. Our hair had been swept into low, loose buns, our faces painted and powdered. Jamie was last in the chair. We'd be slipping on dresses and walking down for the ceremony in half an hour.

The time, combined with the fact that she'd be posting to social media all day but couldn't be bothered to answer a call or return a text, had Jamie near her breaking point.

"You could never be a bridezilla. You're justifiably frustrated." I crouched in front of a row of dresses, two cornflower blue, one white, to give them one last pass with the steamer. "Though I do think it may be poor form to murder someone on your wedding day. Even if they deserve it."

Upending a bottle of champagne, Lina filled Jamie's glass to the brim. "I'll murder her for you. Doing a murder on the bride's behalf is fair game, right?"

She peered at me over her shoulder. Seems I was the arbiter of wedding etiquette. I wasn't sure how qualified I was for the role, but I'd happily lend my stamp of approval, and even make up some justifications. "It's our sacred duty as bridesmaids, actually. It's…historical, a time-honored tradition."

"Weren't bridesmaids like body doubles originally?" Jamie peered at me around the woman loading up a mascara wand before being wrangled back for application.

"Correct. But I think acting as a bridal enforcement squad is in keeping with the spirit of the role."

"Cheers to that." Lina lifted the bottle in salute, then drank directly from it.

A hint of a smile tugged the corner of Jamie's mouth. "Y'all are the best. I love my cousin. I do. And giving my mom and aunt a win felt necessary at the time, but I knew from the beginning this was a mistake. You two should have been maids of honor. You practically were anyway."

With no wrinkle left unturned, I rose from the floor and packed up the steamer. "We were perfectly happy being unofficial."

"Yeah. I had a different answer all ready to go there."

Jamie released a light burst of laughter, and Lina caught my eye with a satisfied smirk. Making Jamie feel a little better in a stressful situation was our job, and I was glad we were succeeding. I was also glad the mascara was finished before her little outburst.

With a final swipe of pink over her lips, the makeup artist finished with Jamie and equipped her with instructions and products for freshening up later.

The photographer's head popped into the suite. "Hi, ladies. Are we ready to put on dresses?"

Jamie's shoulders fell on a frustrated sigh. "Well, we can't wait around for her. The hair and makeup ships have sailed. She has her dress with her, wherever she is. I think we have to keep going without her."

I nodded our affirmation to the photographer and gently laid a hand on Jamie's arm. "I think that's best, too. I'm sure she'll make it."

"And if she doesn't, then screw her."

"Lina!" Somehow casually discussing this woman's murder seemed fine, but "screw her" was crossing a line.

"What? It's the truth." She stepped directly in front of Jamie, clasping her shoulders and squaring them up. "Listen. If she doesn't get her shit together and show up, you're still marrying Nico today, right? That's all that really matters. A rogue bridesmaid—yes, bridesmaid, I'm fucking demoting her myself—can't even touch that. If she makes it, great. And if she doesn't…"

"Screw her." So much for crossing a line. I was now cosigning.

It was a distinctly Lina pep talk, sweet sentiment delivered with a bit of an edge, and it was exactly what Jamie needed to hear. Tension slipped from her shoulders and a tentative smile broke across her face. She shook her head as if to clear it.

"You're right. Today is about me and Nico. That's all that counts." She reached out, grabbing each of our hands and clutching them tight. "Thank you. Both of you. Of all the amazing things Nico has given me, you two are really high on the list. Thanks for letting me into the group."

"We couldn't imagine it without you."

We pulled each other in for a fierce group hug and I willed my misty eyes not to ruin my makeup. Even with waterproof mascara, tear streaks could do a lot of damage. I was determined to wait until the ceremony to make a mess of my face.

Lina sniffed then cursed, dissolving the emotional moment in laughter. "Okay. Let's get this woman dressed and go watch Nico lose his mind when he sees her."

EVAN

I hear I got a new partner to escort and that she's pretty fucking hot.

I bit my lip, trying fruitlessly to contain a smile.

Jamie's cousin had appeared five minutes ago as we arrived in this little holding area. Evidently she had her own hair and makeup people who she simply couldn't do without, and informing Jamie of that fact had slipped her mind.

I hadn't known whether to brace for a brawl or a meltdown as she offered this up as a perfectly reasonable explanation, but Jamie seemed positively serene as she promptly and officially demoted her. Lina and I were now Maids of Honor. I would be walking with Evan, Lina with Remy, and Amber with Jack.

A shakeup this late in the game seemed a little gratuitous regardless of this woman's offenses, but I wasn't about to question Jamie's handling of the situation. And with Lina's death glare trained on her, Amber didn't seem too eager to question it either.

I was even less inclined to argue now that I was getting flirty text messages from my new partner.

That literally just happened. How did you find out?

Lina texted us.

Of course. Whether it was motivated by her practicality or her love of vengeance, there was no way she would let this news go unshared.

> So what do you think? Do I have a shot?

> I guess you're charming enough.

> You guess??

> Do you need a reminder of how charming I can be Violet?

> Absolutely.

Those telling little dots lingered for an inordinately long time before his one-word answer came through.

> Shit.

My peal of laughter drew inquisitive looks. *Nothing to see here. Just my foolish boyfriend playing with fire and getting burned.*

> This thing starts in like two minutes and now I'm pitching a tent.

I fought back another fit of giggles. *How unfortunate.* I hadn't started this little exchange, but I had certainly won it. Sadly, the gloating would have to wait till later.

> Good luck with that! I love you! 😊

> I can't decide if you're the best or the worst. Either way I love you too.

> See you at the altar sweetheart.

My heart skipped at the last message.

He obviously didn't mean it *that* way. It just happened to be where we'd see each other next. It was silly to imagine…everything my mind was currently trying to imagine. We weren't even close to that. I wasn't sure we should ever be close to that. And yet as I read and reread it, that's where my thoughts pulled me.

See you at the altar sweetheart.

A flicker of longing flared in my belly.

"Vi." My head snapped up as Lina waved me over to where the coordinator was putting everyone in line.

Grateful for the well-timed interruption to that train of thought, I dropped my phone into my pocket—gotta love a dress with pockets—and hurried over to take my place between Lina and Jamie. Music swelled in the room beyond. We did last checks on hair and makeup and dresses, blew Jamie one last kiss, and then, one by one, we were off.

I stepped through double doors into a grand ballroom. Smoky, abstract wallpaper framed by black moldings lined three walls, while to the right, a bank of windows with gauzy coverings flooded the space with light. Glittering art deco chandeliers hung from high ceilings. A path of petals led through the rows of guests to an arch dripping with white blooms, a secret garden cropping up in the middle of a glamorous speakeasy.

No sooner had I reached the aisle than my gaze found him, the sight of him knocking the air out of my chest.

He stood at the end of the aisle, dashing in a grey suit and cyan tie, chestnut hair swept neatly back from his face, piercing brown eyes locked on me as if I was their only purpose in life. Slowly, a smile unfurled across his lips, pushing dimples into each of his cheeks in turn.

Every lightning bug he had ever conjured in me illuminated at once. They raced down my spine and danced in my vision. They wrapped themselves around my heart and squeezed so tightly I feared it would stop beating.

On shaky legs, I walked down the aisle toward him, and that silly little imagining sparked by his text message roared into a full-fledged fantasy. I could walk down an aisle meant for us, and he'd look at me like that. We'd make promises of forever, and I'd feel that smile against my mouth before we kissed as husband and wife.

I felt a surge of emotion, and it probably should have been fear or anxiety or apprehension, but it unequivocally was not. It was excitement. Certitude. The bone-deep, roots-in-the-ground feeling that this was exactly right.

Locations and careers and caretaking and kids—they were a sticky mess. But suddenly this piece didn't seem too messy. So much of my life was a list of things I couldn't or shouldn't do, couldn't or shouldn't have, but maybe I could take this one thing for myself and the rest would be okay. Maybe I could marry the man who looked like he was about to sprint down this aisle to have me in his arms.

I felt my own smile spread, and his grew impossibly wider. We were our own feedback loop of grinning, sappy happiness.

It wasn't until I reached the end of the aisle that I sheepishly remembered we were, in fact, at someone else's wedding. I was a freshly minted Maid of Honor, for Pete's sake. I needed to at least try to focus on the happy couple.

I pulled my attention away from Evan and gave Nico an enthusiastic thumbs-up over my bouquet before taking my spot beside Lina.

Jamie glowed as she came down the aisle. Nico did, in fact, lose his mind when he saw her. They exchanged rings and personalized vows. He dipped her back in a sweeping kiss at the end.

I cried and smiled and clapped at all of the appropriate moments, but I couldn't stop myself from stealing glances across the aisle to where Evan's gaze remained fixed on me.

And every single time, my heart fluttered.

And every single time, the desire burned brighter.

Maybe I could.

———

Lina stumbled off the dance floor to the bridal party table where I was sitting. "The anti-chafing shorts are earning their keep tonight."

I handed her a glass of water and, obligingly, she pounded it.

Toasts had been made, cake had been cut, and we were deep into the party portion of the evening. Lina had been living on the dance floor, as was her way, and I had been living mostly in this chair, as was mine.

I had actually gotten out to dance several times, and for being at the end of an extraordinarily long day, my body was holding up remarkably well. I was under no illusions that I wouldn't be laid up for most of next week, but if my status right now was any indication, it might be relatively mild.

Lina returned the glass to the table. "You holding up? Need anything?"

We'd lived together through college and for a couple of years after. She'd seen a lot, and she knew better than most what my situation looked like.

It wasn't always easy being friends with someone with a chronic illness. It was a lot of missed plans, a lot of early nights, a whole lot of accommodation, and too little communication. Most people didn't understand. Even fewer wanted to sign up.

But Lina had been one hundred percent in from the very beginning. As soon as my health issues started spiraling, she stepped up to be my rock. Even now, she was looking out for me. If I needed to bail, she'd smuggle me out. If I needed an assist, she'd be ready to provide it. And if I needed to dance, she'd shake her ass with me all night without telling me I shouldn't.

"Nope. All good."

"Ladies." Jamie appeared, looking slightly less polished but somehow even happier than she had at the start of the evening. "My husband and I have a surprise. I'm here to get you."

Lina smirked. "How many times have you called him that in the last four hours?"

"Fifty-six."

"Nice."

"I do my best. Now where's Evan?"

"I don't actually know." He'd been stuck to my side most of the night, but he'd gone to the restroom about twenty minutes ago and hadn't returned. I was starting to get a little worried he'd fallen in, to be honest.

We all scanned the room. "There. It looks like Nico's already got him." Jamie pointed to where Nico, Remy, and Evan were crossing the room toward the bar. "Let's go!"

She was very excited about this surprise. Grabbing Lina and me by the wrist, she dragged us across the room, not that we were resisting, but we could hardly keep up.

We rounded the end of the bar, joining the guys in front of a secluded bistro table holding six shot glasses and a bottle of peach schnapps.

Nico took Jamie's hand as they turned to face us. "It's not a celebration unless it's schnapps-a-bration."

"We are not calling it that." Evan patted his shoulder on his way toward the table. "Rem, let's line 'em up."

Maybe it was a weird thing to get sentimental about, but as Remy poured the liquor and we all gathered around, I was feeling decidedly sappy. Judging by the giant smiles circling the rest of the table, I wasn't the only one.

Evan lifted his shot, and the rest of us followed. "To the happiness, the love, and the many terrible shots that your marriage has in store. To Nico and Jamie."

Cheers rang out, and we drained our glasses, the cloyingly sweet liquor the perfect punctuation to the moment, and Nico pulled us into an aggressive group hug before demanding we adjourn to the dance floor.

We paired off. Nico sang into Jamie's ear, making her glow with happiness. Remy spun Lina in a surprisingly deft move as they talked and laughed.

And Evan...Evan held me close, swaying our hips to the beat. Joy fizzed through me.

"I have a surprise too. Are you ready to get out of here?"

I pulled back to see his face. It was definitely his I Have A Plan Face, excited and calculating, but there was an extra smolder in his eyes that told me this very well might be a sexy plan.

Sign. Me. Up.

"Yes. I just need to grab my stuff from the bridal suite."

"It's already moved."

"To the car?"

He shook his head, the corner of his mouth hitching. "Upstairs."

CHAPTER 24

VIOLET

Sultry music and a heady floral scent enveloped me as soon as I stepped through the door of our suite, charging the air like a thunderstorm rolling in on a summer night.

With a hand to my lower back, Evan ushered me further into the room. Picture windows framed a breathtaking nighttime view of downtown. Plush velvet furniture created a small sitting area while a large four-poster bed beckoned from the corner.

And on every available surface…dozens and dozens of violets.

They were woven around flickering candles, scattered across the crisp white linens of the bed, piled on tables, and trailed across the floor. The skin behind my ears tingled, as if with each bloom, he was whispering my name directly against the spot.

How? Part of me wanted to ask the question, but I couldn't bring myself to interrogate whatever magic he'd weaved into this perfect space.

A spread was set in the living space, champagne chilling in a bucket, an enormous slice of wedding cake, a platter of fresh fruit that was clearly an excuse for the bowl of whipped cream that accompanied it, and tucked to the side, several bottles of water, my heating pad, and naproxen.

But he didn't take me to it. Instead, he pulled me in the direction of the bathroom. It was a statement of minimalist luxury with slate tile, dark wood, and chrome fixtures glowing warmly in the light of dozens of candles. To the left were the sinks and a makeup vanity, to the right an enormous walk-in shower. And in the middle of the room, the star of the show, a free-standing white tub with steam curling up in sensual invitation.

Candlelit baths were becoming a habit, and I couldn't say I was opposed. "This feels a little like déjà vu."

He stepped in close behind me, his desire crashing into my back like a wave. His lips skimmed my neck, leaving the skin prickling.

"More like fantasy fulfillment."

"Baths are a fantasy for you?"

"Since that night at your house? Hell yes." His fingers found my zipper and eased it down. "I wanted you so goddamn bad I could hardly breathe. But you weren't for me, not yet."

My dress fell to my feet, my bra seconds behind it. Need pooled low in my belly.

"So I walked away when all I wanted to do was stay and undress you. See the water slide over your skin. Watch you get all lathered up and spread soap across this gorgeous body."

My nipples pebbled as his fingertips skated down my sternum then over my belly button to the lace of my panties. He pushed them over my hips, and they joined the puddle of clothes at my feet.

Standing in front of him completely naked while he was fully dressed was impossibly erotic. My breathing was heavy, my nipples ached, wetness gathered between my legs. He hadn't even really touched me, and yet just the scrape of his clothes against my sensitized skin had me clenching in anticipation.

His lips grazed the shell of my ear, his voice low and rough. "Will you let me watch now?"

Oh. Absolutely yes.

I swayed into him, and he chuckled as he steadied me. Walking me forward, he helped me step into the tub, and I sank down into the steaming pool. The water had the familiar silkiness of Epsom salts. This very sultry bath was doing double duty. I remembered the setup in the other room. He'd brought water to hydrate, meds to reduce inflammation, the heating pad and bath salts to soothe aching muscles and joints. This whole setup was doing double duty, romance and seduction and quiet care all rolled into one.

A wave of affection and hope rolled through me. This didn't make me feel like a drain. This didn't make me feel like my body difficulties were in the way. He was seeing all of me, loving all of me at once. And, at least in this moment, he didn't seem at all burdened by it.

As if in answer to my thoughts, he leaned over me, tipping my chin and slanting his mouth over mine. I felt it all—the care and affection, the love and the lust—all layered together and pouring through the most delicious kiss.

Finally, he pulled away and stood. His tie hung undone around his neck. Working down the front of his crisp white shirt, he unfastened each button, pulled it free of his charcoal slacks, then rolled up the sleeves. But he didn't remove it, and he didn't move to join me. Instead, he pulled the vanity chair forward and sat, elbows on knees, looking like sex incarnate.

His shirt gaped, framing that firmly muscled torso. His hair, once tidy, was now falling artfully over his forehead.

"You're not joining?"

Shaking his head, he ran a thumb across his lips. "I meant it when I said I wanted to watch."

He nodded toward a loofah and body wash on the ledge near the tub.

What a tease.

He'd riled me all up and put me in this bath alone. Well, the joke was on him because he was as alone out there as I was in here, and I was about to put on one hell of a show.

I loaded the loofah with body wash until it was foamy in my hands. Lifting a leg out of the water, I swiped the suds across my skin, working up one side and down the other. Slowly, methodically, I soaped my other leg, followed by my arms, my neck, my shoulders, my belly. His eyes tracked every move, his gaze hot, searing me everywhere it landed.

Releasing the loofah, I leaned back, pulling pins from my hair and letting it tumble over the side of the tub. I gathered suds to run soapy hands over my chest. I cupped my breasts, grazing my nipples with my thumbs while I massaged the underside with my palms. My peaks stiffened as I caught them between my fingers and tugged, feeling the answering pull at my center. Evan's sharp intake of breath matched my own.

I rolled my head to the side. He looked devastated—undone by need, by me. I ached to push us both further.

"You want to see what I do in the bath?"

I moved my hand down my belly, finding that swollen bundle of nerves with my fingertips and giving it a hard stroke.

"Fuck." He sounded as desperate as I felt.

I rubbed myself in tight little circles, my legs spreading wider as I started to build. I quickened my pace, chasing my pleasure while he watched me climb. My eyes fell closed. Water lapped at my breasts. My fingers thrummed over my clit, and the hot coil in my core tightened. I reached for the edge.

A hand closed around my wrist and yanked it from the water. My eyes flew open in time to see my fingers disappear into Evan's mouth. Closing his lips around them, he sucked, and I felt it as if his mouth were between my legs. Even in the water, I could feel my arousal flooding the spot.

His eyes, dark and wild, locked with mine. "Come here."

————

EVAN

She clutched my hand as I helped her from the tub, water dripping from her naked body.

Her skin was flushed pink from the bath and her near-orgasm, her hair a cloud of fire tumbling over her shoulders. She was beautiful. Brilliant. Sweet and strong and sexy. My whole fucking heart outside of my body, pinning me with lust-soaked green eyes.

"Your turn." She sank to her knees on the rug in front of me.

Fire churned in my stomach. I felt feral, white-knuckling self-control that had been in danger of shattering all day. She'd walked down an aisle to me, for god's sake, and I hadn't begged her to tack on another marriage to the ceremony. I made it through dancing with her pressed against my body and that spectacular, masochistic bath. But this might push me over the edge.

She unfastened my belt and opened my slacks. I lifted my hips when she gripped my waistband, letting her slide my pants and underwear down my thighs. She grabbed me as I bobbed free, already painfully hard. Begging for her.

Leaning forward, she settled her mouth right at the base of my cock and breathed deep, a little moan of pleasure catching in her throat on the exhale.

Fucking hell, she's gonna kill me.

She pressed the flat of her tongue to me and slowly dragged it up, licking the underside of my shaft all the way up to the bead of moisture gathering on the tip. She sucked my head into her mouth, flicking her tongue around the flared rim. Sparks shot down my spine.

She parted her lips, that perfect O wrapping around me, taking me deeper. My hand tangled in her hair, my hips lifting to meet her as a groan broke in my chest.

Adding her hand, she gripped me tight and moved it up and down my length with the stroke of her mouth, building my pleasure along with her pace. Already, the pressure was multiplying, pulling sensation from the rest of my body and concentrating it under her touch. But as incredible as it felt, it wasn't how I wanted to come.

My dick gave a throb of protest as I pulled her off, dragging her up my body to straddle me over the chair. With one hand bracketed across her still-damp back and one clutched at the back of her neck, I pulled her flush to my body and brought that wicked mouth to mine. She opened immediately, and my tongue swept in to savor her, devouring her sweet moan.

Her fingers knotted in my hair while I trailed kisses down her neck to a puckered pink nipple. I sucked it into my mouth, and her head fell back as I ran my tongue over the rough little bud. God, she tasted good, every part of her a slight variation on her flavor. And I was the lucky bastard who got to sample every single one.

I moved to the other breast, nipping at the underside before pulling that nipple between my lips like I had the first.

"Ev." She squirmed on my lap, canting her hips and rubbing her wet slit against my length.

Goddamn.

I dug my fingers into her hips, grinding her down, chasing her heat. She rocked with me, sliding me through her slick folds. Every pass threatened to tear me apart. I was painfully hard, literally aching with need for her.

I panted against her breast. "Condom. In my pocket."

She froze, and I immediately followed suit, worried she was hurting. But when I looked up into her eyes, there was no edge of pain. Just desire, clear and bright.

"I have an IUD. We don't have any STIs. I don't need it if you don't."

My heart lurched then took off like a shot. She didn't want to use a condom. I'd never done that before, and to my knowledge, she hadn't either. The thought of me and Violet without barriers, doing something that was only ours, that would only ever be ours—it had that white-knuckle control slipping away fast.

My voice felt like gravel. "I don't need it."

Her hands framed my face, anchoring me in her gaze. "It's us. I want to feel you."

I was done.

My mouth crashed to hers, quick and rough, before I stood, setting her on her feet and spinning her to face the vanity. With a gentle hand between her shoulder blades, I bent her forward, and she gripped the edge of the counter to brace herself. I kissed the freckles running down her spine and she trembled, tipping her hips up in invitation.

"So eager." I smiled into her skin.

Taking myself in hand, I ran my head along her seam, down over her clit, and back up to her entrance. Blood rushed in my ears as my heart pounded against my ribs. I pushed in by degrees, savoring every exquisite inch, working steadily deeper until I was fully seated inside of her.

Nothing—*nothing*—had ever felt as good as Violet clasped hot and tight around me. My entire body was a live wire, electricity radiating out from where we connected. It was a miracle I didn't finish right then.

Breathing through the barrage of sensation, I let my hands roam, loving the way she arched into my touch. My hands settled in the dip of her waist, and I held her still as I dragged myself back through her channel and surged forward. She grunted when I hit bottom. My eyes snapped to hers in the mirror and held.

Right here like this, we were as close as two people could be. A feeling of completeness hit me like a bat to the chest, obliterating everything that wasn't this connection with her. It was everything. She was everything. And I had no more restraint.

"Hang on, baby."

I tightened my grip, thrusting into her hard, and she pushed back to meet me, pulling a groan from us both. I moved in her, with her, sinking inside her again and again, losing myself to her friction, to the push and pull of her wrapped around me, to her eager little noises. Steam and sweat slicked our skin. Her breasts swayed. Her lips parted. But her eyes never left mine in the mirror.

She was close. Her delicate muscles fluttered around me in a way that had my balls tightening and my dick swelling, each pulse of her pussy drawing my release closer to the surface. I levered her farther back into my hips, dipping low and rolling up into her, hitting exactly where she needed me to give her that push over the edge.

Her eyes screwed shut as she clamped down around me like a vise. Her back arched and her body shook, her orgasm ripping her apart. Banding my arms around her, I pulled her trembling body to my chest, burying my face in her hair, holding her while wave after wave racked through her.

Everything.

"Violet. I love you."

She whimpered, and I broke, my orgasm thundering through me, and I emptied my release into her in hot bursts. I clutched her like a lifeline in the downpour of our shared climax, struggling to let go even after the storm subsided.

Eventually, I slipped out of her, and we swayed on our feet. I grasped the edge of the counter as I took in the sight of us in the mirror.

We were ravaged. She was a sex goddess, her hair wild and her makeup smudged, exposed skin pink and puffy in all the right places. I, on the other hand, with my shirt open and my pants around my knees, looked like I'd been caught in some kind of weird sex tornado that rumpled my hair and blew off half my clothes.

"I can't believe we did all of that and I'm still dressed."

She pulled her lip through her teeth. "It's kind of hot."

Tipping her head back, I peered down at her. "You have a kink we need to discuss?"

She giggled and spun to face me, smacking my bare chest. "No. Well, not that one anyway." I felt my eyebrows hit my hairline as she cackled.

"But seriously." Stepping close, she circled her arms around my waist. "That was incredible…and I love you too."

Contentment thrummed through me. I took her face in my hands, brushing gentle kisses over her swollen lips.

"Feeling okay?"

"Yeah. A little tired, but surprisingly okay. I guess a bath can work wonders."

"Or you're all hopped up on sex endorphins."

"Or that." She placed a kiss right over my heart. She had to know it belonged only to her. "We better get cleaned up before they wear off. I also need to take meds and eat about half that cake before I go to bed."

"Anything you want." *Anything.*

CHAPTER 25
VIOLET

I sat in the middle of my living room floor, books and knickknacks scattered around, stuffing them into half-full boxes. The email that would determine where these boxes landed, as well as the trajectory of my entire career, was due any day.

Just an average Thursday! No existential crisis whatsoever!

I'd given myself as many recovery days as I could after the wedding. I stayed with Evan, let him take care of me. But it had been almost a week now, and while my tiny place wouldn't require too long to pack, I couldn't put that chore off any longer. I'd come while he was at work today, trying to get as much done as possible before he came to get me for dinner at his mom's tonight.

While I was sure the short turnaround between acceptance announcements and the program start date would be daunting for most, my relocation situation was particularly bonkers. My end date here didn't give me much buffer. In two weeks, I would either have all of this in storage while I left my whole support system to take a running leap into my dream career, or I'd be moving it in with my dreamboat boyfriend while building my life here at home.

Admittedly, both options seemed fantastic, but it was a lot of change in a short time and a lot of uncertainty around huge, life-defining conditions. I decided to allow myself the angst. It was stressful not knowing where you were going to be. Even more stressful not knowing where you *should* be.

Doubt whispered in the back of my mind. Should I even be considering this fellowship anymore? When I applied, it seemed like a perfect solution to problems I desperately needed to solve. I'd needed a fresh start, needed to escape my soul-sucking work situation, needed to feel inspired again. More than that, I needed to take control of my life, do something for myself that I could be proud of.

I was already taking steps in the right direction to fix a lot of those problems—even without the internship. My relationship with Evan was a factor for sure, but it was also the more active role I'd been taking in my own life. I was stepping up, feeling less and less like a bystander, and challenging the notion that I had to keep my life small and take whatever the universe gave me.

And now there were real, exciting work opportunities presenting themselves that could meet my needs while keeping me here at home. I wouldn't have to turn my life upside down. I wouldn't have to be separated from my whole support system. I wouldn't have to delay my move-in with Evan, wouldn't have to put us through the strain of long distance. Wouldn't have to miss him. I could get what I needed and stay here where I was happy and safe.

*And yet...*my feet ached to jump.

Yes, it was scary. And yes, it would be hard. But it would also be a giant, thrilling dream fulfillment. It would be trusting myself, choosing myself in a way I hadn't since I was nineteen.

It wasn't the safest option or the most practical. There was a good chance I was being foolish and would regret it immediately. But I knew I had to try.

My laptop, aka my constant Email Watch companion, dinged. It sat open on the coffee table, a new email at the top of the inbox. Scrambling across the floor, I pulled it into my lap and stared at the subject line, reading and rereading as tears blurred my vision.

Congratulations…

My hand shook as I hovered over the link, afraid to click it, as if somehow that word would vanish when I actually opened the email, as if maybe it was a silly misunderstanding or a trick of my watery eyes. I wasn't quite ready to read the letter that would clear it all up. But my excitement outpaced my fear and on a shuddering breath, I clicked.

Congratulations on your acceptance…your application and submission were standout entries…we look forward to having you with us…

The tears were no longer content to remain in my lashes. They fell in heavy drops down my cheeks, getting lost in the corners of my wide-sprawling smile. I tumbled to my back, legs kicking and arms flailing, happiness too big for my body looking to make its escape.

I was in. Out of hundreds of applications, they chose mine. They saw enough promise to give me an opportunity, and I was going to take it.

My phone buzzed from somewhere nearby. Locating it under a pile of throw blankets, I brought it to hover over my face.

Mom.

The woman had impeccable timing as usual. It's like she could sense that anything at all might be happening in my life from four hundred miles away and she was on call 24/7 to make sure it was put to a stop. Add that kind of diligence to the daily care of a chronically ill kid, and it would be too much for anyone to handle. No wonder I almost destroyed her. I had relieved her of the latter, at least, but she would never give up her post on the former.

I was going to have to tell her. The acceptance was real, and I would be moving across the country in a couple weeks. She deserved to know. As much as I was dreading it, as much as I was a little resentful that this conversation would mar my excitement, I couldn't bring myself to keep it from her now.

I sat, needing all the spine I could get for this conversation, and swiped to answer the call.

"Hey, Mom."

"Violet. How are you feeling, honey? I know you had that big wedding on Saturday. Is Evan taking good care of you?"

"Of course he is, and I'm feeling fine."

"I know how it gets when you do too much."

"It wasn't too much, Mom. It was a great day, and I took some time to rest after. I'm doing good, I promise."

"All right. I worry about you, you know."

"I know." I was done with small talk, if her chastising me about my health could be considered small talk. "You have really good timing, though. I have some good news to share."

Despite the "good news" lead-in, I could already feel her anxiety climbing through the phone. This was not going to go well. It was never going to go well. But I'd pushed it off as long as I could, and now it was the end of the line. I braced for impact.

"I applied for a writing fellowship, and I just found out I was accepted. It's a six-month program in Boston that starts in a little over two weeks. I'm actually packing up my apartment right now. Anyway, it's a really great program and a huge honor to be selected…"

The silence was loud, and it stretched as she made sense of my revelation.

"What about work? Where are you going to live? How are you going to pay for it?"

"I'll be putting in notice with Gemma tomorrow, and I'll live in the housing provided by the program. It's a cute little studio apartment in the same building with the other fellows. It's all paid for on scholarship by the people who host. Kind of a charitable investment in the arts. It's such an incredible opportunity—"

"How could you possibly do that, Violet? Go up there all alone with no one to care for you? And I'm sure these fellowship people will have expectations of you if they're giving this all for free. What happens when you can't keep up with whatever they're wantin' of you?"

The words slashed across my chest. I knew this was coming. Could predict with disturbing accuracy the objections to being on my own, to taking on too much. But no amount of knowledge seemed to immunize me to the hurt.

"And what about Evan? That boy already does so much for you. Is he gonna be okay with you running off for six months? Is he gonna wait around? How is that any way to treat him when he turns himself inside out for you?"

My mom loved me. She wanted me to be okay. But she had a special gift for plucking the deepest insecurities from the depths of my psyche and giving them a voice.

You're not enough. You're too much.

You can't take care of yourself. You're a burden to others.

You can't do it. It's foolish to try. You're hurting people.

Stay small and be grateful for what you're given.

"You just gonna throw away your life? Your job and your relationship and everything to go gallivanting—"

"Enough, Mom." The words snapped off my tongue like a lightning bolt, bright and charged and stunning. "I'm not throwing away anything. My current job is terrible, and I'm leaving it regardless. Evan loves me. He supports me, and we'll be okay. And believe it or not, I can do this. I can take care of myself, and I can be successful. If that turns out not to be true, at least I'll have tried instead of wrapping myself in bubble wrap and letting life pass me by."

"I'm only trying to take care of you, Violet." Her voice was all quiet indignation, more defensive than contrite.

But it took the fight right out of me. This was far from done, but I didn't have any more energy for it today. I couldn't convince her to see this from my perspective, and I no longer had it in me to try.

"I know you are, Mom. Look, I've got to go get ready, but we'll talk more this weekend. Okay?"

Fortunately, she conceded. We said our goodbyes and I collapsed back to the floor, drained of energy and nursing some fresh wounds.

I told myself that she was wrong. About me, about Evan, about everything. But when her voice and the one whispering in the back of my mind sounded so much alike, it was hard to be totally sure they weren't right.

————

EVAN

Here

We were running late. We were supposed to be at his mom's house basically right now, but he'd gotten hung up at the office, so I was going to jump into the moving car as he sped by in an attempt to minimize our tardiness. Donna Marshall did not suffer a lack of punctuality, even when the offender was her only son.

I hurried down the stairs and out the door onto the sidewalk, surprised to see Evan rounding the hood of his car.

"Hey. I thought—"

He scooped me off the sidewalk, arms around my waist, spinning me in sweeping circles while he kissed the hell out of me.

Well.

Eventually the spinning ebbed, followed by the kissing, and he sat me down on my feet, dropping one more peck to my lips. "I love you. Get in."

Hurrying me to the car, he pulled away from the curb before my seatbelt was even fully fastened. He sat forward in his seat, thumb tapping on the steering wheel, three dimples out in full force. It was simply impossible not to smile at his grinning face.

"What's going on with you?"

"The reason I got caught at the office." He glanced at me, the wattage of his smile broadcasting exactly what he had to share.

"You got it."

He nodded, and I shrieked, slapping him on the shoulder, his answering laughter rolled through the car.

"Paul and Luce pulled me into a meeting. The city's going with us. My design. My building's gonna be downtown. It's…" He shook his head, looking a little awed. "Fuck. It's unbelievable."

"It's completely believable." Reaching across the console, I took his hand, squeezing it tight. "What about the promotion?"

His smile was wry. "Not official, but…"

"In the bag?"

"Between the award and this, I have a really strong case. Luce told me tonight I have her vote. Add her support to Paul and Nancy's, and I think it's pretty much a done deal."

We sat there together, savoring the moment, excitement and happiness filling the car to bursting. We'd celebrated so many victories together over the years, but this one felt different. We weren't just each other's biggest cheerleaders now. We were also a team. It was *our* life we were building.

I wanted to add my good news to our little party. Celebrate another team win. I took a breath to speak.

"The schedule is going to be intense for a while. Thank god you're moving in."

Oh. I guess that part wasn't ideal. Long distance got that much harder when working around not one but two demanding schedules. It was an unpleasant reality to mar this moment, but we'd still be able to figure it out.

"I don't think I've ever been happier, Vi. It's all happening. And the best damn part is you. Starting our life together." He pulled my hand to his mouth to kiss my palm.

I should have loved those words, but I found my heart sinking. It was a lovely sentiment. And it wasn't wrong, but it wasn't exactly right either, not the way he meant it. I needed to tell him, but bringing it up now would wreck his joy, and I couldn't form the words.

It would be okay. We'd go do this dinner and I'd figure out how to tell him without it feeling like a cloud of doom. We'd talk about it tonight, tomorrow at the latest. He'd get out his notebook, and we'd make a plan, and everything would be fine.

CHAPTER 26
VIOLET

My childhood home was a hotbed of angst. It's not that it wasn't a loving place or that I didn't have plenty of happy memories there as a young kid. But the pleasant moments were so covered up by the years of mysterious illness and unanswered questions and fraying patience and suffocating protectiveness that even stepping in the door felt like putting on a too-tight sweater…that itched.

This home, though, this home exuded warmth. Sure, it needed a little attention, but no amount of peeling paint or crumbling pipes or whatever else was on the to-do list here could take away from the peaceful, joyful, supportive place Donna had created for her family. Was it any wonder that they were all fighting so hard to keep it?

Even as an outsider, I felt buoyed as soon as I walked through the door. And after that happy, hard, uncomfortable car ride and the resulting weight that had settled into my chest, I could use all the buoying I could get.

We stepped into the cozy living room, and Lauren's head popped out from behind the wall separating it from the dining room, a devious look on her face.

"Oh, hi, big brother!" Her voice was too loud, too bright. This obviously was not for our benefit. "You finally made it."

Donna's disembodied voice boomed from behind her. "Is that Evan? What time is it?"

"Traitor." Evan good-naturedly pulled his sister into a headlock/hug as we crossed through the dining room. "Yeah, Mom. We're here. Sorry we're late. I got caught at the office."

She appeared at the mouth of the kitchen, wiping her hands on a dish towel. "Well, I knew it wasn't Violet causing you to be late to a family dinner. This angel would never do me that way." With a covert wink, she hauled me into a fierce hug before rounding on Evan, hands on hips. "My son, on the other hand…"

He didn't wait for her invitation before wrapping her in his strong arms, pressing her face to his chest. She swatted him but he held tight, muffling her laugh. "I am beside myself with shame. I'll never let it happen again."

Finally, she squirmed free and primly smoothed down her salt and pepper bob. "Well as long as you feel properly guilty, you can pour me a drink to make up for it."

"Yes, ma'am." Evan kissed his mother on the cheek and moved toward the sideboard bar as she retreated back to the kitchen.

"He gets off so easy." Lauren rolled her eyes, equal parts exasperation and affection shining through the gesture, before reaching out to me for a hug of her own. "It's so great to see you. It feels like it's been forever."

"I know. Nico and Jamie's wedding stuff made everything so crazy."

The sound of smallish feet tearing down the stairs and through the living room was joined by Tabitha's enthusiastic bellow. "Uncleeee Evannnnn!"

He set aside a wine glass and decanter in time to catch the colorful blur careening at him. Tabbie was nothing less than a fashion icon dressed in rainbow-striped tights, a black tutu, a My Little Pony T-shirt, and a Batman mask that couldn't hide the adoration on her little face as she wound her arms tight around his neck.

He made a show of being crushed by her strong hug, coughing and stumbling as she howled and squeezed tighter. My heart tumbled in my chest, a sensation I didn't at all want to evaluate. But I was fortunately saved from having to examine it too closely by a shout of my own name, and the reappearance of the blur moving in my direction.

I crouched to hug her. "Looks like you let your Uncle Evan go just in time. I was afraid he wasn't going to make it."

She popped a hand on her small hip. "He's a drama queen."

I bit my lip, clamping down on my smile. Lauren was less successful, slapping a hand over her mouth that did nothing to contain her snorting.

Donna didn't even try to hold back, her open laugh roaring from the kitchen. "Ain't it the truth, baby."

"Hey! Wait a second. I'm not sure I care for being ganged up on like this." He dropped to his haunches beside me, gently tugging on Tabbie's ponytail. "You turning on me, kiddo?"

Her face as somber as it could be, Tabitha laid her hand on his shoulder and gently shook her head. "Sometimes the truth hurts."

With that, nobody was containing their laughter.

———

"Batmans don't belong at this table. Mask off, ma'am." Tabbie dutifully handed over the mask to her mother, more concerned with the food spread than her ensemble.

We gathered around, passing dishes as she passed judgment. The pork chops were "good but not as good as steak," the "scallop potatoes" were "AMAZING," and the roasted asparagus was "kinda blech," an opinion that earned her a light chiding from her mom and a covert nod of agreement from her uncle.

We tucked into the meal, which was all amazing if you asked me, the first few minutes filled only with yummy noises and Tabitha's quiet "dang it" when she tried the asparagus and accidentally let a yummy noise slip.

When we'd made a healthy dent, Evan straightened in his chair. "So the reason we were late tonight was actually because I was getting good news." Utensils lowered as all eyes moved to him. "The city is building a municipal building downtown. Paul and Lucia gave me the pitch. And tonight..." He reached for my hand under the table, making us that team again and making my stomach rock with unease. "I found out I won it."

The table erupted, even Tabbie jumping in with cheers she didn't fully understand.

I smiled—of course I smiled—but it felt a little too stiff on my face. What was wrong with me? This news had been elating an hour ago. I was so proud of him, happy for him—for us.

There was a tension between his big dreams and mine that was feeling far more real and a fair bit scarier than it had up until now, but surely it wasn't too big for us to handle.

The weight of his hand was heavy in mine. *A team.* That had to be the issue. We were supposed to be a team, and I had withheld information that was important to us both. I'd chickened out, and now I was feeling guilty for not being open with him. I'd feel better once we talked.

I swallowed down a small wave of nausea and worked to fortify my smile.

"It also turns out that Luce is retiring. And this makes it likely that they'll make me department head."

"As they damn well should." Donna beamed over her glass of wine.

"I'm proud of you, brother."

"Uncle Evan wins everything!"

"And the best part is that the promotion will come with a signing bonus big enough to cover the repairs on this place."

Donna's smile faltered. "Baby. That's not your job. The bonus is great, but this is not where you need to spend it."

"Of course it is, Mom. You can't lose this place."

Lauren shot up from her chair. "Hey, Tab. Let's go work on dessert."

Tabbie looked skeptical. "Mom, we're in the middle of a conversation, and I think it's gettin' good."

"Which is exactly why your time is up, ma'am. It's now or never for cake."

"Ugh. I can't quit cake." Looking positively beleaguered, she slunk out of her chair and Lauren shuffled her into the kitchen with a backward glance to mouth "proud of you" toward Evan.

Releasing my hand, Evan rested his forearms on the edge of the table, leaning toward his mom, his voice low and intense. "This place is home, Mom. For all of us, but especially for you and Lauren and Tabbie. I can't let you lose it when I can help."

"That's very generous, and I love you for it, baby, but I've been working on things of my own, and I've got it all handled. You don't need to worry."

"Of course I—"

"Tonight is not about that anyway. Let's focus on celebrating, and we'll talk about this another time."

He wanted to argue. I could see him gearing up to fight, but Tabbie's "who wants cake?" rang from the kitchen, and his mom's expression begged him not to push, so on a sigh, he nodded his concession.

This was nowhere near over. Helping them stay in this house was more important to him than the building and the promotion put together. He'd want assurances that they were in no danger before he'd be willing to step back. But he'd gotten that stubborn streak from the woman sitting across from him, so if she didn't want his help, the showdown would be epic.

For tonight, anyway, they'd called a truce. We'd keep the focus on good news, and they'd duke it out another day.

Lauren caught my eye from the kitchen, and I nodded that the situation was safe for reentry. The sound of plates clinking echoed in the still-tense silence. Fortunately, the mood recovered remarkably quickly when Tabbie bopped in with a giant slice of chocolate cake, Lauren on her heels carrying four more.

Tabbie sat her plate in front of Evan as he pulled her onto his lap. "I put a sparkler on yours. It isn't a birthday, but you can still make a wish if you want."

She enlisted her mom to light the sparkler and sang "Uncle Evan Wins Everything" at the top of her lungs before instructing him to blow it out, which he dutifully did to a round of cheers.

She insisted this cake was The Very Best Ever, and I could not say she was wrong. I briefly wondered if bathing in this frosting would be frowned upon, but ultimately decided against pushing the bounds of etiquette.

When our plates were clean, Tabbie leaned in close to Evan with a chocolate-smeared mouth and an urgent whisper. "What did you wish for?"

He whispered back. "I wished that there was somebody around here who knew how to throw a proper tea party."

Eyes wide, the corner of her mouth curled in delight. "I'm the queen of tea parties."

Lauren and I had taken dish duty so Evan could get to the tea party. Now I was on my way to attempt an extraction so we could head home.

I paused at Tabitha's half-open door, hanging back to take in the charming scene.

Evan and Tabbie and a host of stuffies were gathered around a small white table. They had dressed for the occasion. Tabbie perched on a chair, donning an oversized tiara and what appeared to be a vampire cape. Next to her, Evan sat cross-legged on the floor, sporting a very extravagant 1920s-style fascinator and dripping in plastic jewelry. They both tipped white-and-blue patterned teacups to their lips, pinkies held high. He said something that had her dissolving in a fit of giggles.

Warmth suffused my chest. It was utterly adorable, and I was not above swooning over this sweet man with his niece.

"God, he makes it hard to give him shit when he's just out here being the best uncle ever." I glanced over my shoulder to find Lauren peering in behind me. Her smile was wry, but it didn't hide the glisten in her eyes. I could only imagine what seeing them together meant to her. "She's so lucky to have him. I'm a damn good mom, don't get me wrong…but I don't know… It's like he's built for it."

He was. His nurturing spirit, his tenderness, his patience, his willingness to be silly—they were exactly what the best uncles—the best dads —were made of. I'd always seen it in him, always thought of him as made to be a father.

Guilt pinched my middle.

"I can't wait to see him with his own." She hitched a laundry basket up on her hip and continued down the hallway, tossing a conspiratorial wink over her shoulder that turned the pinch of guilt into a punch.

She wouldn't see him with his own. He would never have his own.

I'm taking that from him.

My chest cracked in two. My eyes snapped back to him, looking for reassurance, desperate for some sign that this wasn't the worst possible thing I could do to him, but I knew I'd never find it. He'd wanted to be a dad since he was a kid himself. That hadn't changed. All that had changed was his willingness to give it up to be with me.

Suddenly dizzy, I clutched the doorframe to hold myself upright.

How had I let this happen? I'd known this since the beginning. Hell, I'd panicked about it in the beginning. But then it was Evan and lightning bugs and trust and sex and a fantastical future that shimmered on the horizon, and somewhere I lost track of reality. I let myself be whisked away by fantasies of taking this for myself and conveniently forgot what I'd be taking from him to do it. Bitterness flooded my mouth at the selfishness.

Being with him felt right. I loved him. Wanted him. So that was it? I was going to tie this man to a life he didn't want? Potential kids weren't even the only front I was failing him on.

Exactly what did I think was going to happen to every other messy piece of this?

He would pause excitedly planning our lives together and wouldn't be brokenhearted when I announced a six-month separation?

He would spend his life caring for me, supporting me, working around flares and limitations, and wouldn't feel resentful? Wouldn't start to look at me and see a chore instead of a partner?

He would give up his desire for children and not think of it as the biggest regret of his life?

I'd laugh at the absurdity if it wasn't choking me.

The mismatch of lives moving in different directions was bad enough, but that part, at least, was potentially overcome-able. The destructive force of long-term caretaking duties wouldn't be. I had to look no further than what my mom endured and the way my relationship with her still strained under the weight of my illness to know that was a fact. But even if I could believe it would magically be different with him on that front, kids were the full stop.

Lauren was right. He was built for this, more than anyone I'd ever known. And I knew better than anyone how much he wanted it. As much as I had once upon a time.

As much as I still do.

But he could still have it, and I wouldn't be able to live with myself if I was the one who took it from him.

CHAPTER 27

EVAN

Something was off.

Vi had gone quiet, her movements stiff and stilted. Initially, I thought she must be hurting, but she said she was fine, and while she was notoriously bad about downplaying how bad she felt, she never flat-out lied about it.

That left being upset, but I couldn't for the life of me figure out what might have caused it. I'd spent the car ride back to my place running the evening over and over in my head but coming up empty. Everything was good—great even—and then out of nowhere it wasn't.

She'd barely said a word the whole way home, barely touched me since dinner, given quick, unconvincing answers when I asked, in as many ways as I could think of, what was up. That was the piece bothering me most. She never shut me out. When something was wrong, we talked, and right now it was radio silence.

Unease simmered in my gut.

We made it through my front door, and she sat her bag down as I emptied my pockets on the entry table. I didn't want to keep harping, but I didn't feel like I could let this go. I reached out, my hand grazing her waist, ready to pull her close and figure out whatever this was, but she didn't let me. She stepped away, putting distance between us and leaving my extended hand empty. The simmer of unease rolled into a boil.

Moving into the living room, she turned to face me, her brow knitted, nose wrinkled. She looked like she was bracing for impact, which did nothing to calm my anxiety.

"I have something to tell you." Her fingers tangled in front of her as she took an uneven breath. "I got the fellowship. I found out this afternoon. I should have told you but…" She finished on a shrug.

Oh. That was…great, of course.

That familiar blend of pride and nausea I'd felt every time I'd thought about this was hitting critical mass with the revelation. This was a huge achievement. I was excited for her…and terrified of what might happen if she went.

I hated myself for the mixed-bag reaction. I should be celebrating for her like she did for me. Besides, I was getting ahead of myself. A lot had changed over the past couple of months. Her getting in didn't necessarily mean she was leaving.

"Vi. That's incredible. I'm so damn proud of you."

Her lips pulled into a tremulous almost smile.

"You're talented. You deserve for that to be recognized. No matter what happens, getting in is huge."

The smile slipped. "What do you mean, 'no matter what happens?'"

"I mean whether or not you take it. It's awesome that you got in, but you don't have to go now. You have other options."

A reel of emotion played across her face—confusion, hesitation, distaste—none of them the reaction I wanted or expected. "Other options to explore if this didn't work out. I'm not going because I have to. I'm going because I want to."

She was talking like she'd already made the decision. Like she was already out the door. And everything here was a backup, an afterthought. My muscles were strung tight, tension churning in my gut.

"So moving in together, that was just an option to explore if this didn't work out? I didn't realize this was only Plan B we were working on."

"That's not what I…" Her eyes squeezed shut in frustration. Well, she could join the damn club. "This was always the plan. You've known that since the beginning."

She was right. It had been the plan, but a helluva lot had changed since it was made. I guess that didn't make as much difference as I thought it did. Suddenly I was out on this limb by myself.

"I thought it would be a conversation at least." Thought the life we were building here would be worth considering, not dismissed like it was never more than a consolation prize.

"This program is once in a lifetime."

It was also halfway across the country and required leaving her whole support system. How the hell was I going to take care of her from thousands of miles away? She'd be going it alone, something she should never have to do.

"I'm sure it's great, but it's also a lot to take on. Do you really think it's the best situation for you?"

Her brows knotted together, hurt and disbelief painted across her face, like I'd betrayed her somehow. "You don't think I can do it."

Goddammit. That wasn't—

"Well, good news, my mom beat you to the You Can't Do This speech, so you can save yourself the trouble."

A bitter taste filled my mouth. Her mom suffocated her, hovered like she was incapable, never supported her, never believed in her, never recognized that she was the smartest, strongest, most amazing woman on the planet. I *was not* her mom. But I wasn't about to apologize for acknowledging reality or for giving a shit about her well-being or for wanting to be the one to make sure she was okay.

"No. I know you can do it. I just don't know if going up there all alone with no one to take care of you—" I stepped toward her, reaching out, hoping to close the distance, but she held the space, leaving me empty-handed again as she folded her arms over her chest.

"I can take care of myself."

Sure. No need for me at all. "Really? So you didn't need me after you crashed yourself into the ground at Jamie's bachelorette? And you didn't need me in the wedding aftermath?"

She reared back like I'd slapped her. Tears welled in her eyes.

Shit.

"I know taking care of me is a lot, but I never expected you, of all people, to throw it in my face."

I hated making her cry, hated that she thought I was trying to hurt her. I did my best to moderate my tone. "I'm not throwing anything in your face. I love taking care of you. I'm trying to sign up to do it forever. All I'm saying is that you need it. It's absurd to pretend you don't." My stomach churned at the thought of her thousands of miles away, alone and in pain, too far for me to help make it okay. "I think it's reckless to run off where nobody—"

"Evan." Something cold slid down my spine at the way she said my name, a sense of dread moving in with it. "We need to end this. Us."

My brain scrambled to make sense of the words. *End this? As in, break up?* That...how was that even part of this conversation? We were talking about whether she would stay here or go to Boston. Where in the fuck had ending this come from?

"Why would you say that? Look, we'll figure this out."

"There's nothing to figure out. This is how it has to be."

Her mouth was drawn into a solemn line, her gaze firm but distant. She was serious. She was actually talking about leaving. Not temporarily-long-distance leaving, permanently-not-together leaving.

My heart slammed against my ribs, panic hammering through my veins.

You don't have to leave me. I can fix it, build you something you'll love.

"It doesn't. Please, move in with me. If you don't want the other job, don't take it. Write full-time. With the promotion, I'll make enough to support us while you do. Tell me what you want and I'll do it. Just… stay with me. Let me take care of you—"

There was a tremble in her voice as she cut me off. "That's not your job. I don't want that from you."

It was a hot blade through my middle, opening me wide. I knew if I looked down, I'd see my heart and soul falling from my body at her feet, but I couldn't tear my eyes from hers, her lashes clumping with moisture. What a stupid fucking thing to notice when I couldn't even breathe.

This couldn't be happening. Five hours ago, we were kissing on the sidewalk. She seemed happy.

"It was never going to work. I'm sorry."

No. No no no.

"Violet. Don't." I was choking on my words, on the lump that formed in my throat as hot tears stung the backs of my eyes.

"I should go." She stepped close to me for the first time since we'd walked through the door, her familiar honey scent rolling my stomach.

I wanted to grab her, to pull her close and not let go till I'd made this right, but I couldn't move. I stood completely paralyzed, my brain screaming at me to do something, while my world crumbled around me.

"Bye, Ev." She pressed her lips to my cheek, soft and warm, damp from the tears that were now rolling freely down her face. That tender kiss seared my skin like a brand. I had no doubt that I'd feel the mark for the rest of my life.

I hung on every sound as she walked past me—the soft fall of her footsteps moving away from me, the clink of her bag as she took it from the table, the creak and click of the door as she left me alone. I wanted to chase her down the driveway, to beg her not to go. But I'd done that once before, and I knew how it ended. When someone decided they wanted to leave you, there was no convincing them to stay.

It was done.

Whatever had me paralyzed dissolved with her absence, and I collapsed to the couch, head between my legs, fighting through waves of nausea.

She didn't want me. Whatever I was offering wasn't enough.

She left me.

It was never going to work.

CHAPTER 28
VIOLET

You are extremely capable and can definitely handle this.

The problem with lying to yourself was that it was difficult to overcome your own skepticism.

I lay flat on my back in the middle of my living room, eyeing the stack of boxes that was feeling more and more like a mountain every second.

My movers had come and gone, all my furniture and long-term keep boxes hauled away to a storage unit. All that was left were the eight boxes and two contractor bags of personal items that were coming with me to Boston.

All I had to do was get them down to my car, a task that seemed completely doable when I planned all this out a week ago, but now, after days of packing and stacking and too many tears and not enough sleep, my body was having none of it. My hips ached. My knees throbbed.

I was marooned in this empty apartment. I hadn't even gotten to how I was going to survive a 2,000-mile road trip when I couldn't get eight boxes and two bags down three flights of stairs.

This on-my-own thing is off to a great start.

The door buzzer sounded, and my heart took off, like it had with every door buzz and every phone call and almost every text over the last week and a half.

It is not him. He wouldn't buzz, he'd come straight up…or maybe he wouldn't anymore. *It doesn't matter. You don't even want it to be him.*

I needed to get better at selling myself lies.

Peeling myself off the floor, I hobbled to the speaker and pressed the button.

"Hello?"

"Hey." A masculine voice, a familiar one, but not the one I wanted. Didn't want. *Dammit.* "It's Remy. Can I come up?"

I forced brightness into my voice. "Hey! Of course. Come on up."

I pressed the button and opened my front door, leaning on the frame till he crested the top of the stairs. He didn't stop when he made it to me, didn't even pause to say hello, just tugged me into a warm, comforting hug, very nearly dissolving me into a puddle of tears right there in the doorway.

I'd felt so lonely since that night with Evan, so isolated. I'd pulled into myself, avoided contact, unsure how to interact with everyone in light of the breakup and my leaving. I should have known better. I had friends besides Evan. Friends I could count on. Friends who would show up if they thought—*unless…*

"Did he send you?" I pulled back to see his lips purse, the Remy equivalent of a grimace.

"No. I just know everyone's gone and I thought you might need some help today."

I released him from the hug and waved him inside with me, covertly dashing away a single escaped tear. He was right about the low-on-reinforcements situation. Nico and Jamie were on their honeymoon. Lina had to go out of town for work. Evan was unavailable to me for obvious reasons. It was a little strange how he wrote himself out of "everyone," as if he were some kind of alternate, but I was too grateful for his presence to pick at it.

"Thank you. Honestly? Your timing couldn't be better. I was just trying to figure out how to get this stuff," I gestured to my very small mountain that probably looked more like an anthill to him, "down to the car."

With a silent nod, he set to work, stacking and carrying while I opened my door, pushed the button to let him back in, and uselessly observed the manual labor. Fifteen minutes later, it was done. The mountain had been relocated, presumably now piled into my Ford Focus hatchback.

On his last buzz-up, I snagged two water bottles from the refrigerator, hydration the best I could offer, but he didn't return empty-handed.

He came to stand next to me at the island, placing two shot glasses and a bottle of peach schnapps on the countertop. My heart warmed.

"We didn't get a chance to do this for you." He poured the liquor into the two tiny glasses. "It deserves to be celebrated."

It was incredibly thoughtful, an assurance that I still had my support system, still had my traditions. It was a message I desperately needed. I'd been worried that the implosion of my relationship with Evan might have blown up our friend group right along with it. I was racked with guilt and fear and awkwardness that fueled my self-imposed exile. But Remy wasn't going to let me languish. He came to help, came to celebrate, came to remind me that I had people. And I knew without a doubt if the others were in town, they'd be here too.

My hand shook a little as I took my shot from the counter. "Thanks for this."

He raised his glass. "To the best this fellowship has ever seen." Clinking our glasses, we downed the shots on a shudder. "Jesus Christ, you guys couldn't have chosen something drinkable for this ritual?"

"I don't know. I think the disgustingness really adds something."

The corner of his mouth tugged up as he grabbed one of the bottled waters I'd set out and downed half of it in one go. I was pretty sure it had more to do with washing the schnapps away than any labor-related need. He hadn't even broken a sweat. The only sign of his exertion was his dark brown hair, usually immaculately coifed but now ever so slightly out of place.

Rem was a good-looking guy. Okay, an incredibly good-looking guy. Even through my decade-long Evan haze, I could recognize that. He was classically handsome in that movie star way, all square jaw and strong brow. He was wickedly smart, reliable, taciturn but exceptionally kind. Truly, he was a catch, but it occurred to me that beyond a few one-off dates to events, he'd never brought women around…or men, for that matter. It was curious. I wondered if he was happy.

I was in no position to go digging through someone else's love life when mine was in shambles. And I was sure he wouldn't appreciate the scrutiny, so it would be inappropriate to launch that attack on a day he'd shown up to rescue me. My brain's desire to distract itself from my pile of problems was no excuse to harass him.

Eyes on your own paper, Violet.

He cleared his throat, bringing me back to the present. "So how are you holding up? Really?"

It seemed I was the only one with a no-harassment policy.

Why did I think friends were nice again? Was profound loneliness really so bad?

Ugh. Yes, fine. Friends, good. Loneliness, bad. It was lovely of him to ask, and I did probably need to talk about it. Sharing is caring and all that.

I sighed—in defeat or in relief, I couldn't quite decide. "Terrible? Scared of moving. Scared of being completely out of my depth with this program. Hell, scared of being completely out of my depth with life. I couldn't even get my stuff down the stairs on my own. I'm not actually sure I can do this." The floodgates were open. I couldn't have stopped now if I tried. "And I miss him so bad, and I'm not sure if he'll ever talk to me again. And fuck, Rem, he's my best friend, and I don't know what to do without him. And I know I made the right decision—the right decision for both of us—but right now I think I may hate myself for it."

My breathing came in ragged pants as he stared at me, his face completely expressionless, the silence stretching for a long moment before he broke it. "That's…a lot."

A rusty laugh burst from my chest, and another followed, peal after peal, making it feel lighter for the first time since I walked out of Evan's apartment. It wasn't even funny, but the release of it felt so good that I let it keep coming, let it rack me until a cry sprung up in its place. I let that rack me too, the release just as good, just as necessary.

Remy let loose a string of curses under his breath, and then he wrapped me in his arms again, issuing sweet but slightly awkward pats to my head. A nurturer he was not, but he was here giving it his best, and I was grateful. Eventually the wave of emotion ran its course, and I gathered my wits, pulling back and scrubbing my face clean.

"Sorry about that."

He handed me a paper towel from a rogue roll on the countertop and stuffed his hands into his pockets. "I won't pretend to know what to do about you and Evan. That's…well outside of my area of expertise. But I do know that you're going to be okay on the other things. You're more capable than you give yourself credit for, and needing help with some things doesn't take away from that. There's also no program in which you could be in over your head, so don't let it intimidate you."

Well, I'll be damned. Remy, whose primary goal was saying as few words as possible in every scenario, had given me a full-blown pep talk, and a good one at that.

"Thanks, Rem." I felt more optimistic than I had in days, enough that a small smile pulled at my mouth.

He nodded, his allotment of words spent. We walked to the door in comfortable quiet, and he gave me one more quick embrace before disappearing back down the stairs.

———

Four days, four disgusting hotel rooms, 1,955 miles, and not a single bowl of ramen along the way, but I made it. If I thought my body was struggling after packing, it was decimated after that road trip. I needed to take longer, go slower, let myself rest along the way, but that wasn't in the cards. This was the reality, and I had to find a way to make do.

I took my stiff body and negative thirty spoons to find the registration desk in the lobby of the fellow apartment building. A beautiful young woman with dark skin, coily hair, and presumably infinite spoons beamed at me from behind a folding table.

"Hey! Howahya? You checkin' in?" Her voice was bright and musical, with a heavy Bostonian accent. I loved her already.

"Hi. Yes. Violet Ward."

She consulted her tablet, made a couple of taps, then began gathering packets and papers from the table and passing them to me. "Welcome, Ms Ward. I've got you marked down as arrived. Here's your key and your parking pass, and this page is your room info. You're on the fifth floor. Elevators down that hall on your right." An elevator. This woman was a goddess. "This packet here's got information about the area—market, restaurants, parks, hospitals—anything you could need. And this one's got all your program info—your mentor, your schedule, a map, and lots more about what to expect. My name is Stella. I'm the fellow liaison, and you can find my contact at the front of that packet as well. You need anything at all, you let me know, and I'll take care of ya."

I mustered a smile through the fatigue. The goddess Stella deserved my best. "Thank you so much."

Gathering my papers, I started back toward the front door but hesitated. Even with the elevator, there was no way I was going to be able to unload my car. She'd said to ask if I needed help, but the thought of going back with this request racked me with anxiety. What would they think of me? That I was a princess who thought she was above moving her own things? That if I couldn't manage this, I probably shouldn't be here?

I hated this. Hated asking them to go out of their way for me. Hated feeling like a burden. But I didn't see any other choice.

I turned back toward the desk. "Stella? I'm so very sorry to ask, but I have a…medical condition." I stumbled over the words. I didn't use them a lot, didn't want to make my situation out to be a bigger deal than it was. But in this case, it seemed as necessary as it was uncomfortable. "I'm not really able to unload my boxes from my car. I realize it's a lot to ask, but is there any way I could get some help?"

I held my breath. *Please don't hate me.*

"Of course we can make that accommodation." The ease in her voice caught me off guard. "Which is your car?"

"Uhh…the blue Focus."

"Got it. Leave your keys with me and head up to your room. I'll call the guys and have them unload for ya. It may be a few minutes. Is that okay?"

Is that okay?? She was actually asking me. As if I were the one being inconvenienced. "Yes. Whenever they can get to me. I don't want to be any trouble."

"Oh, it's no trouble at all. We're glad to accommodate our fellows with medical needs or disabilities."

Just like that, my request had been granted. It wasn't treated as an annoyance or an unreasonable ask, but a perfectly natural thing for me to need and them to provide. I was inexperienced at requesting these kinds of things, at least not from people I didn't know, and even then I tried to limit it, not wanting to put people out. But according to Stella, at least, I needn't have worried.

I thanked her again and set off to find my apartment, half reeling from how easy that was. The elevator, miracle of modern technology and savior of aching joints, carried me to the fifth floor where I located my unit, turned my key in the lock, and stepped into my new home.

It was…charming. And not because I'd just spent four days in atrocious motels. I guess I'd been expecting something more akin to a dorm room, spartan and utilitarian. This was not that.

To the right was an eat-in kitchen with navy blue cabinets and butcher block countertops, a round table, and four chairs. To the left, a living room complete with sofa, side chair, and coffee table. And at the back, a neatly made bed with a wood headboard and crisp white sheets. All artfully decorated in a mid-century aesthetic. The walls were lined with windows and bookcases, and I wasn't sure which I was more excited for. Whatever this place lacked in size, it made up for in comfort and homeyness. I loved it already.

I'd taken a beating over the last couple of weeks. Ever since I found out I was accepted, everything had been a struggle, and I was feeling every inch of it. My body was battered, my mind fatigued, my heart heavy. But since I'd stepped through that door, every single thing had been basically perfect, exactly what I needed.

I'm supposed to be here.

A lance of pain speared through me. I wished Evan would have seen that. It wouldn't have changed our situation. I had to let him go no matter what. But his lack of confidence had been a blindsiding injury. He'd always believed in me—often more than I believed in myself—encouraged me to reach, told me I could do anything. And then suddenly he was jumping on the *Violet's incapable* bandwagon.

Well, he and my mother could enjoy the ride alone because I was declining to get on board…at least at the moment. The truth was it came in waves, but for now, indignant felt a lot better than bruised, and I refused to ruin my exemplary arrival experience with another crying jag, so indignant it was.

Spreading my heap of literature across the dining table, I gingerly planted myself in one of the chairs. I'd familiarize myself with the neighborhood and think about ordering groceries later. For now, I was eager for information on the program. It started tomorrow, and since I hadn't arrived earlier in the weekend, the sense of lagging behind weighed on me.

I flipped open the folder to the first-page contact sheet.

Fellow Liaison: Stella Sullivan

Mentor: Miranda Shultz

On a gasp, I reared back, as if the words had jumped up and bit me.

Miranda Schultz is my mentor.

It made sense if I thought about it practically. Mentors were probably assigned based on genre and demographic fit. But practicality be damned. This was magic.

On instinct, I reached for my phone and pulled up my text thread with Evan. Even now, my first impulse was to share this news with him, but the phone was a brick in my hand as I reread the texts we'd exchanged when I made it to town, the first since that night at his apartment.

Made it here safely.

EVAN
Thanks for letting me know.

Punching the lock button, I flipped the phone face down on the table. He was not the appropriate recipient for my exciting stories. Not anymore, or at least not for now. Stupid tears threatened again, but I refused to give in.

I belonged here. Miranda Schultz was my mentor. And I had more magic to chase.

———

I made it a whole week before I fully crashed.

Travel was a trigger. Road trips, in particular, were a trigger. Lack of sleep was a trigger. Long days were a trigger. Too much physical activity was a trigger. Stress was a giant trigger. It was honestly a miracle that I'd lasted this long.

A cocktail of adrenaline and angst and excitement had powered me through those first days. I'd met Miranda, met my cohorts, gotten acquainted with the format of the program, learned the basics of the neighborhood, and promptly spiraled into a monster of a flare.

Now I was curled up in my blanket cocoon, meds on board and curtains drawn, attempting to dull the pain by distracting myself with sitcom rewatches. Those efforts were failing.

This sucked. I wanted to be starting my second week with gusto, wanted to be learning, working. I was missing my first official meeting with Miranda to talk about my manuscript ideas. My body was, once again, sabotaging me, stealing the things I wanted.

Except…

She'd gotten me here. I'd put her through a lot, and she'd held on for as long as she could.

"What if it were me?" Evan's voice echoed in my memory. *"Being sick is not a failing…You're doing your best…I wish you were as kind to yourself."*

I had done my best. And maybe that was good enough. Maybe it was time to give my body—myself—a little grace…or even appreciation.

It was not lost on me that Evan's voice was the one in my head. As it turned out, the best friend influence didn't disappear with a breakup. I'd spent many hours over many restless nights trying to decide whether I was more angry or hurt, and it was decidedly both, but mostly I just missed him.

My phone alerted a received email. A response from Miranda. Sending the email to cancel this morning had me sick with guilt. Canceling our first meeting would look awful. She might think I wasn't serious about this program or not cut out to be here. At best, such a late cancellation was inconsiderate. She'd probably think I was wasting her time or that I'd be trouble going forward.

> *Hello Violet,*
> *So sorry you're unwell. I do have some experience with chronic illness and completely understand the difficulties and the need to recover.*
> *Please take care of yourself and take all the time you need. Your health comes first!*
> *Don't worry about the meeting. We'll get started when you're feeling better.*
> *Can't wait to work together!*
> *Miranda*

If this email was to be believed, she thought…none of that. As far as she was concerned, my illness and the impacts of it were normal, understandable, easily worked around.

She wasn't the first who'd treated it that way. I'd received accommodations with a smile throughout this entire week. I thought about Stella. About the guys who joked with me as they brought up my things. About my friends—Nico, Jamie, Lina, Remy…Evan. They never treated this like a burden.

Maybe my view of myself wasn't the only thing that was off. Maybe other people's perception wasn't what I thought it was either. My parents, Gemma, Rob—maybe they were the outliers, not the rule. Or if they were the rule, maybe the rule was wrong.

I…did not have the spoons for this line of thinking. To even go down that road, I'd need a lot more energy, a lot less brain fog, and probably a therapist, none of which was available to me today. I pulled the blanket tighter around me, securing comfort rather than a shield. I was still exhausted, still in pain, but I felt remarkably more peaceful.

Being this sick was not ideal, but it was fine. I would do what I could. People would understand and help. I would feel better soon. And it would be okay.

I'll be okay.

CHAPTER 29

EVAN

I wonder how far I could drop-kick that snowman.

He was staring me down from the countertop in the break room with his jaunty hat and superior grin. *Smug little bastard.*

I stirred my coffee and gave him a death glare, definitely in the holiday spirit.

I'd made it three months without Vi. The first month I spent cycling between depressed and cranky. I thought I was improving by the end of month two, but she didn't come home for Thanksgiving, and my plan to try to reestablish at least some kind of real communication between us was trashed. Lina went to Boston over the holiday, so now instead of talking to Vi directly, I'd spent the last two weeks trying to pry information out of Lina. It was turning me into a real fucking Grinch.

I generally kept it together around here. Aside from a professional reputation at stake, promotion news would be coming down soon, and I had way too much riding on it to lose the job because I kicked a snowman.

I left him to accost others with holiday spirit and retreated to my office. Sipping my coffee, I turned my phone over in my hand.

Don't do it, man. No good comes of it.

Who was I kidding? Of course I was gonna do it. I was a masochist.

I opened my text thread with Violet and reread every message we'd exchanged since she left.

There were six. Six goddamn messages in three months.

VI

Made it here safely.

Thanks for letting me know.

It had been a huge relief. I'd been so damn worried about her alone on that trip. Would the hotels be safe? Would she have a flare and get stranded? I'd been damn grateful that she was willing to let me off the hook, but I was still reeling and couldn't manage any more than a quick thank you.

Happy Birthday. I hope you're having a really good one.

Thanks. It's been good. Out having drinks with the guys. Hope you're doing ok.

That was a lie. It hadn't been good. I'd spent it at Remy's with him and Nico, crying into my whiskey. She never responded.

Happy Thanksgiving Vi.

You too, Ev.

I could hear her voice saying my name when I read it, and it gutted me all over again.

That was it, the sum of our communication. And my most pressing issue.

I missed every part of her. Her smile and her laugh and her eyes and her hair. The crinkle of her nose and the smell of her skin. Hot nights and lazy mornings. Missed it all so much that my heart physically ached with every beat.

But more than anything else, I missed my best friend. That piece hurt so bad I thought my heart might give up and stop beating altogether.

If I couldn't have anything else with her, I had to find a way to rebuild that, had to find a way for us to be friends again. A helluva lot closer than acquaintances that exchanged six text messages in three months.

The problem was I had no idea how. Or if she even wanted to. She was the one who'd left, the one who decided she didn't want this anymore. How far did that extend? It was hard to believe that she'd be out on our friendship after ten years, but she wasn't exactly out here building bridges.

A message popped up on my work computer.

PAUL

Head to the conference room, Evan. The executive team needs to see you.

Congratulations.

My pulse took off like it had been shot out of a cannon. This was it. And he said congratulations…

Holy shit.

I was going to be the department head. I was going to be able to take care of the house.

And all I wanted to do was call her to share the news. That beat-stopping pain squeezed in my chest.

Not right now, dammit. Go get your promotion, then celebrate…then cry in your whiskey.

———

I was yanked out of a painfully vivid Violet dream by three small wrecking balls, six pairs of wide, excited eyes staring back at me as I blinked into consciousness.

"Uncle Evan, it's Christmas morning!"

Fucking early on Christmas morning, judging by the dim light coming through the living room windows, but the exhilaration in Tabbie's voice was enough to grow my Grinchy heart, especially combined with the unrestrained joy on all three of my niblings' faces. *Too damn cute for their own good…or mine.*

"Heck yeah, it is. Did you already check the tree? Did he show?"

Tabbie rolled her eyes. "Of course I did. Do you think I'm an ama-cher or something?"

She was clearly ringleading this expedition, as usual. It made sense. First, this was her house. Second, Taylor's kids were younger than her, Mia by six months, but Dylan was only two. But third, and the real crux of the matter, Tabbie was the ringleader of any circus she was involved in, anyplace with anyone. Fortunately Mia and Dylan seemed content to let her run the show. They had this kind of cousin pack dynamic that they slipped right into no matter how infrequently they actually got to spend time together.

It was great that we were all under one roof for Christmas this year, even if I had volunteered to sleep on the couch so Taylor and Adam could take the guest room and all the kids could be contained in Tabitha's room…which was clearly light on containment.

"He did come." Mia's voice was an urgent whisper. "He even knew me and Dylan were here."

I snagged Dylan and lifted him to sit on my stomach, and he grinned at me around a pacifier that had become the bane of Taylor's existence. She kept taking them away and he kept producing them from some-where. It was driving her bonkers, which was both hilarious and not my problem. As Cool Uncle, I reserved the right not to kill the little magician's vibe.

"All right. Here's what I'm thinking. It's Christmas, and no parents are up so we gotta make it count." They were practically vibrating at my words. "How do we feel about waffles?"

A cheer blasted from all three before they started adding their own requests to the mix.

"With whip cream?"

"And chocolate chips?"

"Banana!"

I laughed. *And damn, it felt good to laugh.*

"Whatever makes your heart sing, little man." I ruffed his hair. "You know what else we need? Christmas Hot Chocolate." Another cheer, this one even louder. "Okay. Okay. But you gotta keep it down, or you're gonna blow our cover."

Levering myself up and setting Dylan back on his feet, I herded the whispering, giggling mass of footie pajamas toward the kitchen, feeling a faint smile pull my cheek. It was foreign. As was the absence of the urge to kick a snowman or punch a Santa.

I wouldn't quite call it happy, but it was closer than I'd been in a while.

We were deep into our waffles and hot chocolate when Mia shoved an enormous bite (waffle with chocolate chips *and* chocolate syrup) into her mouth and talked around it. "Why don't you have any kids, Uncle Evan? You're really good at kids."

"'Cause his girlfriend moved away. Her name is Violet and she has red hair and she's super cool." Tabbie licked whipped cream from her fork, casually wrecking my shit without even knowing it. "I kinda miss her actually. Uncle Evan, do you miss her too?"

My throat closed up and my stomach rolled. I doubted *"so much that it feels like it's going to crush me sometimes"* was an appropriate answer, but it was the only one I could come up with at the moment.

They stared at me—of all times to wait patiently for an answer—while I worked to clear my throat, trying to get it working while I came up with something to say. Neither effort was going particularly well.

The stairs creaked, saving me from the miniature inquisition. Plates and cups and conversations were immediately abandoned as all three of them rushed into the living room to see who'd emerged. Happy voices flowed from the other room, but I still couldn't catch my breath.

I needed to get it together. If the mere mention of her name by a five-year-old was enough to take my legs out from under me, I wasn't doing great.

Lauren poked her head around the entrance to the kitchen. "Hey. Everyone's up. It's tree time." Her face fell, presumably in response to the internal crisis I must have been broadcasting. "Are you okay?"

I attempted to school my expression. I'd talk to her about this later, but I was not about to ruin Christmas with my misery.

"All good."

She looked skeptical but didn't pry.

"Let's go party."

A party was the last thing I wanted, but as my family gathered, my tension loosened and the ache eased.

The kids went wild over every new package, big or small, theirs or others'. Mom took a thousand pictures. I flipped Lo off when she mouthed "Taylor's my favorite" to me after opening a particularly thoughtful gift. I passed out rounds of coffee and hot chocolate with Tay, assembled toys with Adam.

And I only thought about Violet about six hundred more times.

———

The sun was high in the sky by the time I found an opportunity to talk to Mom alone. She was tucked under a light blanket on the back porch, a cool breeze moving through the wind chimes. I approached from behind and dangled a glass of eggnog in front of her face.

I was always game for beverage delivery, but this particular refreshment was strategic. I had a gift to deliver, and I wasn't totally sure how it would be received. I figured a little holiday libation couldn't hurt my position.

"Well, if it isn't my favorite child." She accepted the offering and patted the space next to her on the porch swing. "You've earned a spot next to me…until I need a refill, at least."

I took her invitation and sat with a nog of my own, passing her the red envelope that had been burning a hole in my pocket all morning. "I didn't want to give you your present in front of everyone else."

"A secret gift." She sat her glass on the small table next to the swing with a wry smile. "Your sisters may see this as cheating, but I'm willing to allow it."

I forced an uneasy chuckle. This topic hadn't gone all that well the last time I'd broached it. I understood her hesitation, really I did. But I was hoping that in the spirit of the holiday, she'd have a better reaction, be more reasonable about accepting help.

Lifting the flap of the envelope, she slid the contents free. She didn't even read the letter, her eyes zeroing in on the check like it was a homing beacon while her brow furrowed and the corners of her mouth tugged down.

"What is this?" Her voice was tight. No amount of eggnog was going to ease the way on this one.

I took a deep breath, bracing for the fight. "Two weeks ago, I officially got the promotion to department head." Her chest puffed up. Even when she looked like she was about to throttle me, her pride in me was clear. I fucking loved her for that. "The bonus came through last week. It's for the house, Mom. For you. This should cover—"

Stationary swatted at my head. Repeatedly. My mother was engaged in a full-on melee, words landing between each blow. "What is the matter with you?"

"Ouch. Shit." I used my arms to protect my head as best I could with a half-full drink and fled to the porch railing. "Jesus, Mom."

She waved the offending check at me. "I told you not to do this."

"Please take it. I know you don't like it, but I couldn't handle it if you lost the house and I could—"

"I'm not losing the house, son!"

"I…what?"

"I've been working on my own solutions. I got special financing though my connection at the credit union, and I negotiated with the Neighborhood Association to start paying me for the work I'd been doing on a volunteer basis. God knows they can't afford to lose me. It'll be plenty over and above my regular income to start getting this place in order. Not that it's any of your damn business."

I stood there, mouth gaping open like a beached fish.

"I told you I had it handled. You think you're the only one around here who can make a plan? That I'd been sitting around here for months with my thumb up my ass? Do you not think I'm perfectly capable—"

"Of course I don't think that. You're probably the most capable person on the planet."

"You're damn right I am. So why, even after I told you I had it, did you feel the need to run roughshod over me to fix it yourself?"

Something tugged at my middle, guilt and something else I didn't want to examine too closely. "I'm sorry. I didn't mean to."

"I accept your apology, and I thank you for it. But you did do it, and what I want to understand is why." She cocked her head, holding me in an assessing gaze, disassembling me. She would take me apart and uncover the answer before I even knew what hit me.

"I guess I thought you needed the help." I hedged.

It did not appease her. "Why do you feel the need to make yourself the fixer of everything for everyone?"

"Not everyone."

"Everyone that matters to you. You fix like it's your job."

The words snapped between us, prodding at sore spots I didn't even realize existed. Why were people always harping on that? Acting like it was somehow wrong. Of course helping my people was my job. What the fuck else would my job be? "That's because it is."

"Why on Earth would it be your job to fix everybody's everything? We don't need that from you."

It was a brutal echo of Violet's words the night she left.

"That's not your job. I don't want that from you."

That's what she said when she walked away. She didn't want my help. She didn't want me. Now my own mother was saying the same.

Rejection sliced me down the middle, gutting me all over again. Taking care of people—that's who I was. It was the best I had to offer. And it was nothing anyone wanted.

"Then what fucking good am I?"

Silence fell heavy between us. All I could hear was my own breath sawing in and out of me, stinging all my ragged edges.

"Evan." Her voice was kind but firm, a soft censure. "You are a helper by nature, and that's a beautiful thing. The people in your life rely on you and that's good, too. Though, after your dad…I probably relied on you too much."

"Mom."

She lifted her hand to stop me. "It sounds like somewhere along the line you started to believe that was the only thing you were good for. That your ability to fix, to take care of people and things, was what made you valuable. And maybe if you didn't do those things or didn't do them well enough, we'd have no use for you at all."

She was cracking me wide open, pulling me apart where I stood. As ridiculous as it sounded when she said it out loud, it was exactly what I'd been feeling. Like she pulled it directly from that yawning pit of fear in my gut.

Dropping her handful of papers to the swing, she came to stand in front of me. Held my eyes like she was about to impart wisdom, and I better damn well listen up. "But here's the thing, baby. It's bullshit."

I huffed a silent laugh. Wisdom indeed. Mom was never one to mince words. Which made her next ones all the more potent.

"We don't want you because of what you do for us, we want you because of who you are."

My heart thumped with gratitude. I knew it was the truth. It may take some time to internalize, but I was starting to recognize it now, could see how messed up my perspective had been.

But she wasn't done. She pinned me with a pointed look. "Now about you gettin' all highhanded—if you're not careful, you'll let fear get the better of you, stop trusting people to love you. You might even start treating folks like puppets instead of people."

Shit. "Apparently I already am." On a guilty sigh, I turned toward the yard, elbows on the railing. "I did it to you." *And it wasn't the first time.* My heart dropped into my stomach. "I did it to Violet too."

"Mmm." She leaned next to me. "Wanna tell me about that?"

"I tried to convince her to stay instead of taking that fellowship. Tried to fix it for her. Tried to decide what was best for her instead of supporting her." I drove my hand through my hair. "Fuck. It's no wonder she left me."

I'd basically forced her away. I got scared, let my fear of her leaving, my fear of her not wanting or needing me, take control. I stopped listening, tried to force my own agenda. Hell, I all but told her I didn't think she could do it.

I broke us.

Mom snagged the glass of eggnog from my hand and took a long sip.

"Well, baby, what are you going to do about that?"

CHAPTER 30

VIOLET

I HESITATED ON THE SIDEWALK, HALTING AT THE STOOP OF THE MOST picturesque brownstone. Miranda and I had grown close over the past few months, but crashing a family holiday could still be an imposition.

I'd gone round and round with myself this morning and briefly considered bowing out, saving us both from the burden of her obligatory invite. But it occurred to me that she didn't feel "obligated" enough to invite any of her other fellows, so the obligatory invite theory collapsed pretty quickly—and the bow-out plan along with it. The most obvious explanation was that she invited me because she wanted me here, and since I wanted to be here, I pushed down the lingering bubble of awkwardness bouncing around in my belly and made my way up the stone steps.

The building was beyond lovely—bay windows and iron railings and ornate moldings and a glossy black front door.

He'd love this.

The awkward bubble burst, and the familiar weight of missing him settled right into place. Even after months apart, it remained stubbornly present, materializing like clockwork every time something reminded me of him. Which maybe wouldn't be such a problem except that, after a million years together, basically everything reminded me of him, launching me into the angry-hurt-sad circuit that was becoming painfully routine.

I'd let it get out of hand yesterday. Lina had pushed hard for me to come spend Christmas with her family at the lake house, but even being in the same city as him felt impossible, so I'd insisted that I wanted to experience Christmas in Boston, that I was dreaming of a cozy holiday at home. At the time it felt almost true, certainly the lesser of two evils. The reality was much less Cozy and much more Crying Through Every Christmas Movie We'd Ever Watched Together.

But today was a new day. And fortunately, it wasn't giving me much time to ruminate. The front door swung open as I crested the top step, Miranda's face beaming in welcome. "Come in, come in. It's freezing out there, and you're not rated for these temperatures."

She was not wrong. Texas hadn't prepared me for winter in the Northeast. It was a whole new world of winter wear and hand warmers and violent shivering. I hurried in as she shut the door on the chill and took my coat, her sleek black bob swinging as she spun to place it on a hook.

Her home was as elegant and charming on the inside as the out. Traditional, but in a way that felt warm and timeless rather than stuffy and dated. It was a perfect fit for the woman herself. In her tapered-leg denim, soft cream sweater, and the most stylish house shoes I'd ever seen, she was simultaneously impossibly chic and effortlessly casual.

Evidently, even after months of working together and a burgeoning friendship, I was still working with a fair bit of hero worship.

"I'm so glad you made it. Abby's been after me to have you over ever since that night we all got drinks." I followed her through the house to a beautifully renovated kitchen where meal preparation was in full swing.

Abby stood at the stove, more casually dressed in jeans and a sweat-shirt, her short-cropped blonde hair falling over her forehead as she worked. She stirred, then tasted, then nodded her approval. The smells alone had me approving right along with her.

"Violet!" She left her post, wiping her hands on a kitchen towel that was flung over her shoulder before squeezing my arm in an affectionate greeting. "We're so glad you came. I've been telling Miri—"

"I told her. You've been appropriately credited, dear." Miranda kissed her wife's cheek. "Violet, do you want a glass of wine?"

"I'd love one." She peeled off toward a bar area while Abby shuffled me toward a stool at the island. "Thank you so much for having me."

She waved me off. "Miri's loved working with you, and after I met you, it was obvious why. We've wanted to have you over for ages. Boxing Day's the perfect occasion, right?"

"I…have no idea. I don't think I've ever known anyone who celebrates Boxing Day. I guess you could say I'm unfamiliar with the customs."

Her light laughter floated through the kitchen as she returned to her work. "We are too, to be honest. It actually started as a joke. When we were figuring out all the Jewish/Christian stuff at the beginning of our relationship, celebrating both Chanukah and Christmas was non-negotiable. Then we were already doing so much December celebrating, we decided we had to throw in Boxing Day as well. Sort of a "no holiday left behind" thing. It was just a silly thing at first, but somewhere along the way, it became our favorite. We make a giant meal, bake with the kids—or at least we did when they were younger, teenagers have less interest."

A tall, lanky boy, about sixteen by my best guess, appeared around a corner. He was the spitting image of Miranda with dark hair and deep brown eyes. "What do teenagers have less interest in?"

"Baking with your mothers."

"Oh, yeah. I definitely don't have any interest in that." His smile was wide and teasing. "Interested in the cookies though. At least you still have that."

Rolling her eyes and fighting a smile herself, she clutched her chest with both hands. "Well, then I guess I can go on living."

He patted her head in a patronizing gesture, and she shooed him away, finally giving in to her grin. "We have a guest. Now pretend you're not a heathen and introduce yourself."

"Yes, ma'am." He extended his hand over the island, and we shook. "Hi. I'm James."

"Violet. I'm one of your mom's mentees."

"My favorite mentee. And my friend." Miranda approached with three wine glasses, distributing one to her wife and one to me before taking a sip of her own.

"That's cool. So you're a writer, too?"

"Trying to be."

"She's a very good writer. You'll be buying her book before long."

"That'll be a relief." James leaned toward me conspiratorially, eyes wide and brows lowered. "Right now she only lets us buy hers."

"You should be so lucky." Miranda's faux outrage was spoiled by her huffed laugh. Pushing buttons was clearly a whole love language for this kid, one his moms spoke fluently. "Dinner's almost done. Go grab Grace and set the table."

He nodded and started to leave, but peered over Abby's shoulder on his way by to deliver a parting jab. "Huh. Bold choice on the runny gravy. Should I set out straws?"

Abby was appropriately scandalized. "It's reducing!"

"Hey. It's not a criticism." He put his hands up in surrender. "You do you. I'm just trying to make sure we have appropriate utensils."

Swatting at him with her towel, she drove him from the kitchen and returned to her gravy. "Damn. It really is runny. Miri, could you grab me the cornstarch?" She gestured toward me with her spoon. "Please don't tell him. I'll never hear the end of it."

"Your secret is safe with me."

With the gravy thickened, I helped carry family-style platters to the dining room where James and his younger sister Grace, a fourteen-year-old with pink hair and effortless style, had the table set.

We took our seats and passed the dishes, loading our plates with classic Christmas fare. This was the holiday I'd missed yesterday. I was surrounded with family, accepted into it even if only for the day, and the food smelled so heavenly I couldn't wait to dig in. I was unbelievably grateful that I hadn't bailed.

Setting aside my silverware, I unfurled my napkin and heard Abby's shriek and the kids' booms of laughter as a straw came tumbling out of it into my hand.

———

Dinner was all but finished when I excused myself to go to the restroom and had disbanded completely by the time I returned, so I set off toward the kitchen to make myself useful with cleanup.

I was halfway down the hall when I caught sight of Abby at the sink. The water was running, but she was hunched over, arms braced, head bowed. I recognized the posture immediately. She was in pain.

I picked up my pace to help, but James beat me to it. I watched from the kitchen entry as he took the rag from her hand and gently guided her toward a stool, pulling it out for her and helping her sit before taking her place at the sink.

"She has fibromyalgia." I started at Miranda's voice beside me.

She looked toward her wife, and the pieces clicked into place. From the very beginning, she'd been so understanding of my condition. She even mentioned experience with chronic illness when I canceled that first meeting. This was that experience, a wife with fibromyalgia.

"I love the way they take care of her. James, especially, is so attentive."

Of course she loved it. They weren't even mine, and my heart was toasting right up at the sight of this teenage boy seeing and caring for his mother so tenderly. Their relationship was beautiful, with teasing flowing into affection and affection into care so easily that you could hardly differentiate them.

And now that I was looking for it, I could see how it had permeated the whole evening. It was in the way Miranda had grabbed the heavy dishes to bring to the table, leaving the light salad bowl for Abby to carry. In the way Grace had popped up to grab Abby a refill of water when she ran low. Obviously, in the way James had helped Abby to a seat and taken over on dishes. And not a single time had it felt like a chore. It was just there, tangled up in the love and laughter of family.

They adored one another, Abby no less. And why wouldn't they? She was wonderful and she was theirs. Why wouldn't they be grateful to have her? Why wouldn't they be glad to help when she needed it? And why wouldn't my people do the same for me?

They would. They did… He did.

Why was it so easy to believe all this good for Abby with Miranda, but not for myself with Evan, even when he'd been showing up with it for years already? Why was it so obvious to me that Abby could be a great mother, but not that I could be?

"Are you okay?"

"Fine." I shrugged dismissively. "Having a few Earth-shattering real-izations is all."

With a knowing chuckle, she nodded down the hall. "Come on. The kids have got cleanup. Let's go in here."

She led me through double pocket doors and into a study I would dream about forever. On one side, a beautifully carved wooden desk. On the other, a couple of oversized armchairs with a small table between them. And on every wall, floor-to-ceiling books, interrupted only by an unlit fireplace.

This is where she wrote. I'd love to say I knew because I could feel the creative energy suffusing the space, but really it was because I knew that if I had a space like this to write in, I'd plant myself there and never, ever leave.

"So. Seems like you were having a bit of a moment back there." She gestured toward the chairs, and we sat. "Now I may be totally off base here, but might that have something to do with some life experience you share with my wife?"

Wow, she was perceptive. With not much more than a look and a few words from me, she'd zeroed in on the issue with perfect accuracy. I'd be willing to bet she had more than the general topic clearly identified, but perhaps she was keeping it vague on purpose, leaving the door open for me. I could choose whether or not to walk through.

This wasn't generally the kind of thing I felt comfortable talking about. I'd only ever shared it with Evan. But suddenly, the need to talk was burning a hole in me. And Miranda felt like an exceedingly safe place to share. She'd become my mentor far beyond the roles assigned to us by the program, and she had ample relevant experience in this area.

I let my thoughts tumble out. "I think I've spent a lot of years telling myself what I couldn't have. What my presence meant for the people in my life. And I think I'm realizing it was bullshit all along."

Her burst of laughter filled the cozy space as she shook her head. "Internalized ablism is quite the thing."

I would never have thought to put it in those terms, but that's exactly what it was.

"I'll confess I've suspected you struggled with it. Abby did for a long time. We were married with two small children when she was diagnosed. I had carried James, and she carried Grace. The pregnancy triggered it for her. Suddenly there we were, with a toddler and an infant and a major medical crisis and no answers. And when we finally did get those answers, they made life look completely different than we'd planned."

My heart ached for Abby. Our stories may be different in the details, but there was a lot there I recognized. I knew about struggling to get answers, and I knew about grieving the life you'd wanted.

"Her view of herself fundamentally changed. She no longer felt like herself. Said she was sticking us with a lemon—her words, not mine. But to us, she was still everything we wanted and needed. It took her a while, but eventually she began to see herself clearly again."

It certainly didn't seem like Abby was mourning anymore. It was clear that she loved her life, and that she felt loved and valued by her family.

"What helped her?"

"Me, I hope." Her mouth tipped in a smile. "I know our kids did. Therapy. Community with people who understand her experience."

That's what this was. She was paying that forward. Trying to help me like others had helped Abby. My heart swelled with gratitude, a lump in my throat along with it.

"For a long time, I've thought of myself as a liability. I was so sure I was going to use people up. I could never be what my friends or family really needed—certainly never what a husband or kids required. And it's not like I came up with those ideas out of nowhere. I've had experiences that confirmed it." Even now those memories left little slices across my heart. But they didn't cut quite as deep. And they weren't the only memories I had to go on. "But I've also had plenty that disproved it."

"But those can be harder to believe."

"Yes. Exactly. I think I've been trying to. I feel like I've been chipping away at it for a while now. But tonight...I don't know. It's just so obvious when it's happening with someone else right in front of you."

"What if it were me?... I wish you were as kind to yourself."

The truth of Evan's words settled into my bones. If it were Evan, I'd give grace. If it were Abby, I'd never doubt her worth. I deserved no less from myself.

CHAPTER 31

EVAN

The last two days were a blur.

I'd tried to enjoy the rest of Christmas Day with my family, but after that spectacular ass-kicking Mom delivered, I struggled to stay focused, so I bailed early and spent the evening on my couch, marinating myself in whiskey and inspecting every second of my relationship with Violet through fresh eyes. I did not care for the picture coming into focus.

I spent hours trying to parse what made me an attentive, supportive, and helpful boyfriend vs what made me a control freak with abandonment issues and a hero complex. The lines were blurrier than they probably should have been. Separating them would require more work…with less booze in my system.

Starkly clear, however, was the fact that my misery over the last four months was self-imposed. The breakup, the virtual collapse of our friendship—it was all on me.

I hurt her. Didn't listen to her. Didn't support her. I tried to make her smaller.

For years, I'd despised everything and everyone that made her feel like she had to be smaller, but the second I was uncomfortable, there I was, trying to keep her close, keep her contained. I'd promised her to want it too much with her, and then I'd abandoned that promise when I got too scared to see it through. It was a fucking betrayal. And I hated myself for it. So I'd poured another whiskey over it. And when I still hated myself, I added another.

The next morning, I woke up with a nasty hangover but fresh resolve. I had to fix this—the irony of which was not lost on me, but of all the things that had not been my job to fix, this absolutely was. I had to get to her and try to make this right.

After three ibuprofen, five glasses of water, and a greasy breakfast, I'd gotten to work. I mined Lina for information, packed a bag, and booked a plane ticket—but not a hotel. Maybe that was optimistic, but yesterday, I'd been feeling optimistic.

Today, I was not.

Today I was sitting in the parking lot of her building, staring at a bagful of takeout ramen and questioning my life choices.

Lina mentioned that she hadn't found a place she loved for ramen, so I dove down a rabbit hole researching. In that optimistic haze, her favorite meal represented the perfect olive branch. Now it just felt like lunch.

My head thumped against the steering wheel. Fuck, I had not thought this through. This was where a lack of planning got you—trying to win back the love of your life with noodles. What an excellent time to abandon one of my core personality traits. I thumped my head against the steering wheel three more times.

It was too late now. I was here, and I sure wasn't driving away from her.

I stared at the front door, wishing I had more to go on, more control of the situation. But that wasn't how this worked anyway. As uncomfortable as it made me, I knew deep down that I couldn't plan my way out of this with all the time in the world. I just had to put myself out there and hope that she'd be willing to talk to me. We'd take it from there.

Grabbing the bag of food and throwing the door open, I plowed through the parking lot and into her building, before taking the longest elevator ride of my life up to her floor, my organs rearranging themselves the entire way. By the time I made it to her door, my heart was in my throat and my stomach was on the floor.

I knocked, pulse pounding as I heard movement inside. She must have checked the peephole, because her olive-green eyes were wide as the door swung open, her round lips already parted in surprise.

The air evaporated from my lungs. After all of these months apart, she was the most beautiful sight I'd ever seen. A goddamn oasis in the desert. In the ten years since we met, I'd never gone this long without seeing her, and in that moment, I knew I'd do literally anything to keep from doing it again.

"Evan?" She pulled a chunky green sweater tighter around her body, protecting herself from the cold or from me, I wasn't sure. Whatever it was, I ached to drive it away, to pull her into my arms and feel her melt into me, warm and safe. But that was about six dozen undefined steps away, so I tucked my free hand into the pocket of my coat instead.

"Hey."

"How did you… What are you doing here?"

She was understandably surprised, but beyond that, I couldn't tell how she felt about my being here. I wanted to respond appropriately, but I was lost, like my ability to read her had been cut off with our separation. The disconnect fed my unease as I searched for the right words.

"I brought you ramen." I lifted the bag. Maybe if I led with the food, I could buy myself time to figure it out. "Lina said you hadn't found a place you loved."

Her face screwed up in confusion. "You came all the way to Boston to bring me ramen?"

"No. That's…" *Ridiculous.*

I was fucking this up. She was bewildered, and I was giving her nothing. I pushed a hand through my hair, like somehow it would calm the chaotic thoughts swirling around my head. It didn't help shit. But I took a deep breath, and it did.

Tell her why you're here.

My heart was threatening to throw itself out of my chest, but I let my hand fall, let my arms spread at my sides, opening myself to her in every way possible.

"I don't have a plan, Violet. I have no idea what the next step is beyond this bag of takeout and you opening that door. All I know is that I'm miserable without you in a thousand different ways. I don't know how to be without you, and I don't want to know."

She blinked as her eyes went shiny. I was making her cry again and still had no idea what she was thinking. Panic beat a driving rhythm through my veins.

"This is completely my fault. But I'm asking you—begging you—to talk to me. Let me apologize. See if maybe we can work this out—"

My words were cut off by the thud of her body crashing into mine, her arms wrapping around my waist, her face buried in my chest. Without a moment's hesitation, I dropped the takeout to the floor and returned her embrace, the scent of honey and home filling the first full breath I'd taken in months.

Relief threatened to buckle my knees as tears clouded my vision. This right here is what I couldn't live without. I could face whatever came next, as long as she was in my life.

A sob racked her body.

"Sweetheart." I ran my hands over her back, her hair, desperate to console her now that I could again. "It's okay. We're okay." My own tears fell as I repeated it like a mantra into her hair, maybe as much for my own comfort as for hers. "We're okay."

I lost all track of how long we stood there, holding each other like our lives depended on it, but eventually her breathing evened and our grips loosened.

"Do you want to come in?" She hadn't moved her face, so her voice was muffled in my layers of clothing.

I allowed myself a chuckle at how damn cute she was, but not the kiss I was dying to place on the crown of her head. We weren't there yet.

"Yes. Please."

We disentangled ourselves, dashing a few remaining tears away and collecting the miraculously intact takeout.

The apartment was small but homey, filled with cozy things that made the space feel like hers, the way my place had started to before she left. The way I hoped it would again.

"Are you hungry? According to the internet, this is the best ramen in Boston."

The corner of her mouth tugged, the barest hint of a smile that felt like a ray of fucking sunshine.

"I'm good for now." She placed the bag on the counter and met me in the living area, humming with nervous energy. Her fingers tangled, her nose wrinkled, her gaze not quite meeting mine. Reuniting was one thing, working shit out was another. We both knew that what came next wouldn't be easy. As much as I hated to see her worry, I was more than a little relieved that my ability to read her seemed to be coming back online.

I took two steps toward her to close the gap between us, my hands circling her upper arms. Finally, her eyes met mine, anxious but open. It was all I could ask for.

"I'm so sorry, Vi. I got scared. Scared of you leaving. Scared of you not needing me. It was never about thinking you couldn't do it, I swear. It was about thinking I couldn't. I should have backed you up. Should have given you whatever help you wanted. Should have told you that

I love you. And that you're brilliant. And that I couldn't wait to watch you succeed."

I needed more. More contact, deeper connection. I moved my hand up to cradle her face. She didn't pull away, so I pressed forward.

"I put my fears and my idiotic need to be the fixer over what you needed. And I know that wasn't a one-time problem. You said it would never have worked, but I can do better."

She grasped my wrists, pulling them gently from her face, but it didn't feel like a rejection, more like she needed me to hear what she was going to say next.

"That wasn't why I said that. You did hurt me that night, and I won't argue that it wasn't an issue, but that's not why I ended it. I already planned to before we even got home."

I rocked back on my heels.

What the fuck?

Apparently I couldn't read her at all. This was a rejection, and it had been all along. She was what? Letting me down easy? It felt anything but. All the wounds I'd been trying to patch up for the last four months were tearing wide open. I started to pull back, but she held tight, keeping me in place.

"I thought I had to let you go. I thought I was being selfish by forcing you to take care of me forever and keeping you from having kids. I thought you'd run out of patience at some point or realize you'd sacrificed too much."

My heart broke in a whole different way hearing her say that. I knew she worried about those things, but I had no idea it was that bad. "Vi."

"I don't think that anymore. Or at least I mostly don't. I'm working on it."

"You aren't. You could never be."

"I'm starting to believe that. A lot has changed for me here. I'm feeling more confident."

I could see that confidence shining in her small smile. If she let me, I'd spend my life trying to boost it.

Happiness and what looked like a little excitement flickered in her eyes. "A big part of that is believing that I could be a good partner, a good parent even."

She didn't say *"with you"* but that didn't stop hope from springing.

"I want it to be with me." Clasping her hands in mine, I pulled them against my chest. "I know I have work to do. It's been brought to my attention that I can be overbearing at times."

She laughed, small and breathy but real, and an anvil slid off my sternum. "I've done a lot of thinking about where that comes from, and we can talk about all that later, but for now what you need to know is that I promise I'll change it. I'll always want to take care of you—"

"I'll always want you to."

She was saying yes. "Thank fuck."

I dropped my forehead to hers, and she tipped her chin up to meet me.

"I'm yours, Violet. I have always been yours. I will always be yours."

———

VIOLET

My heart took off at a dead sprint as his mouth captured mine.

He was here. I still couldn't believe it. The moment my heart was ready for him, he appeared as if it had called him. Which of course was utterly fantastical, but as love stretched between us like a million sparkling threads, insistent and indestructible, it seemed impossible to imagine it happened any other way.

He. Was. Here. And he was mine. Joy shimmered through me, overwhelmingly bright and impossible to contain.

His hands slid up my throat to my face, delving into my hair as he tipped my head to take the kiss deeper. His lips opened mine as his tongue slipped in to tease me. Tingles cascaded down my body, the base of my throat, the backs of my arms, the inside of my thighs.

Breaking away, he kissed down the column of my throat, then buried his face at the crook of my neck on a deep, shuddering breath.

"Every day. I needed you every goddamn day."

I knew the feeling. My heart and body had ached for him constantly, and now that he was in such close proximity, they were demanding an end to the deprivation. "I need you now."

I felt his smile spread against my skin.

His jacket fell to the floor, and he slid my cardigan off my shoulders to join it. Mouths followed hands as they removed his shirt and then mine, touching and tasting, savoring every inch of newly exposed skin. The feel of him beneath my palms, warm and solid and actually here, was almost too wonderful to bear.

Lips trailed down my sternum as he sank to his knees in front of me. His tongue traced the edges of my bra, lifting goosebumps over the swell of my breasts, then laved each nipple through the navy mesh. They stiffened and strained against the fabric, pebbling under his lips as he licked and sucked.

I whimpered in protest as he nipped down my stomach, but it dissolved quickly into pants of desire when he slipped his hands under my waistband, sliding my leggings and panties over my hips and down my legs in one excruciatingly slow motion as his mouth mapped every dip and curve.

It was the sweetest torture I could imagine. Anticipation pulsed between my legs as my fingers tangled in his soft hair.

His hands trailed up the backs of my calves, catching one knee and lifting it over his shoulder, opening me to him as he nipped and sucked the sensitive skin of my inner thigh. I trembled as he worked higher, closer to where I needed him most. His thumb traced my seam, finding the pool of arousal gathering there, and his restraint shattered.

On a groan, he pushed his face between my legs, mouth finding my wet, swollen center.

Oh, god.

Pleasure radiated through my body as his tongue parted me, his guttural sound of satisfaction the sexiest thing I'd ever heard.

I shook against him, and he gripped my waist to steady me, giving me a gentle squeeze. *"I'm here. I've got you."* My fingers tightened in his hair.

My orgasm was already barreling toward me, every movement of his mouth on me bringing it closer. Tipping my hips forward, I ground against his face, his answering groan pushing me higher.

His lips found my clit and closed around it. For a moment I was floating, suspended in time, weightless and incandescent, before my climax crashed in, the full weight of my satisfaction bearing down on me, pulling me beneath the waves that racked my body.

I crumpled, but Evan was there to catch me, gathering me up and carrying me to the bed where he laid me out and covered my body with his own. He kissed me, tenderly, reverently, while I came down, the taste of me on his lips doing nothing to bring me back to Earth.

He removed our remaining clothing till we were nothing but skin against skin, his hard length pressing into my thigh. I still felt a bit desperate. Even after that devastating orgasm, my need for him was nowhere near satisfied.

I pushed up, and he went willingly, rolling onto his back so I could straddle his hips.

His expression stole my breath. He looked at me like I was everything, eyes wide open and stark with adoration. I'd have known what he was thinking without him saying a word, but he spoke anyway.

"I love you, Violet." He brushed hair away from my face. "Always."

I rolled against him, dragging my wet folds over his erection. His hips bucked, and his eyes rolled back as he bit out a curse. I slid up to his tip, then canting my hips, sank back down, taking him into me, inch by glorious inch.

This was perfect.

Having him buried so deep inside of me. *Perfect.*

Being back in each other's arms where we belong. *Perfect.*

Loving him with all of me forever. *Absolutely perfect.*

His fingertips dug into my hips, and I leaned forward to brush a kiss over his parted lips.

"I love you, too."

I rocked back, taking him even deeper, pulling him to that spot that had another orgasm coiling low in my belly. He lifted to meet me as I ground down. His hands roamed my body, skimming over the dip of my waist and up to cup my breasts. My whole body was sensitized, every touch stinging my skin until I burned, every thrust driving me deeper into a fevered haze.

He pressed his thumb against my clit, making tight circles that sent sharp ecstasy rushing up my spine. His name fell from my lips, over and over, because he was the only thing that existed anymore.

I collapsed forward as sensation overwhelmed me, exploding from my core through the rest of my body with such force that I was sure I would break into a thousand pieces, but Evan was there holding me together, keeping me whole.

He pulled me close, pressing his face into my neck as he murmured words I couldn't understand. He pumped into me, his movements becoming quick and jerky as he found his own release.

We clutched each other tight while we rode out our orgasms, as if we both needed the contact to believe this was real.

Hold me tight and convince me I'm not dreaming. Never let go.

His fingers tangled in my curls, and his mouth found mine once again. He kissed me slow and deep, till our breathing was slow and our bodies were languid.

He ran the tip of his nose down mine. "Thank you."

"For the sex?"

His chest rumbled under me. "I mean, always for that, but no…" He smiled a Three Dimple Smile. "Thank you for saying yes."

CHAPTER 32

EVAN

WAKING UP NEXT TO VIOLET WAS AS INCREDIBLE THIS MORNING AS IT HAD been the previous four. Being pulled into consciousness by the smell of her skin, the warmth of her body tucked against mine—it was heaven. Even the face full of her curls felt like perfection.

She was turned away from me, back against my chest, ass nestled right into my lap where the T-shirt of mine that she was wearing rode up over her bare cheeks, a scenario that was not helping to calm my morning wood. But I refused to wake her.

She'd insisted on staying up late last night so we could kiss to ring in the new year, which had actually turned into us having sex to ring in the new year, and while I couldn't think of a better way to spend it, it did mean that she needed the rest this morning.

That was fine by me. I could lay here holding her for hours and it wouldn't be enough, especially not today.

I gently circled my arm around her waist, slipping my hand beneath the hem of the shirt and pulling her closer. A soft snore rumbled out of her. It was cute as hell and all mine.

I would never get over that.

I loved her more than anything, wanted her more than anything. It ached in my chest with every heartbeat. I was hers. *And she decided to be mine.*

She'd forgiven me. Trusted me. Let me back into her life and her bed, and I was determined never to leave it again, at least not for long.

We had a strong start on that already. We'd been holed up in her apartment like there was a zombie apocalypse outside, but today we had to break the bubble.

She stirred against me, and I peppered kisses up her neck. She hummed and arched in response. "Good morning."

"Good morning, beautiful. How are you feeling?"

She took a moment to answer, and I knew she was running through her morning check. "So far, so good, it seems."

Arching further, she pressed that bare ass that I'd been studiously ignoring against me, the cotton of my boxer briefs doing nothing to dampen the heat.

I nipped her earlobe. "Be careful with that thing."

She wiggled it against me, and I pounced, nipping and tickling and working her up into a fit of shrieks and giggles.

God, I'm going to miss her.

I finished with a sloppy, wet kiss to her cheek, and she calmed, threading our fingers together and echoing my thought back to me.

"I'm going to miss you. I'm not ready for you to go."

"Hey." Turning her to face me, I gathered her close. "It won't be for long this time." I already had two weekend trips planned during the two months she had left here. Then I'd fly back one last time to take her home. Not just home to Austin, home to my place—*our* place.

"I know. But it's hard. In a lot of ways, it was actually easier when we —" She cut herself off, expression horrified. "Oh, god. That's not what I meant."

I kissed her nose where it scrunched. "I know. Go on."

Releasing a breath, she curled further into me. "I've been homesick the whole time, but being here felt easier than being there. Now that's not true anymore, and I'm worried it'll be too hard. I want to be here, but I want to be home with you, too."

I hooked a knuckle under her chin and lifted it to bring her gaze to mine. "You're exactly where you need to be. I should have realized that from the beginning, but I know it now. I've read the work you're doing, heard how you talk about your mentor and the classes. Don't waste a second of this worried about us. I'm here. I'm behind you. And I'll do everything I can to make it easier on you till you're done."

Her smile broke like sunrise and warmed me from the inside.

Of course the next couple of months would be hard. I'd miss her like crazy. But the sick feeling never came. A little discomfort was nothing if I could help her chase her dreams. And hell, it would be a cakewalk compared to what we'd been through.

"We'll be okay. You focus on coming home with a book deal."

She crushed her lips to mine.

———

New Weird Shit entry: lady street performer doing a circus with trained squirrels.

VI

Wow! High marks for creativity. Though I don't know if the animal involvement gains or loses points.

Did the squirrels look happy?

Very. There were no cages (don't ask me how) and they were super cute.

Then 9.

Agreed.

18 hours and counting. See you tomorrow sweetheart.

———

VI

DID YOU HAVE BATH STUFF DELIVERED TO MY APARTMENT?!?!

I did. You don't feel good. Food should be there in five.

Ev...

Don't cry.

OF COURSE I'M GOING TO CRY!!! 😭😭😭

Ok. Not too much then. You don't have the spoons.

Sniff

I'm sorry I'm not there to help. I love you so much.

You helped. I love you. 🤍

———

Holy shit. Last night was...

VI

What are the chances we can reenact that in person when I see you this weekend?

> I feel like I should be concerned that you can no longer speak but since these emojis are going my way I'm gonna let it slide.

VI

> I'm coming home with a book deal!!!!!!!!!!

Calling Vi…

I hadn't made it three steps into the lobby before she was barreling toward me. She leapt into my arms, legs wrapping around my waist, hands framing my face, and kissed me like we were alone even though we definitely were not. All the people milling around this place were getting a show today, and I did not give a fuck. I kissed her back, matching her passion, and squeezed her ass where it filled my hands. If we were gonna do this, we were gonna do it right.

I'd landed at Logan an hour ago with the duffel that was now somewhere near my feet and taken a cab straight here. Now we'd load up her car and drive together back down to Austin. She was coming home. Which meant that I was euphoric enough to not care at all about causing a scene.

We did pull up before things got too out of hand (a minor miracle) and settled for grinning at each other like idiots.

"Should I put you down?"

Her green eyes sparkled. "Or you could load the car like this. Maybe switch me to your back for practicality's sake?"

"As fun as that sounds, I think I'll be more efficient without a human backpack." With a parting kiss, I sat her on her feet. "You packed and ready?"

"Yes. Boxes were finished yesterday, and I packed my weekender after brunch this morning with Miranda and Abby."

"Then let's get to it."

With as little as she'd brought with her, we were packed and loaded in less than half an hour. I closed the back hatch and circled the car, finding her standing by the open passenger door, staring at the apartment building.

Banding an arm around her, I pulled her back into my chest and kissed her temple. "I'm so fucking proud of you."

"I'm proud of me, too." I could hear the smile in her voice. "But I'm also ready to go home."

Spinning in my arms, she threw hers around my shoulders. My heart stuttered.

"Take me home, Evan."

EPILOGUE
VIOLET - 6 MONTHS LATER

"Hey, sweetheart." Evan's voice drifted from the entry.

"In here."

He rounded the corner into the living room where I sat curled up at the end of the couch, my laptop, along with the notes from my editor, long since abandoned on the coffee table. It had not been a great day for concentration…or much else.

He bent over me, greeting me with a lingering kiss.

All right. It was a great day for one thing.

"I talked to the inspector. They're sending over the full report, but no major red flags. There are a couple of smaller things we could ask for, but we can work it out tomorrow."

"That's great."

We were putting a big portion of his bonus and a small portion of my book advance toward a down payment on a house. Our financing was in order, our offer had been accepted, and with a clean inspection report, it was full steam ahead. The place was lovely, a 1970s craftsman that Evan loved for its Good Bones and I loved for its walking distance proximity to Nico and Jamie.

"Are you about to start getting ready? Don't get me wrong, I love the pajamas and messy bun look, but I'm not sure the restaurant would appreciate it as much as I do."

"Actually would it be okay if we stayed in tonight?"

"Uhhh." He blinked, looking unsure.

It wasn't the reaction I expected, but I guess I was springing it on him at the last minute. I kept hoping I'd start feeling better with a little more rest, but now I was out of rest time and my options were get dressed or give up. And I really didn't want to get dressed.

"I'm not feeling all that great."

Concern immediately replaced his hesitation as he sat next to me. "Sweetheart. I'm sorry, I didn't know. What's going on?"

"Nothing outrageous. Just low energy. I don't think a night out is in the cards for me tonight."

"Then of course we can stay in."

"Are you sure? I know changing plans is a pain."

"It's not." He tucked an escaped curl behind my ear. "I'm going to go get changed and cancel the reservation. We can order in. Think about what you want, okay?" I lifted an eyebrow as he stood, shaking his head on a laugh. "Yes. We can order ramen."

———

We'd spent the evening on the couch, eating takeout and watching TV, my feet tucked into Evan's lap. Now I'd been promised dessert.

He crouched by the couch, hands hidden behind his back.

"This is a choose-your-own-adventure dessert. Pick a hand."

"Ooh. I like this game." I rose from my lounging position, very serious about dessert selection, and hummed as I considered my options. "Wait. One hand isn't empty, is it?"

"No. One hand is not empty."

All right… "But are they both things that I'll like?"

"Vi." His tone was only jokingly chastising, but I didn't think I would get anywhere with more questions.

"Okay. Okay." I put up my hands. "Right."

He pulled his right hand from behind his back, producing a pint of ice cream that I snatched from him in triumph.

"I chose wisely."

One dimple creased his cheek as a wicked smile lifted the corner of his mouth. "Did you?"

"Yes?" Though now I was less sure. Was he trying to steer me to something even more delicious? Or was he messing with me? I stared him down, attempting to pluck the answer from his brain, but his grin only grew, providing no answers. "I want to switch."

"Are you sure? There's no going back if you do. You've gotta take whatever's back here."

The more he smiled, the more confident I was in the decision. After all this, he wouldn't stick me with something disappointing. I set the ice cream down on the end table. "Yes. I'm sure."

He nodded and pulled his left hand from behind his back.

A small black velvet box sat in his palm.

My hands flew to my mouth to cover my gasp. My heart fluttered in my chest.

He lifted the lid, and I knew a ring was sitting on the cushion, but I couldn't bring myself to look away from his eyes as they stared, warm and hopeful, into mine.

"You are my everything. My best friend. My favorite person. The love of my life." He pulled the ring from the box. "And I'm asking you to add one more thing to that list. I love you with all of me, Violet. Be my wife?"

The lightning bugs were so bright, I would swear I was made of them. Tears filled my eyes. I nodded, unable to find my voice, but it was enough. He slipped the ring on, the weight of it on my finger, in my heart, feeling exactly right.

I threw my arms around him, joy radiating around us as our lips met. It was the best moment, the most perfect proposal—*oh noooooo.*

I reared back, grasping his shoulders in panic. "Oh my god, I ruined your proposal."

"You didn't ruin anything." He stroked my arms, but I would not be calmed.

"But this was not the plan! I know you had one. What was it?"

He shook his head. "Vi. It doesn't—"

"It does. Tell me what it was. I'll go find your notebook."

He sighed and moved to sit on the couch, pulling me into his lap. "We weren't actually going to a restaurant. I had a picnic set up at the park..." I moaned like he was killing me because he was. "String lights and champagne..."

It sounded entirely magical. Of course he had planned an amazing proposal. I hated that I'd ruined it for him, for us.

"We have to do that. Or...I don't know...pretend we did that."

"Absolutely not."

"Why? It sounds perfect. We can have a redo."

He clasped my face in his hands, halting my protests. "We don't need a redo. I want to marry you. In the park with champagne or on the couch with takeout. Feeling great or feeling shitty. When life goes according to plan and when it doesn't. It doesn't have to be perfect. It just has to be us."

I melted into him. He was right. Who needed perfect when we had each other?

"It'll always be us."

THE END

Evan and Violet have found their happily ever after, but their story isn't over!

*You can find their bonus epilogue at the link
and see them again in the next installment of the
ATX series, The 5 Second Rule, in which Lina meets her match.*

https://dl.bookfunnel.com/jqriqahrbc

ACKNOWLEDGMENTS

First, thank you to every reader who picks up this book. The fact that you even exist is splendid and surreal. This story has so much of my heart and I am beyond grateful to you for choosing to spend your time with it.

Thank you to my editor, Dawn Alexander, for helping this story (and this author) find its way, and to Kimberly Hunt and Emily Laughridge for refining and polishing it into its best self. Thank you to Amanda Montgomery and Sanjana Basker for their brilliant insight. And thank you to Enni Tuomisalo for bringing Evan and Violet to life with her lovely cover.

Thank you to my wonderful family and dearest friends whose support and encouragement in this big, new endeavor has meant more than I'll ever be able to say.

Finally, thank you to my husband, Ross—the first to tell me to do this and the first to call me a writer. My first sounding board, first reader, first hype-man, and endless encourager. Thank you for making me feel like the biggest me. And thank you for carrying me when I need help getting there.

ABOUT THE AUTHOR

Kandice Hemenway is an author and romance enthusiast from Fort Worth, Texas. She writes sweet, sexy romance pairing heart and heat with positive representation of diverse experiences, especially those of chronically ill folks like herself.

She loves a big plate of pasta, a hot cup of tea, a thorough checklist, and anything olive green. Her favorite places are the mountains of Colorado and her very old house in Texas. She firmly believes in snuggling under a blanket no matter the weather. And there is nothing more important to her than her people.

www.ingramcontent.com/pod-product-compliance
Lightning Source LLC
Chambersburg PA
CBHW030141310726
48970CB00005B/1539